22
SECONDS

James Patterson is one of the best-known and biggest-selling writers of all time. His books have sold in excess of 400 million copies worldwide. He is the author of some of the most popular series of the past two decades – the Alex Cross, Women's Murder Club, Detective Michael Bennett and Private novels – and he has written many other number one bestsellers including non-fiction and stand-alone thrillers.

James is passionate about encouraging children to read. Inspired by his own son who was a reluctant reader, he also writes a range of books for young readers including the Middle School, Dog Diaries, Treasure Hunters and Max Einstein series. James has donated millions in grants to independent bookshops and has been the most borrowed author in UK libraries for the past thirteen years in a row. He lives in Florida with his f

Maxine Paetro is ⬚⬚⬚⬚⬚⬚⬚⬚⬚⬚⬚⬚⬚⬚⬚⬚ James Patterson on the b⬚⬚⬚⬚⬚⬚⬚⬚⬚⬚⬚⬚⬚⬚⬚ te and Confessions series, ⬚⬚⬚⬚⬚⬚⬚⬚⬚⬚⬚⬚⬚⬚ novels. She lives with her h⬚⬚

Meet The Women's Murder Club

EXCLUSIVE PROFILES by Our Crime Desk

LINDSAY BOXER

A homicide detective in the San Francisco Police Department, juggling the worst murder cases with the challenges of being a first-time mother. Her loving husband Joe, daughter Julie and loyal border-collie Martha give her a reason to protect the city. She didn't have the easiest start to life, with an absent father and an ill mother, but she didn't shy away from a difficult and demanding career. With the help of her friends, Lindsay makes it her mission to solve the toughest cases.

CLAIRE WASHBURN

Chief Medical Examiner for San Francisco and one of Lindsay's oldest friends. Wise, confident and viciously funny, she can be relied on to help whatever the problem. She virtually runs the Office of the Coroner for her overbearing, credit-stealing boss, but rarely complains. Happily married with children, her personal life is relatively calm in comparison to her professional life.

CINDY THOMAS

An up-and-coming journalist who's always looking for the next big story. She'll go the extra mile, risking life and limb to get her scoop. Sometimes she prefers to grill her friends over cocktails for a juicy secret, but, luckily for them, she's totally trustworthy (most of the time...). She somehow found the time to publish a book between solving cases, writing articles for the *San Francisco Chronicle* and keeping together her relationship with Lindsay's partner, Rich Conklin.

> **When your job is murder, you need friends you can count on**

YUKI CASTELLANO

One of the best lawyers in the city, she's desperate to make her mark. Ambitious, intelligent and passionate, she'll fight for what's right, always defending the underdog even if it means standing in the way of those she loves. Often this includes her husband – who is also Lindsay's boss – Lt. Jackson Brady.

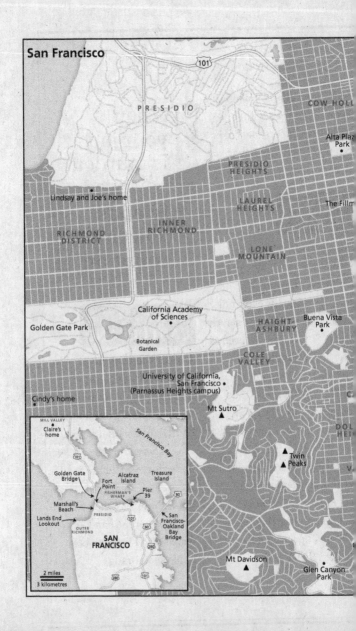

San Francisco

PRESIDIO

COW HOLL

101

Alta Plaz
Park

PRESIDIO
HEIGHTS

Lindsay and Joe's home

LAUREL
HEIGHTS

The Fillm

RICHMOND
DISTRICT

INNER
RICHMOND

LONE
MOUNTAIN

California Academy
of Sciences

Golden Gate Park

HAIGHT-
ASHBURY

Buena Vista
Park

Botanical
Garden

COLE
VALLEY

University of California,
San Francisco
(Parnassus Heights campus)

Cindy's home

Mt Sutro

DOL
HEI

MILL VALLEY

Claire's
home

San Francisco Bay

101

Golden Gate
Bridge

Fort
Point

Alcatraz
Island

Treasure
Island

FISHERMAN'S
WHARF

Pier
39

Marshall's
Beach

80

Lands End
Lookout

PRESIDIO

101

San
Francisco-
Oakland
Bay
Bridge

OUTER
RICHMOND

80

SAN
FRANCISCO

280

Mt Davidson

Glen Canyon
Park

Twin
Peaks

V

2 miles
3 kilometres

101

280

101

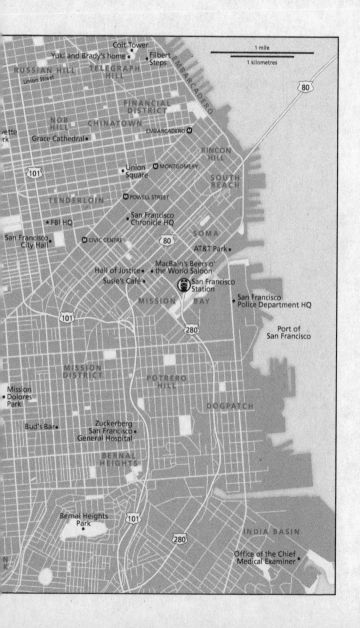

A list of more titles by James Patterson appears at the back of this book

JAMES PATTERSON
& MAXINE PAETRO

22
SECONDS

PENGUIN BOOKS

UK | USA | Canada | Ireland | Australia
India | New Zealand | South Africa

Penguin Books is part of the Penguin Random House group of companies
whose addresses can be found at global.penguinrandomhouse.com.

First published in the UK by Century in 2022
Published in Penguin Books 2022
001

Copyright © James Patterson 2022
Excerpt from *The Perfect Assassin* © James Patterson 2022

The moral right of the author has been asserted

Typeset by Jouve (UK), Milton Keynes
Printed and bound in Great Britain by Clays Ltd, Elcograf S.p.A.

The authorised representative in the EEA is Penguin Random House Ireland,
Morrison Chambers, 32 Nassau Street, Dublin D02 YH68

A CIP catalogue record for this book is available from the British Library

ISBN: 978–1–529–15869–4
ISBN: 978–1–529–15870–0 (export edition)

www.greenpenguin.co.uk

Penguin Random House is committed to a
sustainable future for our business, our readers
and our planet. This book is made from Forest
Stewardship Council® certified paper.

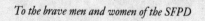

To the brave men and women of the SFPD

22
SECONDS

PROLOGUE

One

CINDY THOMAS WAS working at the dining table she'd bought at a tag sale down the block. It was cherrywood, round, with a hinged leaf and the letters *SN* etched near the hinge. She traced the initials with her finger, imagining that the person who'd left that mark was also a journalist suffering from writer's block—and Cindy was as blocked as a writer could be.

Her full-time job was as senior crime reporter at the *San Francisco Chronicle*. She'd been covering the violent murders of a killer unknown. And then, at the end of his crime spree, caught by the police, this unrepentant serial monster had asked her to write the story of his life. And that's what she was doing—trying to do—now. It would be easy for her agent to sell this idea for a true-crime thriller about Evan Burke. He was a savage and highly successful at getting away with his kills. According to him, he was the most prolific killer of the century, and Cindy didn't doubt him.

She had no shortage of quotable and illustrated research.

Because Burke wanted Cindy's book to secure his place in

criminal history, he had provided her with notebooks, as well as photos of his victims, alive and dead. He'd given her his maps to his victims' graves, which, when opened by homicide cops, had turned up bones, clothing, and other evidence of Burke's crimes. He'd been convicted of six murders, which in his mind was insufficient, but the prosecution was plenty happy.

Right now Burke was in solitary confinement at San Quentin State Prison, in the maximum-security wing. And at the same time, he was inside Cindy's head night and day. Thoughts of Burke's victims—what he'd done to those young women—never left her. She wasn't getting enough sleep and the writing she had done so far showed it.

Henry Tyler, Cindy's boss and mentor, and publisher of the *Chronicle*, had said to her, "This book is your big shot. Take it." And he'd given her two days off a week with pay so she could work on the book at home. Home was the small three-room apartment she shared with her fiancé, Rich Conklin, a homicide inspector who'd been a key member of the team that had captured Evan Burke.

Rich was giving her total support. He did the laundry. He read her pages for accuracy. He consoled her when the bloody murders made her cry. And since Cindy had commandeered the dining table for her book-in-progress, Rich had taken to eating his breakfast over the kitchen sink.

It was incredible to have Rich backing her up, but in a big way, he couldn't help her. It felt to Cindy as though her brain had jammed on the brakes—and it wasn't all about Evan Burke.

Outside, in real time, the city she loved had been divided by a restrictive new gun law that had sparked violence among the citizens of San Francisco. Lindsay Boxer, Cindy's closest friend and Richie's partner, had gotten burned while upholding this law.

Lindsay had recently been benched for an indeterminate time while an officer-involved shooting she'd been part of was investigated. There was no telling if the city would side with her and return her gun, badge, and police authority, or make her an example to help the mayor.

Cindy felt sick for Lindsay. And in trying to help her, she had only made things worse.

Two

CINDY CLOSED HER laptop and shoved it aside, making room on the table for her crossed arms. She put her head down, thinking again about her call to Lindsay last night. When Cindy had asked how she was feeling, Lindsay had lied, saying, "I'm fine. I'm not worried, so don't you worry, either."

But Cindy *was* worried that Lindsay was being made a target for upholding this new law, even though anyone in Lindsay's place would have taken the same shot.

Cindy had written about the incident in her crime blog, sure that support would pour in. That hadn't happened. So many crazed and furious readers had jammed her inbox that Henry Tyler had called her on her cell phone, sounding upset. Raising his voice, which he almost never did with her.

"You're looking for trouble," Tyler had said. "Stay out of this."

"What, Henry? It's no different than what I write every day."

He'd made himself perfectly clear. Her half-page blog post had thrown gas on the fire caused by the new gun laws in effect in San Francisco and other large cities across the country.

A national resistance movement was mobilizing.

They were calling themselves Defenders of the Second, and their motto was "We will not comply."

Tyler had ended his tirade, saying, "Full pay while you write your book, Cindy. It's a gift. Until it's done, you're off Crime and on the Weekend section. Now go. Write."

Cindy hadn't cried, but she'd wanted to. Henry was right. She'd missed the big picture and made the blog post personal.

Just then her phone rang again. She grabbed it from the dining room table and said, "Hello?"

A man's voice shouted into her ear, "My gun is my business. Read the Consti—"

Cindy clicked off. *How did the bastard get my cell phone number?*

She had to go out. Somewhere. She dressed quickly in jeans, a cardigan, running shoes, and Richie's leather flight jacket. She checked that the stove was off, fluffed her hair, and closed the curtains. Last, she stuffed her laptop into her backpack along with her police scanner and dropped her phone into her pocket.

Cindy headed out, walking east on Kirkham, squinting into the morning sunshine. At the end of the block, she turned north toward Golden Gate Park. There was a bakery called Sweets down the street, and she had an idea to bring fresh-brewed Sumatran coffee and cookies to Lindsay. Being together, commiserating, could cheer them both up.

Cindy texted for an Uber to pick her up at Sweets, on the corner of Twenty-Fourth Avenue and Irving Street, then drive her to Lake Street to see Lindsay. The bakery was in sight when a black sedan pulled up to the curb.

"Ms. Thomas?"

"Right. Give me a second, will you? I'll be quick."

The driver called out, "There's no parking here."

"Five seconds."

Cindy turned her back on the driver as he drove at walking speed behind her. He called her name again. She turned, impatient now, and was surprised to see three men, boys really, get out of the car.

"What's the matter? Look, forget it…," she said to the one who had been driving. The words were just out of her mouth when she saw a gun in the driver's hands. She looked into his eyes as he growled at her, "Get in the car, bitch. We need to talk to you about your friend Lindsay Boxer. This is on her."

Shocked by the threat, Cindy yelled loudly, "Get away from me."

She was reaching for her phone when a fist came at her and slammed into her face. There was a split second of sharp pain, but the lights were out, and Cindy went down.

PART ONE

NINE DAYS EARLIER

CHAPTER 1

A LIFELONG VETERAN of US intelligence agencies, Lindsay Boxer's husband, Joe Molinari, now worked from home as a high-level consultant in risk assessment, port security, and advanced cyber threats.

When Joe had a contract, the Molinaris were flush. At the moment, Lindsay's SFPD salary paid the rent.

Joe's phone rang at 7 a.m. as the morning sped toward its chaotic climax. The caller ID read *Steinmetz FBI*. Steinmetz was section chief of the FBI's SF field office and Joe's former direct report. Joe picked up the phone on the second ring.

As Lindsay called him from the other room and their precocious almost-four-year-old daughter charged into his home office crying because she didn't like her outfit, Joe heard Steinmetz's booming voice in his ear.

"Rise and shine, agent."

Jesus, he thought. He shushed Julie and said, "Craig. Everything okay? Can I get back to you in a half hour? I'm in the middle—"

"I need you today and tomorrow," said Steinmetz. "Could be for much longer."

Hesitating, Joe ran his hand through his hair. He was reluctant to pick up a potentially dangerous FBI case. And two days could turn into two months. But it wouldn't be good for business to say no to Steinmetz.

"I can meet you downtown by nine," he said.

As Joe dressed, Lindsay told Julie she looked fantastic, to just go with it, and dished her up a bowl of Cheerios. Joe made eggs while Lindsay toasted bread, and when the plates were clean, Lindsay emptied her mug of coffee into the sink and asked, "Did Steinmetz give you a clue?"

"Couple of days' work, maybe more."

Lindsay looked at her watch. Joe knew she had a meeting at eight. "Cool. We'd better get going."

Lindsay buttoned Julie into her coat. Joe leashed their aging border collie, Martha, and when the family was out on the street, Joe kissed his wife before she zoomed off in her blue Explorer. He and Julie walked Martha to the corner and back, and he still got the kiddo to the school bus in time.

Joe's car was across the street.

He switched off the alarm, started the engine, and headed downtown. Fifteen minutes later he found a parking spot on Golden Gate Avenue a block from the imposing government building that dominated the area. Joe checked his watch as he cleared the metal detector in the lobby. He was five minutes to the good.

He'd only just taken a seat in the reception area when Craig Steinmetz came through an interior doorway.

He said, "Molinari."

Joe walked over to Steinmetz and they shook hands.

"What's it been? Couple of months?" the chief said to Joe.

"Right, and yet still fresh in my mind."

14

It had been an abduction. Guns fired. An agent had been killed.

Steinmetz sighed. "I know, Joe. This is a different type of assignment, if you choose to accept it."

Joe followed Steinmetz to his office, which, despite the section chief's rank, was classic FBI decor. Two flags flanked the desk: the Stars and Stripes on one side, and on the other, the Department of Justice flag with its eagle on a shield over a field of blue. The President's photo hung on the wall opposite the desk. There was a corner bookshelf, four blue chairs, a two-seat sofa, and a coffee table. No knickknacks or personal pictures, just the absence of distraction.

Steinmetz went to his desk.

Joe took the chair across from Steinmetz, who asked, "You remember Mike Wallenger?"

"Sure. We were a team for a couple of years."

"He said to tell you to say yes."

Joe laughed. "That's Mike. Jump first, look on the way down. And still. He breaks no bones. Instincts of a panther."

"True, that," said Steinmetz. "You'll be working with and reporting to him."

"Doing what, exactly?"

"Character name of Alejandro Vega, specializes in gun trafficking and dealing fentanyl on the side. Just served five years for selling drugs on the streets of Guadalajara. He has a family there. *Federales* called to tell me that Vega is very likely coming to our little gun show today, and they could use our help. We want to grab him up and send him home."

Steinmetz pushed a couple of warrants across the desk. One was for search, the other was an arrest warrant.

He said, "Wallenger will fill you in on the details. Be safe."

CHAPTER 2

CHIEF OF POLICE Charles Clapper called the 8 a.m. meeting to order.

His fifth-floor office was packed with forty detectives and uniformed officers. An equal number were banked outside the open door to his waiting room, where they could hear his bulletin on the new gun law.

From where I stood with Rich Conklin, I could see Clapper, the tall, gray-haired man in his fifties, always impeccably dressed and groomed. This morning I saw a stain on his tie and anxiety in his eyes.

I'd known Clapper since I joined the SFPD, and for much of that time, he'd headed up our forensics lab. He was smart as hell, a good leader, and once upon a time, he'd had a sense of humor, which he was losing as he took on the weight of standing on the X where the buck stopped.

Clapper made no introductory remarks, just cut to the mayor's memo, issued early this morning. Once released, it had been read on the predawn news, printed in the papers, and dispatched over the electronic grapevine, where it made stops on handheld devices on the street, in kitchens, on public transportation, and in offices across the city and the country.

I understood why Clapper looked rattled.

California already had the strictest gun laws in the country, but now they'd been tightened further: bans on more semiautomatics, stricter gun registry and sales requirements. Automatic weapons were now illegal. So were suppressors and clips that held more than ten rounds, and all guns were required to have GPS so they could be tracked by law enforcement. The number of people who could request "gun violence restraining orders" had been expanded, and "ghost guns" were banned. Anyone arrested in possession of these now-illegal weapons could expect jail time.

Last night, in defiance of the new law, a throng of rowdies, both locals and out-of-towners, had gathered outside Oracle Park. They'd been armed with AKs and semiautomatics and had grown increasingly defiant, chanting "We will not comply" as their ranks swelled. Cops and the SFFD had dispersed them with warnings and a blue line.

"We'll be buying back weapons at eighteen publicized locations," Clapper said, tapping a clipboard. "This lists the fair prices we'll be offering in the form of grocery and big-box-store gift cards in exchange for weapons. And you'll learn where you can sign out a cruiser with the setup kit.

"I'm asking you all to sign the schedule to man the buy-back stations. This is a chance to make friends and reduce the number of weapons in the city. If you haven't heard, a police station in Ocala, Florida, was stormed and the protesters were arrested, sixty of them. They mugged for the cameras and promised payback if their guns were impounded. Which they were. Similar protests have gone on in Texas, Oklahoma, and Wisconsin."

It was still fresh news that cities around the country had put similar gun restriction laws into place, and protests were sparking up like wildfires.

Even police were divided on the issue.

Half the cops I knew were glad to get excessive firepower off the streets. It was also true that the other half agreed with the protesters, who took the new law as an attack on their rights under the Second Amendment.

Clapper said, "Anyone with issues about gun control, keep them to yourself. I expect you all to do your duty as law enforcement officers and to watch your backs. Questions?"

There were none. Clapper ended the meeting. His office and anteroom emptied. Along with my friends and colleagues in Homicide, I clattered down the fire stairs to our squad room.

Our new gun law had shut the door on military-style weapons. I sent up a silent prayer that the protesters wouldn't batter that door down.

CHAPTER 3

HOMICIDE LIEUTENANT JACKSON BRADY'S office was a one-hundred-square-foot glass enclosure wedged into the back corner of the squad room. He could see I-80 through his window and the entire bullpen through his walls, and I could see him clearly from my desk fifteen feet from his door.

Today, as nearly always, he wore his platinum-blond hair banded in a short pony, a denim shirt, blue tie, blue jacket, jeans. His intense blue eyes were focused on his desk while he spoke on the phone. He was in what I thought of as his "blue study."

The office—and the job of lieutenant—had once been mine, but I had stepped aside so that I could work homicides hands-on. For now, my friend and partner, Rich Conklin, was bringing a new member of our squad up to speed, and Brady had me working as his backup officer in charge.

This involved managing case files, assigning manpower, and, if Brady was otherwise involved, answering his phone. When he ended his call, I took five paces to his office, knocked for effect, and opened the door.

"Boxer?"

"We have to talk, Lieu."

"Not really. You've been sighing hard enough to blow down my walls for the last whatever."

"Hundred years," I said.

"A week," he said. "But that's you bein' a team play-uh."

Brady had come to the SFPD from Miami PD, bringing a touch of Southern drawl with him. I slumped into a side chair, put my gum-soled shoes up against the side of the desk.

"I want to work the gifts-for-guns program with Alvarez."

"She signed up?"

I sighed. "She will. You know Alvarez is a good team play-uh."

He gave me a look but had to smile.

"What's up, Boxer?"

"I need to get out of this place."

"Fine," said Brady. "Tell Conklin I need him to help me."

I left Brady's office before he could say, "Keep me in the loop."

Alvarez, recently of Vegas PD, Vice squad, was a gung-ho, good-looking thirtysomething, and she was all in. She leaned back in her chair, pumped her fist, and said, "Yesss."

I told Conklin he was temporarily assigned to my desk outside Brady's office, and he wasn't overjoyed. "Don't forget to write," he said.

It took an hour plus to gain possession of a van, learn the buy-back protocol, and drive to the Walmart parking lot in Daly City. I parked the van not far from the store's front doors, slid open our side panel, and set up a market tent and a card table on the asphalt. As ordered, Alvarez and I wore SFPD windbreakers over our Kevlar vests.

Alvarez checked out the camera inside the van with its view of the table, and I put out signs and a couple of folding chairs.

"I'll get coffee," she said.

Great idea.

I sat in a folding chair in the morning sunshine. Shoppers pushed their carts full of merchandise and some small kids to their cars. A woman of about seventy came toward the van, and when she got to the card table, she showed me a bunch of crumpled newspaper inside a plastic bag.

"I have something to sell," she said, handing me the bag.

I unwrapped her old S and W .22, showed her the price chart. She nodded and I gave her twenty-five dollars in a supermarket gift card.

"Thanks for the grocery money," she said.

Alvarez returned with black coffee and four packets of sugar for me, milky latte for herself.

We toasted with our coffee containers.

"To getting guns off the street," she said.

To which I added, "It's a good day to be a cop."

CHAPTER 4

MIKE WALLENGER WAS briefing Joe Molinari in the car. He wore a red cap inscribed *Defenders of the 2nd*, the name the gun-law protesters had adopted. His canvas jacket, jeans, steel-toed boots, and three-day-old beard completed the look. Like Joe, he had his gun in a hip holster under his jacket, and his badge was hooked to the opposite side of his waistband.

Joe's undercover guise was what he'd worn to meet Steinmetz. Khakis, striped sweater, one of the new, lighter Kevlar vests under a black-and-orange Giants windbreaker. Loafers. He was Everyman.

Wallenger took a card out of the console and passed it to Joe. It was a mug shot of a dark-haired man in his late thirties with a tattoo of a dragon on the right side of his neck.

"That's our subject, Alejandro Vega," Wallenger said. "He buys guns in Mexico, largely military surplus, and sells them in the US. He's been out of jail for a week."

Joe said, "So he served his time, went home for a conjugal visit and to restock?"

"So it seems. That's all I know except that he's our problem."

Joe said, "Okay. Tell me the plan."

"I've kept it simple," said Wallenger, negotiating the turn at Geneva Avenue. "When we get to the show, we'll locate Vega's booth. I'm your neighbor with gun knowledge, and you're looking to buy an automatic handgun for protection. Money's no object. You want the best. And if Vega doesn't offer what we like, you just keep asking what else he has.

"If he puts out an illegal weapon, I'll pull my piece and step in with a warrant. You put him on the floor and cuff him. I'll call our backup, and they'll confiscate his goods and search his vehicle."

"Mike. You asked for me. Why?"

"'Nobody does it better…,'" Wallenger sang.

"Oh, man. Please stop. I used to like that song."

"No joke. You don't look like a Fed."

"Yeah," said Joe. "Pasta. Homemade. I put on a few pounds."

"That's a good thing. Vega will not be able to pass up this gun show. And we look like customers. He won't make us."

"I'm glad for the opportunity, Mike."

Wallenger grinned and said, "The pleasure is mine."

He parked the unmarked blue Honda sedan in the huge lot off of Geneva Avenue outside the Cow Palace, the convention center where the much-anticipated gun show was being held. The lot was three-quarters full and the doors had only opened in the last hour.

Joe got out of the car and zipped up his Giants windbreaker.

Wallenger said, "You go in first."

While his partner checked in with the backup teams, Joe went through the revolving doors to the convention center. He showed his badge and gun to security, then cleared the magnetometer.

Joe took in the vast dimensions of the place, the volume of the innumerable would-be gun shoppers milling among the hundreds of sellers' tables and, incidentally, blocking his view. He narrowed his focus, scanning table by table, hoping his gaze would fall on the man with the dragon tattoo.

But Vega was a needle in a haystack of needles.

It was Wallenger who spotted him.

CHAPTER 5

ALEJANDRO VEGA'S TABLE was at the end of a middle row, equidistant from the front and rear exit doors.

Mike Wallenger nodded to Joe, a signal to move in. Joe put his hands in his pockets and drifted to the edge of the crowd of about a half dozen men who were browsing Vega's table of long guns and military weaponry. With Wallenger at his back, Joe stared down at the display laid out on green felt. It all looked legal. Vega sensed that he had a buyer and looked up.

Joe said, "Hey there. I'm looking for a handgun, fully automatic, with the best suppressor you have."

A bearded man wearing a hunting jacket over plaid flannel, standing at the table to Joe's left, said, "Wait your turn, huh?"

But Vega said, "Hang on."

He reached under his table, seemed to dig around without looking, and pulled out a Glock handgun. Joe saw solder seams. The gun had been worked on, upgraded from a semiauto to a full auto.

Vega screwed a suppressor onto the muzzle and said, "Isn't this sweet? It's my own piece, but I might be ready to let it go."

"That's just the one," said Joe with a touch of awe in his voice.

He was leaning forward to get a better look and felt his windbreaker rise over the badge on his hip, where it caught the eye of the bearded guy in the hunting jacket standing next to him.

"Al," the hunter shouted over the rumble of the crowd. He pointed at Joe. "He's a Fed."

Vega didn't hesitate. He already had the Glock in his hand, and he aimed it at Joe, saying, "Don't think about it. Don't even think about taking me in."

Joe said, "Hey, hey. Calm down. I'm off duty. Just looking for a personal piece."

He surreptitiously dropped his hand to his holster, but Vega had the advantage. Joe thought fast, running through his options: what could he say to Vega to get him to drop the Glock? He thought about grabbing the gun, wrenching it out of Vega's hand. And he also thought that if a bullet was discharged, he could be shot. Security could fire on the sound of a gunshot. He could easily imagine wounded bystanders.... That could set off a bloodbath.

Joe said, "No one is going to hurt you. Just put the gun down on the table."

Vega was still aiming at Joe's head, eyes darting to the front doors, back to Joe, to the hunter next to him, maybe seeing him as a potential hostage.

"I'm not going back in," Vega said.

Wallenger stepped in at Joe's left, shoving the hunter out of his way. He faced Vega over the table, his gun locked, loaded, and pointed at the gun dealer. With his left hand, he flipped up the edge of his pullover so Vega could see the badge.

"Put the gun down, Mr. Vega. Hands up. No one wants to hurt you."

Joe kept his eye on Vega's automatic Glock, which might be loaded, but was momentarily distracted by movement out of the corner of his eye: a man in black striding up the aisle on his right, yelling into the rumble of the crowd, "Drop the gun!"

Joe turned toward the voice, but before he could say, "FBI," the man in black, reasonably picturing a crime in progress, raised his weapon. Joe took instinctive action, tackling Wallenger to get him out of the line of fire. Wallenger fell, taking down Vega, with a couple hundred pounds of Joe on top of the pile. The table collapsed under them, sending all three crashing to the floor. The table and the scattered array of guns fell all around them.

Leaving Vega to Wallenger, Joe quickly rolled into a sitting position, now with his gun in his hand. The man in black held a badge in his left hand, but it was unreadable from where Joe sat. Keeping his gun at his side, Joe shouted "We're FBI!" at the precise moment that the man in black fired. Joe felt the blow to his chest, then another in his midsection.

The shooter yelled, "Everyone stay where you are!"

Joe heard an unintelligible voice booming over a megaphone. His thoughts were scrambled. He didn't know if he was alive or dead.

CHAPTER 6

JOE COULDN'T SEE. He fought to understand the last six seconds, to assess the pain in his chest.

He opened his eyes. He was on the floor, sagging against what could be a large canvas sack. From this viewpoint he saw Wallenger cuffing Vega and a scuffle of security men in black busting up the crowd.

Wallenger yelled to Joe across the crumpled table.

"Joe. Are you hit? Joe? Hang in there for me, buddy. Medics are on the way."

The shooter was a man Joe recognized as Fred Braun, SF division of ATF. He was in his fifties, medium height and weight, muscular, eyes close together, giving him the sharp, focused look of a predator. Wallenger stood up and Braun spat, "This is an ATF bust, you idiot."

"Give me a break, Braun," Wallenger shouted. "Vega is ours."

Braun said, "You know what the *F* in ATF stands for?"

"He crossed the border and state lines with weapons," Wallenger said. "You know FBI's charter?"

Joe put the turf war out of his mind. He wasn't sure if the bullets had penetrated his gear, but he didn't feel blood running down his body. He thought he could stand up. He also thought that he could be having a heart attack.

A young FBI agent, Charles Schaming, came over to Joe, felt for a pulse, and asked him questions, made him follow his finger with his eyes.

Joe said, "Help me up."

Schaming said, "Just lie still, will you, Agent?"

"Help me up, damn it."

"You know moving could kill you," Schaming said.

"I'll kill you if you don't...."

Schaming put his hands under Joe's armpits and hefted him into an upright sitting position. He unzipped Joe's windbreaker and extracted a flattened bullet from the front of the vest. He showed it to Joe. It had only penetrated the windbreaker, but Joe knew that the bullet's punch alone could stop a heart.

"That's good," Joe said. "Help me get this thing off."

"Lean forward, okay?"

Joe thought he'd faint as he did as Schaming told him to do. The second bullet fell onto the floor.

Schaming picked it up and handed it to Joe. "A good luck piece," he said. "A pair of them. Joe. Joe, how ya doing?"

Sirens whooped in the near distance, adding high notes to the echoing din inside the cavernous hall. Vega was constrained, on his feet, with two FBI agents roughly escorting him out to a car in the lot. ATF secured the rest of the scene.

Braun was on his phone as EMTs examined Joe, asked his name, birth date, address.

"How do you feel?" Wallenger asked.

"I'm good. If you all unhand me, I think I can do a forty-yard dash."

Wallenger asked the paramedic if Molinari was good to go.

The paramedic said, "He refused. I can't make him get into the ambulance."

"Lean on me, pardner," Wallenger said, putting an arm around Joe's waist.

Joe struggled to match Wallenger's pace as the two agents joined the flow of people crowding through the exit doors. Outside on the pavement, Wallenger said, "We're right over there."

Following Wallenger's finger, Joe saw the unmarked blue sedan that had been their ride to the Cow Palace only forty-five minutes ago.

As if from another dimension, he heard Wallenger say, "You took those bullets for me, you lunatic. I think you own me now. And by the way, thank you."

"Welcome, dear."

Joe stumbled toward the car, reached for the passenger-side door handle. Wallenger was saying they should make a stop at the emergency room—when Joe passed right the fuck out on the asphalt.

CHAPTER 7

DR. ROB LIU, the attending physician in Metro's emergency room that day, had examined Joe. Peering at the large bruise spreading across Joe's torso, he'd spoken one word. "Impressive."

"Bullets just bounce off me," Joe had said.

"I'm going to give you a CAT scan, then we'll talk again."

Three hours later Joe's chest was taped and there was a small, shrink-wrapped sample pack of painkillers in his pocket.

Wallenger was waiting in the hospital lobby. He'd ditched the *Defenders of the 2nd* cap and was wearing a jacket marked *FBI*. He told Joe that they'd been slow-walking Vega so that Joe could interview him. That the gun dealer was mute, in custody and chilling in holding.

He added, "You look worse than Vega."

"Then let's work him over so I can go home to bed."

"Your ribs. Any breaks?"

"Mostly just a bloody bruise the shape of the lower forty-eight."

Wallenger strapped Joe into the passenger seat.

When the seat belt tightened across his chest, Joe said, "Watch it."

"Sorry, Molinari. Seat belts are the law."

Wallenger started up the car, and as he drove away from the hospital, he brought Joe up to the minute.

"Steinmetz checked in with the federal cops in Mexico to arrange transfer of our prisoner. He got first licks on Vega for a couple of hours, but all Vega said was, 'Lawyer.'"

They got stuck in traffic heading toward I-80 and the Bay Bridge, but by four fifteen Butch and Sundance—as they'd been called when they were partners—were back in the FBI building at 450 Golden Gate Avenue. Steinmetz took Joe to the observation room with its mirrored window offering a wide view of the interrogation room. Vega was alone, cuffed to a metal loop in the center of the table, humming a tune.

Steinmetz said to Joe, "All we have on him is that automatic Glock, but once we turn him over to the *federales,* he's not our problem. See what you and Wallenger can get out of him. Maybe he's sitting on a stash somewhere."

Wallenger held the door for Joe, and the two agents took seats across from the prisoner. Wallenger took the lead in the interrogation, giving Joe a chance to observe.

Vega said, "I have a dual citizenship, you know. My mom is *Americana.* I demand an attorney."

"Where's your passport?"

Vega looked at his hands.

"You're not a citizen," said Wallenger. "You're a tourist. How about taking the pressure off yourself? Instead of making up shit, tell us what we want to know."

"Right," said Vega. "And you won't deport me?"

"We'll put in a good word with the cops across the border."

Vega stopped playing, saying only, "Lawyer, lawyer, lawyer."

Wallenger pushed away from the table and said he'd be back in a moment with extradition papers. When the door closed, Joe moved his chair closer to Vega and asked questions using the tried-and-true method of interrogation: empathize, make the subject your friend, offer a way out.

He said, "Alejandro, you can call me Joe. I know today has been brutal, so let's work out a deal you can live with. You tell us what we need to know, and I'll be your spokesman to the *federales*."

Just then Steinmetz entered the room, saying, "You're our guest for the night, Vega. Tomorrow we're taking you home."

"My home?"

"Jail. Should feel like home."

Steinmetz left the room and two security guards entered to take Vega to his cell. The captive turned his eyes to Joe, saying, "Joe? I need a minute with you. I've got something you want to know."

CHAPTER 8

I WAS HUNGRY and rain soaked when I came through the front door to our apartment, calling out, "Mommy's home." Joe was lying on his back on the bare floor with our geriatric border collie, Martha, curled up next to him, twitching inside a dream. Julie was in Daddy's recliner watching a documentary about pelicans. She scrambled off the chair, ran to me, and grabbed me around the hips. Martha woofed and struggled to her feet, while Julie was saying, "We walked her, Mom. Before it rained."

"Good job. Why is Dad on the floor?"

"He got into a fight."

Joe said to Julie, "What a blabbermouth. Blabbbbbbermouth."

Julie went back to Joe and squatted next to him, saying, "Blabbbbbermouth. You're the blabbbbbermouth."

She giggled as her father rolled onto his side to look into her eyes. "You cannot keep a secret," he said to our little girl.

She laughed out loud. "You can't, too!"

"Got me. Now. Will someone help me up?"

I walked over and gave Joe a hand. I'm strong, but he's big:

six one, muscular, still built like the college linebacker he once was. I wasn't sure I could manage it, but with some awkward arm pulling and legwork, I got him to his feet. He held on to me. We hugged and kissed. Julie had latched on to the word *blabbbbermouth* and was telling it to Martha, who licked her face.

I asked Joe, "How bad is it?"

"Not bad at all. I'll tell you later. Why don't you change, and I'll order pizza?"

Joe called Pronto Pizza, and Julie returned to the chair. By the time I'd had a hot shower and put on dry clothes, the pelicans had landed and dinner was on the table. Joe had changed his mind about the pizza, and instead we dug into the linguine with pesto sauce. Between bites, Julie told us about her day at school with a dramatic rendition of an *Alice in Wonderland* moment.

"So then the queen says, 'Off with their heads.'"

She radiated pure glee as we laughed along with our Julie Bug.

And then the conversation slowed. My day had been satisfying but not dramatic. Joe wasn't talking except to say, "I could use a glass of wine."

"Coming up."

I cleaned up the table and poured two glasses of Chardonnay as Joe put Julie to bed. He was walking like the Tin Man when he came out of her room and saw me waiting for him on the big old couch. He sat down hard next to me and kicked off his shoes. I made room for him to lie down and fit myself in beside him.

I asked, "What kind of fight?"

"It was nothing," he said. "Turf war with ATF at the gun show."

I ran my hand down his chest and instantly felt the bandage wrapping his midsection.

"Oh, my God. This is nothing, Joe?"

"Hon, can you hand me that glass?"

I reached over to the coffee table, put the glass in his hand. I helped him sit and he drank half the wine down.

"Now start talking," I said. "Or I'm booking you."

He grinned and got comfortable again. "What's the charge?"

"Telling your child but not your wife. That's conspiracy."

"Guilty as charged. Unbutton my shirt," he said.

I did it, getting the full view of a mile of compression bandage around his entire torso. He told me again that it was about the territorial dispute with the head of the local ATF. After I'd wheedled and mocked him, Joe got real. He told me how he'd charged a bad guy with a gun. That there'd been a pileup with fighting. I knew that he was telling me a cleaned-up version of the takedown at the Cow Palace, but I wasn't finished with him. Interrogations are in my wheelhouse.

"This is your only chance to get in front of this," I said in my best interview voice. "Talk now and I can help you. If not..."

"I got shot," he said.

"What?"

"Two 9-millimeter rounds to center mass. Saved by my vest."

After he detailed his block and tackle across the display table and an armed ATF captain firing on him, I understood almost too much.

I said, "You could have gotten shot in the head."

"True. But it wasn't my day to die."

I snuggled up against my dear husband's side, and he very gently drew me closer. I listened to his heart. And I flashed on a time not long ago when he'd had his head split open by an explosion, and so the horror of almost losing him was clear in my mind. Tears came and slid down my cheeks.

"I don't want to lose you, Joe."

"I know. I know, honey. And I'm fine. I wasn't sure for a while. I felt the hits. I blacked out a few times from the pain or the shock. But I've been checked out at Metro. All that's left of the firefight at the OK Corral is a bruise. And an unresolved beef with an ATF captain named Fred Braun."

"Keep going," I said. "What happened after leaving the hospital?"

Joe paused a couple of beats and told me about the interrogation at the FBI office of a Mexican gun dealer, Alejandro Vega.

"This guy...," he said. There was another long pause, and I was about to jump into it when Joe said, "Alejandro Vega is a different kind of cat. What he told me is more than worth the bruising."

CHAPTER 9

OUR BEDROOM IS in the corner of the apartment, with windows on two sides. One of the things I love about this room is the way the two-way, nighttime traffic on Lake Street paints moving streaks of light on the ceiling.

Joe and I were lying close together under the blankets, both of us watching the light show above us, when Joe began to tell me about the interview with Alejandro Vega. I could picture Joe in a small interrogation room, showing his honest face to Vega and Vega trusting him.

Joe said, "Vega wasn't talking. When Wallenger left the room, guards came in and Vega decided I was the cop of last resort. I told him that I had pull with the director, spread a little jam on top, and he bought it. I expected him to lead me to a weapons cache, but no. He told me that he's part of a cartel of street hustlers banding together to run military-grade weapons and high-end drugs from Mexico to California."

"To fill the gap caused by the new gun law?" I said.

"No doubt. But more to the point, Vega's worried that it's known that the FBI has him and he's going to be executed in prison. That his wife and kids in Guadalajara are going to get it, too."

I said, "A very savage warning to others, I'm guessing."

Joe said, "Wouldn't be the first time. According to Vega, snitches pay the price. I told him I'd do my best to get his wife and kids to safety."

"Joe. You're an independent contractor."

He got quiet. When I couldn't stand the silence anymore, I said, "You're thinking about Vega's family."

"No, something else. Remember a couple of years ago when we had drinks at MacBain's with a cop name of Brian Donahue?"

"Brian. Sure. I haven't seen him since he left the force."

"I hate to tell you, Linds. He committed suicide yesterday."

"Whoa. Donahue killed himself? How do you know?"

"Wallenger. He heard that Donahue was found dead in his car. He looked into it, and in his view it was an execution made to look like a suicide."

Could this be true? Had Donahue been involved with a Mexican cartel? I pictured him. He'd been nondescript, average height and weight, about forty-five when I knew him.

Joe said, "He seemed like a good cop and a decent guy. He was putting a couple of kids through college."

"Right," I said. "I never picked him out as dirty. Or suicidal, for that matter."

Joe said, "Wallenger and I are taking Vega to Mexico City tomorrow. Turn him over to the authorities. I'll do what I can for him."

I squeezed Joe's hand and said, "I think Steinmetz got his money's worth, Joe. You're injured. What if you beg off the road trip?"

"Ahh, not if I want another assignment. Besides, I promised Vega."

"I don't like it, Joe."

He said, "I think half a chill pill will help me sleep."

"Close your eyes," I said. "All's well here."

And it was. But Joe was determined to fly Vega to Mexico. I wouldn't feel comfortable until he was safely home.

CHAPTER 10

JOE ROLLED ONTO his side so he could watch Lindsay sleeping. She was breathing softly, her blond hair fanned out over the pillow, clutching a fold of blanket with one hand. He resisted the urge to wake her and tell her that he loved her so much. How lucky he felt that she loved him, too. Grateful that they had married, had Julie, and settled into this life together.

Only hours ago Lindsay had said that he could have taken a bullet to the head. That was true and it was not the first time. Joe had served his country since leaving college and joining the FBI decades ago. He'd never been a thrill seeker. He'd been a justice seeker. He'd taken the job today for the money.

Was that worth it?

It was a long, dark night of the soul for Joe. And an unexpected one.

At dawn he got up quietly and drove to the airport. Mike Wallenger was waiting for him at the Aeromexico hangar, where a small jet would be taking the two of them and their prisoner to Mexico City. Vega stood by the silver plane, handcuffed and shackled, looking lost.

Wallenger said to Joe, "Steinmetz okayed your suggestion."

Joe said, "Good. Thanks, Mike."

All three men boarded the plane and four and a half hours later arrived at Mexico City International.

As they disembarked, Vega, still handcuffed, said to Joe, "In my pocket."

Joe pulled an envelope from Vega's jailbird uniform pocket. The envelope was open and he looked at the contents: a folded letter addressed to "Ana, my beloved wife," along with several thousand dollars in hundred-dollar bills.

He put the envelope into his own pocket as a police van pulled up alongside them. Introductions were made, and the prisoner was turned over to the Mexican authorities. Vega looked over his shoulder at Joe once more, then was folded into the van.

Wallenger said to Joe, "Ready, pardner?"

"Ready as I can be."

"We should be back here at around six."

Molinari and Wallenger got back into the plane and were flown to the Guadalajara airport, where a car waited for them. The driver handed Joe the car keys, and Wallenger typed the address into the antiquated GPS. He enlarged the map, and the two agents studied the graphic road view of Cocula, over an hour's drive from Guadalajara. US government employees weren't permitted to go there, by order of the State Department. And that's where Ana Vega lived with her five kids.

Skirting the city center, Joe drove south on Highway 80. As the landscape became less populated, undeveloped, Joe rationalized that carrying Vega's mail would give them an opening to question Ana Vega about her husband's associates. It might be their only way in.

An hour and a half later, when they were only a mile from their destination, Joe woke Wallenger, who'd fallen asleep in the passenger seat.

"Wake up and smell the tacos," he said.

The road narrowed as they entered the small village. The main thoroughfare was twelve feet wide, banked with two-story buildings in vivid colors of ocher, cinnamon, azure, and green. There were a couple of taquerias and a *mercado* in between the homes. They were a hundred yards from the Vega address when an armored vehicle pulled out in front of them, stopping them cold in the middle of the street.

Wallenger looked behind them.

Another vehicle rolled into the road, this one an old American junker. Maybe a Buick. Two paramilitary types got out. One tossed something back into the junker's open window. With a loud bang and a whoosh, the car went up in flames, and the good guys were blocked from any possibility of retreat.

Joe said, "What the hell is this?"

Wallenger said, "We're armed, Joe."

"What are you thinking?"

"It's the real deal. A Mexican standoff."

CHAPTER **11**

TWO MORE MEN in fatigues and black boots, with ammo belts across their chests and automatic rifles in their hands, got out of the armored SUV in front of Joe and Wallenger. The one coming to Joe's side of the car was five eight, 100 percent muscle, and 10 percent beard. The other man rounded the car to where Wallenger sat on the passenger side. He was six foot, wearing shades and unreadable neck ink. He looked as strong as his partner and was armed the same way. The two who had driven the burning car stood behind the tail fenders with AKs in their arms. Powerful weapons, lethal grade.

Joe had locked the doors and windows, but none of the men in paramilitary gear tried to open them. Instead they aimed their weapons at the windshield, the tall one shouting in accented English, "You two. Out of the car."

Joe held up his badge and shouted, "FBI. USA."

The bulked-up gangster standing next to his window shouted, "Get out. Or I shoot."

Mike said to Joe, "I say where we go next time, Butch."

Joe said, "Don't rub it in, Sundance."

"You'll like it when you hear it."

"Don't talk, Mike. Think."

"I think we should shoot to kill."

"Okay," Joe said. "Except no shooting."

Wallenger raised his hands and showed them to the men in fatigues, and Joe did the same. These men, who were likely Vega's associates, opened the doors, pulled them out, and threw them against the vehicle. They were frisked, relieved of their weapons, and marched toward the armored vehicle parked in front of them. Joe thought about how people disappeared in Mexico all the time. Populations of entire villages were massacred. The two men in a car could be shot and their bodies would never be found.

Wallenger muttered, "Next time we go to the Bahamas. Thought you'd like to know."

Joe sighed. "Are these men working under any authority? Or are they a gang? Vega's gang."

Mike shrugged. The tall one said, "Shut up."

The flaming car exploded as the tall man forced Mike and Joe into the back seat of the armored car. The squat soldier got into the passenger side, turned to see Mike and Joe. Using the seat back as a gun rest, he kept watch on his captives. The two men from the burning follow car got in on either side of their prisoners. The tall one started the vehicle. The engine roared, and the armored car bumped over the rutted road, past the faded, festively painted houses and a small street market, and into an empty field of rocks and clay fronting a disintegrating building at the rear.

The driver stopped the car.

Mike and Joe were jerked out of the vehicle, thrown to the ground, and handcuffed. Joe was hurting bad and out of ideas.

But Wallenger assumed his authority as a federal agent. Knowing their abductors spoke enough English to understand him, he said, "Uncuff us. Our car will be found in minutes. Federal police will arrest you, and you don't want to be discovered holding two abducted FBI agents, cuffed and disarmed. So be quick. What do you want?"

The taller man stood over Wallenger and barked questions that amounted to *What are you doing here? This is restricted territory. Say something smart and you live. Lie and you die.*

"We're seeing the city," said Joe. "We're killing time. Our plane takes us back to San Francisco, and if we aren't at the airport in Mexico City by six—"

The tall man interrupted Joe.

"What do you want with Vega?"

"He's been charged with holding illegal guns. Nothing to do with us. Nothing at all."

"What is this?" The tall soldier held out the envelope with the letter and the cash inside for Ana Vega that he'd taken from Joe when he frisked him.

"I'm doing Vega a favor," said Joe. "Do you understand? He asked me to give it to his wife."

"Where is Vega?"

"In prison," Joe said. "Somewhere in California."

The tall man unsheathed a knife and put the blade against Joe's throat.

"Tell the truth."

Joe said, "That is the truth."

"Where is Vega?"

"I was never told."

One of the men who'd been in the follow car had a radio in his hand. He called out to the tall man with the knife. It sounded to Joe like, "Let's go."

And what would happen to them?

The tall man withdrew the knife, nicking Joe's neck with the blade. He nodded to his partner, and the two of them hauled Joe and Wallenger to their feet and shoved them back into their armored car.

Joe yelled out "Jesus" as he fell against Wallenger, but he wasn't complaining. He hadn't given Vega away. He hoped the gangsters were returning him and Wallenger to their car.

Wallenger said, "They don't want to kill FBI."

Joe clapped his hand over the knife wound to stanch the blood flow and said, "Hope you're right."

If so, there was a fifty-fifty chance he'd sleep in his own bed tonight.

CHAPTER 12

DR. CLAIRE WASHBURN, San Francisco's chief medical examiner, has been my best friend since we were rookies. Since then we have worked on hundreds of cases together, shared secrets, and become godmothers to each other's little girls. I saw her Beemer parked on Harriet Street under the overpass, and I parked next to it.

The entrance to the medical examiner's office is accessible from the breezeway that runs from the back door of the Hall of Justice. I set my car alarm, strode through the covered walkway, and moments later pulled opened the ME office's heavy glass door.

The receptionist hadn't yet arrived, but several late-shift cops were sitting in the row of chairs at the edge of the waiting room, wanting death certificates and releases for bodies stored in the morgue. I didn't see anyone I knew, so I reached under the reception desk and buzzed myself in. I found Claire in the autopsy suite, gowned, capped, and gloved in blue as she did a postmortem on a white female on her table. Bunny Ellis assisted her.

Claire looked up and said, "Lindsay. Was I expecting you?"

"Are you free for lunch?"

"Dinner would be better."

"Okay. One more thing," I said. "Did you do the post on Brian Donahue?"

"I did."

"I've got some questions," I said.

"I'll call you in, say, an hour."

"Great. Susie's at six? All of us," I said.

Claire blew me a kiss and I showed myself out. An elevator in the marble-lined lobby was open, and I took it to the fourth floor, walked down the spur of corridor to the Homicide squad room, and went through the gate. Our squad assistant, Brenda Fregosi, wasn't at her desk, but about half of the day shift had punched in.

Brady's office was dark. Conklin and Alvarez had turned on their lamps and computers but weren't at their desks. I knew where I'd find them. I heard their voices coming from the break room. I stepped in, wished the team a good morning, and helped myself to a freshly brewed mug of coffee.

The three of us sat down at the table for four, and Conklin opened a tin of peanut butter–chocolate chip cookies. Sergeant Cappy McNeil liked to bake. I plucked a small cookie out of the tin and looked at Conklin.

"Rich, remember when we were working the murder of an elderly woman at the Wharf? Carolee something. Williams. And those investigators from Central, Donahue and his partner—"

"Diller," said Rich. "Yeah. Diller thought he was too good to deal with us. What a jerk."

"Did you have a take on Donahue?"

"He didn't say much. He got on his cell phone. Turned his back on all of us."

"That's right. I didn't think much of it at the time."

"I asked about him," said Conklin. "He was hooked on opioids. And then he was off the Job."

"That fits. I just found out that Donahue is dead."

Alvarez asked, "What happened?"

I told my two partners the little I knew: that Donahue had turned up dead in his car a couple of days ago, an apparent suicide.

"I've got a question," said Alvarez. "Central isn't going to investigate?"

Rich said, "They're permanently short-staffed in Homicide. They work cases that happen in their district at night. We get their day cases. More work, more control."

He turned back to me. "So, Lindsay, you're saying there's some question about Donahue being a suicide?"

"Claire will have to call it on the evidence. No sign of violence, no forensics, just a dead former cop who'd OD'd. But I want to check it out," I said. "Maybe I can talk Brady into letting us find out what really happened in Donahue's car."

"I want in," said Alvarez.

"For a total of three," said Conklin.

We high-fived across the table.

Now I only had to convince Brady to make it a go.

CHAPTER 13

YUKI CASTELLANO MET me at the All-Day lot across from the Hall. She climbed up into the passenger seat of my Explorer and we were off to Susie's Café.

An ADA in District Attorney Len Parisi's office, Yuki had just won a difficult case, the jury having come back with a guilty verdict in two hours. My friend was in an excellent mood and had one wish—that her husband, Lieutenant Brady, would take her dancing.

She adjusted her seat belt so that it wouldn't crease her blouse and said, "I thought Brady would have more time for a life once Clapper became chief, but he's still wrung out when he gets home."

"Yeah, he's drowning in an endless paperwork hell," I said. "Plus putting out a dozen fires a day. And now armed militias are gathering in the streets."

Yuki sighed, "He says about four words when he gets home."

"That sucks, Yuki."

I parked on Jackson and we walked two blocks to Susie's.

Opening the front door, we were met with the aromas of good Caribbean-style cooking with a soul-food accent, the din of chatter spiked with laughter, and the plinking of the steel drums.

This place was an instant mood changer.

I waved to Fireman, the bartender, and called out to a few of the regular barflies, then Yuki and I danced our way through the center of our favorite restaurant to cheers and applause. We waved and took our bows, then followed the narrow corridor past the kitchen's pickup window and into the smaller, quieter back room. Luckily for us, our booth near a window was available.

Our waitress, Lorraine O'Day, came over to the table. She's a witty, red-haired woman of about fifty who knows what we like to eat and drink and is well aware that Yuki is an easy drunk, especially if margaritas are in the offing.

"What are we drinking?" she asked.

"Beer all around," Yuki said. "No margaritas midweek."

"Gotcha," Lorraine said. "And I'm bringing you a bonus round of corn chips for the win."

"Mahhhvelous," said Yuki.

I texted Cindy, who texted back, saying she was on her way.

When I looked up, Claire was coming through the passageway. When she reached us, she threw open her arms and hugged Yuki and slid into the booth next to me and squeezed my hand.

Lorraine brought a frosty pitcher of beer with the chips, and then she and Claire had a side chat about the availability of key lime pie. Claire reserved four slices for the table as Cindy slipped into the booth next to Yuki.

"God, I'm hungry. Has everyone ordered?" she asked.

Lorraine brought over the menus and said to Cindy, "Your

timing is perfect, Girl Reporter. Whatever you want, as long as we have it in the kitchen."

"I was thinking I'd go vegan for a while."

"For a story?" I asked.

"For the ten extra pounds around my waist."

"Easy as pie," said Lorraine. "Rice, beans, and greens okay?"

We ordered, munched chips, and during a pause I told my friends what Joe had told me about Sergeant Brian Donahue's suicide. "Correction," I said. "Apparent suicide."

Neither Yuki nor Cindy had heard about it.

Claire said, "As I told Lindsay, I was skeptical about Donahue having committed suicide because his drug overdose was—well, it was miles beyond overkill. Still. That doesn't rule out suicide, but there was no sign of homicide. None."

Cindy jumped in, saying, "I only met him twice, but he looked right past me. Usually a cop will take an opportunity to say, 'I can't comment on an ongoing case and please spell my name right,' but with Donahue, the lights were on, but he wasn't home."

Yuki laughed into her beer, giving Claire the giggles.

I clinked my mug with a fork and said, "More about Donahue, please, Doctor."

Claire cleared her throat and said, "So Donahue practically choked on fentanyl. I've never seen anything like it. Many illegal recreational drugs are cut with fentanyl. That's why we see boatloads of accidental fentanyl ODs. See, it only takes three micrograms of fentanyl to flat-out kill a person."

She touched her finger to a crumb of corn chip on the table and held it up so we could see it. The crumb was minuscule.

Claire said, "This is three micrograms. There was a teaspoon of fentanyl inside Donahue's airways. Half that amount could have killed a herd of elephants. Donahue was streetwise. He had to have known that. So did he take it himself? If not, what happened? There was no indication—"

Yuki asked, "So there was an investigation?"

Claire said, "Yep. The evidence was conclusive enough. No prints, no bruising, nor signs of violence. All indications pointed to suicide. Case closed."

I said, "I asked about Donahue because he may have been involved in something Joe is looking into."

Cindy, paying sharp attention and barely drinking, said, "Keep going, Linds. More on that."

I hesitated, then, within the beery bubble of our clubiness, I spilled the beans.

CHAPTER 14

THREE PAIRS OF unblinking eyes confirmed that it was too late for me to stop now.

I said to the girls, "Joe had heard about Donahue's death and thought he might have been involved in running guns, dealing drugs, possibly connected with a new grassroots Mexican cartel. By the way, that's off the record, Cindy."

"Notes for future reference okay?"

I nodded.

Excusing herself for reaching, Cindy leaned across Yuki and plugged her laptop into the wall socket. She cleared a spot on the table, pushing condiments and her plate to the center, and began to type, her brow furrowed under a tangle of blond curls kept in check by a rhinestone headband. Light conversation went on around her. Lorraine cleared our dinner plates and brought tea and the key lime pie. Yuki showed us a picture of herself having lunch with the mayor, and I followed up with a few words about how worried I was by Joe taking an assignment from the FBI.

About then Claire put down her fork and said, "I have some

news. A little girl from Rosewater Township has been missing since Monday. Katie Caruso. Just turned six. According to the police, there's no explanation for how or why Katie disappeared from her bed in the middle of the night."

We were all right there with Claire. Even Cindy.

Claire went on. "The parents can't explain it and are mad with grief. The police did a thorough investigation, looked everywhere, talked to everyone, and then this morning a long-distance truck driver finds Katie's body in a ditch five miles from her home."

"Oh, no," I said.

Claire said, "Rosewater's medical examiner, Andrea Savino, wants some help with the autopsy. I went to school with her auntie Sam, so she asked me to lend a hand. I'm flying out there first thing tomorrow."

"I heard about that little girl. Terrible story," said Cindy. Then she went back to her laptop. She didn't notice Lorraine asking her if she wanted her tea heated up or if something was wrong with the pie.

"Cin," I said. "Where are you?"

"I'm on a website for crime junkies," she said.

"Find something?" I asked her.

"Nothing on Donahue, but there's mention of another former cop found dead, in Oakland vicinity," she said.

I said, "Another cop?"

"Well, see for yourself."

She turned the laptop to face us.

We saw a photo of a thirtysomething male dressed in work clothes lying near a Ford pickup.

"What are we looking at?" I asked.

Cindy enlarged the picture on her screen.

56

"Can you zoom in on his mouth?" I said.

She said, "Wow. Good catch, Lindsay. Looks like his lips were stapled together."

"Oh, my God," said Yuki. "Is there some text with that?"

"Nothing," said Cindy. "Looks like the one who posted this is currently online. Hang on." She typed and moments later said, "Okay, Hands Up writes, and I quote, 'I don't know his name, but I heard he was a cop. There's a note in his shirt pocket reading, "You talk, you die.""

He was a cop? As I stared at the enlarged photo, I thought he looked familiar. I said, "Cindy, can you forward that to me?"

"This man was found outside SFPD jurisdiction," Cindy said.

"Cin. That's true, but I'd like you to drop it. There may be a connection to Donahue's so-called suicide, and I need to get into that before it's common knowledge."

She said, "I'm a crime reporter! This is a murder!"

"Cindy," I said, "I'm asking a favor. You saying no?"

I reached over and pulled off her signature rhinestone headband.

She grabbed for it, too late. "Hey."

I glared at her. "These two dead men were cops. As a favor to me, Cindy. Send me the photo and that note, 'You talk, you die.' And do not write about it. Please."

She wilted, muttering, "What a bully." She tapped a couple of keys. "There," she said. "Sent and delivered."

"Thanks, Cindy."

"You're soooooo welcome."

We'd all seen this pissed-off look on Cindy's face before, and it might have been warranted, but it was still hilarious. Laughter spilled out of our booth, annoying other patrons, and even Cindy couldn't fight the tickle in her funny bone.

I got up and hugged Cindy and returned her headband.

She said, "Somehow I still love you."

"I love you, too," I said. "And now I owe you."

"Don't worry. I won't forget."

Lorraine topped off our teacups and delivered the check with a plate of little cookies. We whipped out our credit cards and turned on our phones. Yuki texted for an Uber. Claire called her husband, and Cindy shut down her laptop.

I found my car keys and—not that I didn't trust her—checked my phone to see that Cindy had sent me the photo of the cop with the stapled lips. She had. Something was happening just outside my understanding.

I couldn't wait to talk it over with Brady.

CHAPTER 15

WHEN THE ALARM went off at seven, Joe didn't move. He was still bruised, wrapped, and beyond exhaustion since his return from Mexico, so I edged out of bed and took over the morning routine.

I dressed, then woke Julie, shushing her, and said, "Daddy's sleeping very hard."

"Shhhhh," she said to me.

I fed Julie, Martha, and myself, got Julie into pants and a pullover with her favorite soft-soled shoes. We had time to race with Martha to the end of the block and get Julie onto the bus with seconds to spare. I waved at her, and a half dozen other little kiddos waved at me, too. Then I took Martha home. She was a little stiff in the hindquarters, and no surprise, she went back to sleep in Julie's bed. When I kissed Joe good-bye, he put his hand in my hair and mumbled, "Did I fall asleep?"

"Yes, but don't get up. Sleep as much as you can, Joe. Love you."

"Love you, too, Blondie."

I drove to the Hall of Justice on autopilot, thinking about

the strange deaths of Brian Donahue and the unidentified "You talk, you die" man, possibly a cop, in Oakland. Both deaths were disturbing, and I had a feeling I'd seen the Oakland guy on his feet. I have seen, met, and worked with a lot of cops, so that flicker of possible recognition could be wrong. Still. I wanted to open a case file on each and investigate. That was impossible as long as I was Brady's backup officer-in-charge.

While I was taking the fire stairs up to the squad room, an idea came to me. Four flights later that idea had bloomed into a fully formed action plan. I stiff-armed the wooden gate a few yards inside the doorway.

"Morning, Lindsay," Brenda said. "Thirty-one messages for the lieutenant." She handed me a wad of little pink sheets. "And a few for you."

Brenda Fregosi has been the squad's gatekeeper and message hub for most of her life. She is the mother of two, makes pottery in her spare time, and is a trusted and beloved member of the team. There is nothing about the homicide squad that Brenda doesn't know.

Keeping my voice low, I ran my idea past her.

"Of course," she said.

"This is just me talking to you."

"I get it."

"Do you know anyone who could move into your job, say, temporarily?"

"Give me a little time to think about it."

I carried the stack of messages to Brady's desk, then sat down at my own. After running a quick eye over incoming mail, I opened the personnel file of Sergeant Brian Donahue, deceased. His record was solid: twenty years at Central Station, rising from patrol to inspector to sergeant, all in Central's understaffed homicide squad.

I'd reached the last page of the file when the red flags waved me down.

First, an anonymous complaint that Donahue was skimming drugs from busts and crime scenes. Next, that he was stoned during a murder investigation and had terminally compromised the crime scene. He was on the ropes but got a reprieve in the form of a lengthy, effusive, and frankly stunning recommendation from, of all people, our former lieutenant Ted Swanson—the corrupt former head of Robbery and Narcotics, currently serving life in San Quentin.

Based on Swanson's letter, the Internal Affairs Bureau dismissed the complaints against Donahue, and he kept his job for two more years. Until there was another, final red flag.

Donahue was captured on a witness's cell phone pistol-whipping a vagrant. The witness complained and sent the video to the *Examiner*. Donahue was fired; when the vagrant failed to file a complaint, the brass scrubbed the incident from the blotter.

The forensics report dated Monday morning, three days ago, was brief and pointed. The only fresh prints on or inside Donahue's car belonged to Donahue. A half-filled vial of fentanyl was on the seat beside his body. There was fentanyl powder on the front of his shirt, and a small smattering of the drug on his upper lip and chin. There were no signs of a struggle.

Claire's autopsy report on Donahue was also on file and brief. Official cause of death: fentanyl overdose. Manner of death: suicide.

There was nothing left to say. Donahue had been an addict. Had he also been suicidal? The red flags, the forensics, the autopsy, all pointed to an empty life ended in some improbable, mind-blowing death.

Or was it all too neat?

I checked off the details. No suicide note. Car parked safely in front of his house and the only prints were his. Had the car been wiped, fingerprints placed there with the dead man's limp hands? Why hadn't Donahue taken the drug blast in bed, or in an easy chair? It all looked very planned and orderly, but why no note? That would have tied a bow around this organized exit.

He hadn't said good-bye.

I didn't like it.

CHAPTER 16

THE VACUELY FAMILIAR face of the man with the stapled lips was nagging me, pushing to the front of my mind.

Who was he? I needed to find out.

I closed down Donahue's file and opened the photo Cindy had sent me, and I printed it out. Our printer needed toner. The photo was still out of focus, but I looked past the row of staples that had pulled the unknown man's lips into a duck's bill and I studied it.

The victim's face was in three-quarter view. There was something about him. His stuck-out ears. His short-clipped hair. I animated him in my mind and a name came to me. Roy Abend. The dead man could be Roy Abend, a former cop who'd worked at the Hall.

I'd only known Abend casually. I'd seen him in the fifth-floor corridor and at the All-Day parking lot. I'd exchanged a few words with him at MacBain's. He'd had a happy demeanor and a cheerful word for everyone.

I typed Abend's name into the personnel section's search bar and pulled up his thin file from Human Resources. Assigned to the Narcotics Division, Abend had worked for Swanson but had left the SFPD before Swanson's downfall.

I printed out the photo of the note found in Abend's pocket: "You talk, you die." Assuming the stapled DB really was the former inspector Abend, what had he talked about? Had he leaked to the law, or to a buddy who'd ratted him out? Or had he been falsely accused and assassinated to send a message?

A message to whom? How had he been killed and who had killed him?

Brady came in at eight fifteen. I waved, said, "Morning," and he flapped his big paw at me. I gave him time to shed his coat and open his laptop before knocking on his transparent door.

He signaled me to come in and I took a seat.

I asked Brady if he knew about Brian Donahue's untimely death, and he said, "I heard. His funeral is coming up. Want to go?"

"I'd rather investigate why he died."

"The ME called it," said Brady. "Drug overdose. Accidental suicide."

"She had no evidence to the contrary," I said, "but personally, she doesn't buy that Donahue did this to himself."

"Make this good," he said.

Brady listened as I explained what Claire had told me about the extreme load of fentanyl in Donahue's airways.

"Hunh," he said. "I hear you, but that doesn't rule out suicide."

"There was an investigation," I said. "No prints except his, no sign of a struggle. Nothing to work with. Just Donahue lying with his head on the steering wheel, a vial of fentanyl next to his body, a teaspoon of it inside his airways and some on his clothes.

He was unemployed. He left no note. And no one screamed, 'Murder.'"

I kept talking.

"Donahue didn't stink, but he screwed up homicide investigations, and then, get this. He got a five-star review from Ted Swanson."

Brady's eyebrows went up. "What did Swanson have to do with Donahue?"

"Exactly," I said. "Donahue worked out of Central. I saw no shared cases. How did he even know Swanson? But say he did. Say he was working undercover and helped Swanson with a bust. Swanson's recommendation bought Donahue a few more years on the Job, then he brutalized a homeless dude and it was caught on video. That was it for Donahue."

Brady said, "You're sort of building a case for suicide, Boxer."

"Maybe. But there's something else. Brady, did you know Inspector Roy Abend?"

"Five eight, 140, buzz cut, wife named Marjorie, and twin girls about three, and that would be, say, three years ago. Abend was in Narcotics."

"Right," I said. "He worked for Swanson."

I showed Brady my phone and the picture of the dead man with the blue lips, foam pushing out between the staples. "Boss, is this Abend?"

"What the hell?"

"New method of saying, 'You talked.' His lips were stapled together postmortem. And there was a note in his pocket. 'You talk, you die.' Found yesterday in Oakland. That's two dead former cops in seventy-two hours."

Brady stared at Abend's photo.

"Tell me about him," I said.

"Abend told me he didn't like being a cop, Boxer. He turned in his badge. His gun. That was years ago. Last I heard, Abend was a truck driver."

"Boss. I have a suggestion. Hear me out."

CHAPTER 17

WHILE BRADY AND I talked, the phone console on his desk lit up, clamoring for attention. He didn't even look at the flashing buttons, just let the calls go through to Brenda's voice mail as he grilled me on Donahue, Abend, and my big idea.

He attacked every angle but in the end agreed that my time was better spent doing the job I was trained to do. He called Clapper and got approval for what he told the chief was a trial run.

By the end of the day, Brenda had moved to the desk outside Brady's office. Her uncle Bobby, a.k.a. bailiff Robert Nussbaum, retired, was standing behind Brenda's old desk, pinning his grandchildren's pictures to her corkboard.

Mr. Nussbaum wore jeans, shirt and tie, a dark blue jacket with an American flag pin on the lapel. He wore socks with his loafers. What little hair he had was tidy. He was setting out notepads, pens, and a mouse pad when I welcomed him to the homicide squad.

I said, "If you have any questions, need anything…"

"Brenda will coach me," he said. "I'm a quick study. Between you, me, and AARP, Sergeant, retirement stinks. This is what I call a good time. You need anything, give a shout."

"I sure will. How do you want to be called?" I asked him.

"I'm Bobby to you."

I said, "Good to meet you, Bobby."

Twenty feet from our new desk bulldog, two desks faced each other. One was "my" old desk, which Inspector Sonia Alvarez was using, and the other belonged to Rich Conklin. Now those two desks were pushed apart, and a new desk had been placed in the gap, forming three sides of a square.

I took my new seat and exhaled. I was back. Conklin's desk was to my left, Alvarez to my right, and I sat facing down the length of the squad room. I could see every inch of it.

Several of my day-shift colleagues were at their desks under the flickering fluorescent lights. Inspector Samuels tossed paper balls into a wastebasket across the aisle. He sank them all. Inspector Michaels mopped up spilled coffee on his desktop, and a uniform sat on the corner of Sergeant Cappy McNeil's desk, talking to him and his partner, Sergeant Paul Chi. Brady was in his glass bread box at the far end of the bullpen, and Brenda was right outside his walls.

With the morning news muted on the tube overhead, Conklin, Alvarez, and I had a conference about the two dead cops. We had a lot to do. Since Abend had worked in Narcotics, Swanson might have information we could use. Swanson connected the two dead cops and was our last resort and maybe our only mortal hope.

I divvied up the assignments and we bumped fists.

And then we got to work.

CHAPTER 18

EARLY THE NEXT morning Conklin and I drove to the ferry terminal while the sun was still a rim of gold light at the horizon. A marine layer floated above the bay, and we didn't have to wait long for the catamaran to glide into its berth. We boarded her in the light chop and went inside the cabin to get out of the wind and spray.

My longtime partner and I shared a double seat near the bow and talked over the chug of the engine.

"If I didn't say, that was smooth, getting Bobby," Conklin said.

"Wasn't it, though? I think he'll be good."

"Are you ready for Swanson?" Conklin said.

"Never."

Our dislike for Swanson hadn't diminished in the passing years. Ted Swanson had headed up Robbery and Narcotics from a cluster of offices at the far end of our floor. We'd seen Ted often in those days, had liked him, his teams, his family.

He was effortlessly charming, organized, strategic; a great manager; and so sly he was never suspected of turning our own officers into thieves and killers. But the evidence was there. Robberies mounted up. The robbers wore SFPD windbreakers and masks. Cash was stolen from hapless storekeepers and violent criminals alike. Bodies dropped. But no one looked to Ted Swanson until he had to face off against another psychopath, the head of a Mexican drug cartel and a criminal much like him. All of the dead Americans had been cops reporting to Ted Swanson.

Now, despite his charm, Ted Swanson lived with other remorseless killers behind stone walls and barred windows. Poor Ted. My theory, and the reason Conklin and I were paying a call, was that Swanson might be glad enough to see two former colleagues that he would talk to us. Show off. Play his hand.

It was a possibility.

We crossed the bay in under an hour and disembarked at the town of San Quentin's Larkspur Ferry Terminal. From there we approached the nearly two-hundred-year-old prison overlooking the great bay.

There were signs along the way, what to do, what not to wear. We knew the dress code: no gang colors or provocative clothing, just loose jeans, sweatshirts, and SFPD windbreakers, and Conklin and I were in compliance. A guard let us into the fenced area, and we entered the pale stone building with its tall, narrow windows and crenulated towers. At check-in, I produced credentials and papers signed by Brady and by the new warden, Frank Hauser.

I clenched up as guards took me and Conklin through a maze of corridors to a private room, where we waited for Swanson. Anything we said would be recorded, so we sat quietly at one side of the steel table watching the door, which at last creaked open. And there he was between two guards, the crafty, unrepentant convicted criminal serving life without parole. Theodore "Ted" Swanson.

Swanson grinned widely when he saw us, and the smile on his face remained as he was cuffed to the table and seated across from us. My adrenaline spiked to my hairline when the heavy metal door slammed shut, leaving Rich and me alone with a stone killer who used to be a friend.

I wasn't worried that he could flip the table or pull a blade. I worried that Ted Charming could spin a fairy tale and we'd go for it.

CHAPTER 19

SWANSON WAS A blue-eyed, tousled blond in the style of 1950s movie stars. His smile was self-congratulatory, as if he'd just gotten out of bed with a girl who'd written "Teddy, yr the best!" in lipstick on the bathroom mirror.

He was looking at me now, saying, "Wow, what a surprise. Sorry I can't shake hands." He lifted his cuffs a couple of inches and gave us another winsome smile. The dank prison and his dead-end future hadn't changed him. I was grateful to be with Conklin.

"How ya doin', Ted?" Conklin said. "Good to see you."

"You, too, Inspector," said Swanson. "Sergeant. You look amazing."

"Uh-huh. You look better than the last time I saw you."

"When you testified against me? Yeah, that was a bad day."

I said, "We're hoping you can give us some help with the death of a former associate of yours. Brian Donahue."

"I don't see how you get 'associate.' Anyway, why would I help you, Boxer? You told the jury that I was evil. What else? Oh, disgrace to the uniform, psycho killer, that I'd corrupted dozens of police officers—and then you gave some details that buried my ass."

I said, "It's totally up to you, Swanson. In your place, I'd want to give something back."

Swanson snorted, and before he called the guard, Rich jumped in. "Ted? Ted, hang on a sec. You have nothing to lose by helping us, and we can do something for you."

"For example?"

"We'll put a hundred bucks in the store for you."

Swanson laughed. "Wow. A hundred. I don't know what to say."

I said, "We have a hundred from petty cash, and Conklin and I will chip in another fifty each. That's it."

"I was hoping for a night on the town with Kim, my new wife," Swanson said. "But two bills will buy a lot of salty snacks."

"Consider it done," I said.

And then I asked him again about Brian Donahue, the former cop who'd died from an unbelievable snootful of fentanyl. This time Swanson admitted that he'd heard about Donahue's death by overdose.

"He became a more serious user once he was cut from the Job," he said.

Conklin said, "About the letter you wrote for Donahue, sticking your neck out for him when he was about to get canned. Why'd you do that? He didn't even work for you."

"What difference does it make? It's old news."

Conklin smiled, folded his hands on the table, and said, "Let me ask it another way. How would you describe your relationship with Donahue?"

Swanson said, "It was strictly commercial, Richo. I saved his butt so he'd keep buying from me. The few times I actually sat down with Brian were only memorable because he was as bitter as old tires. Whatever his problems were, I didn't ask and I didn't care."

He was looking at his handcuffs, as though he were going down some dark corridor in his mind. And then he was back. He clanked his cuffs against the table and said, "Smartass son of a bitch. Thought he had it all figured out."

I just looked at him and let the silence lie like fog between us.

Swanson laughed. "I read you, Boxer. I guess I was a smartass SOB, too."

Bile climbed into my throat. Swanson was alive, feisty, while cops he'd corrupted were six feet underground. And that wasn't all. Swanson had indirectly created even more damage after his drug and robbery spree ended in a firefight with that Mexican jefe. Dozens of previous convictions had been thrown out because the arresting officers were dirty. Swanson had cast a long and lasting shadow on the entire SFPD.

I pushed these grim thoughts to the back of my mind. I was wasting what little time we had left with Swanson.

"And Roy Abend? You remember him?" I asked.

Swanson said, "Now that you mention his name. He quit after a few months, as I remember."

I showed him the picture of the dead man on my phone.

"Seriously, Boxer. I can't say I recognize him."

I held back a deep sigh. Had we made this trip for nothing more than a mocking interview with this piece of trash?

"So, back to Donahue," I said. "In your opinion, did he kill himself? Was his death a suicide? An accident? Or did someone take him out?"

"Ah, who can say? Guessing, he may have tapped into my

74

connections and got in too deep. I don't know. I wish I had something that would impress you, Sergeant, but I'm living inside a hole on a rock, trying to forget stuff that I didn't pay much attention to at the time. Sorry, compadres."

I didn't speak. Didn't blink.

Conklin said, "Okay, Ted. If a thought occurs to you about Abend or Donahue, we'd appreciate it if you get word to us."

My partner got up and knocked on the metal door. Guards came in and unhooked Swanson's cuffs from the loop in the table. We followed behind them as they escorted him out of the interview room. Moments later, when we were in the high-ceilinged common space below the tiers of cells, I called out loud enough for a few hundred inmates to hear, "Swanson, the SFPD thanks you for your help!"

I thought, *That ought to fix the fucker.*

A guard took us to our next appointment at the Q.

CHAPTER 20

CLAIRE WASHBURN ROLLED her blue clamshell carry-on suitcase to the check-in line at Avia Airlines. She separated her belongings into the provided rubber tubs: her laptop in one, her phone and handbag in another, shoes and jacket in the third. She stepped through the X-ray screener, then collected her things and put herself back together.

Beyond the check-in, a Starbucks kiosk called out to her. She bought a latte grande, found a seat near gate 14, and settled in with the *San Francisco Chronicle*. Twenty minutes later her flight was called. She boarded the commuter jet with a few dozen other passengers and scored a three-seat row all to herself.

Once the plane was airborne, Claire opened her laptop and pulled up her file on Katie Caruso. Since Wednesday's call from Rosewater's ME, Andrea Savino, asking for her help, Claire had been absorbed in Katie Caruso's mysterious death.

Savino had given her a thorough briefing.

She had forwarded the first-grade school picture of the six-year-old, along with a dozen newspaper articles. The articles included terse public statements from law enforcement and a reporter's heartrending interviews with Bill and Karen Caruso, the girl's frantic parents. They'd been unable to explain to the police and the press how Katie had gone missing, but they both felt with all their hearts that their daughter was still alive and calling out to them.

Contrary to their belief that Katie was alive, new facts had been reported in this morning's online *Rosewater Daily News*.

Katie's body had been found Wednesday morning by a tractor trailer driver, Brian Bolliger, who'd noticed turkey vultures circling. He was quoted as saying that he'd almost passed what looked like a pile of trash in a muddy roadside irrigation ditch but had stopped to take a look at the odd color in the icy water of the ditch, which turned out to be the child's blue pajamas. He'd called the police and told them exactly that.

Same paper, same journalist, had reported this morning the painful interview with the child's parents, who now knew that Katie's body had been recovered. They had expressed shock, grief, bewilderment, and guilt at what they believed was their fault for being overworked, preoccupied, not noticing until the next morning that their child had disappeared during the night.

Claire understood. She and her husband, Edmund, were the parents of three grown boys, who'd been rascals as kids but had grown up right. Then, six years ago, they'd had Rosie, who was adorable and trusting and Katie's age.

Edmund could sleep through thunder, sirens, heavy metal music blasting from the house next door. Sometimes, having performed a half dozen autopsies that day, she'd fall into bed beside Edmund and also sleep as if in a coma. If someone lured

77

Rosie outside, or if she went outside on her own, would she or Ed know?

Whatever had happened to Katie, Claire was determined to find the cause and deliver the truth to the police, and if asked to do so, she'd tell the parents as compassionately as she could.

CHAPTER 21

THE PILOT'S ANNOUNCEMENT to buckle up brought Claire back to the moment. She closed her laptop and looked out at the patchwork of farmland and forested rolling hills bisected by Highway 101, which ran north from San Francisco through the small rural town of Rosewater and on up to Oregon.

Where had the child lived? Where had she died? How had her body traveled five miles along that highway, and who had taken her?

The jet descended, bumped along the tarmac, and coasted to the hangar. As stairs were maneuvered up to the plane's exit door, Claire wrestled her bag from the overhead rack, shrugged into her jacket, shouldered her laptop and handbag.

The cabin steward thanked her for flying Avia and ushered her through the hatch to the movable staircase. Claire felt like a hippo dressed as a pack animal, but she kept her grip on the handrail as she descended the stairs to the tarmac and joined the line of passengers making their way through the automatic doors to the concourse.

Claire was passing the luggage carousel when she saw a blond-haired woman in her midthirties, wearing a tailored jacket, straight-legged pants, and blue-framed eyeglasses, holding up a card reading, HI, DR. WASHBURN.

That was Andrea Savino, Sam Savino's niece and the ME of southern Mendocino County.

Claire waved and Andrea rushed toward her, saying, "Wow, I'm so glad to see you. Give me your bags. I'm parked right outside. A small perk of the job."

"I think I would have recognized you even without the sign," Claire said. "You and your aunt Sam could be sisters."

"I love her," Andrea said. "Too bad she lives three thousand miles away." Andrea took Claire's computer bag and the small Rollaboard.

She said, "Claire, I was thinking we should go to the hospital first. Chief Pou will meet us there. He's been working this case since Katie Caruso was first reported missing."

"I've been reading about him in the *Rosewater Daily News*."

"Yeah. The press is going crazy and won't stop until we can go public with how and why Katie Caruso died."

"We all want the same thing. I hope to God we can do it," said Claire.

CHAPTER 22

I HAD SOMEONE else to see while I was at San Quentin. Chris Manolo had worked with me as a CI until three years ago, when he introduced a gun into a domestic dispute and shot his wife. A former small-time drug slinger and sporadic arms entrepreneur, Chris had once been an authority on the traffic of illegal goods. I couldn't know if he was still connected to the contraband grapevine since his incarceration, but Manolo was a wheeler-dealer, so there was a strong possibility.

Manolo was housed in a pod far from Swanson, and as Conklin and I walked there, our designated guard gave us a tour of the prison. Here was Charles Manson's cell. This was where Clarence Ray Allen was housed until his execution at age seventy-six, the last man to be put to death in California. There was Scott Peterson in person, right over there.

Our last stop was a wide-open meeting area where a dozen prisoners were spending time with their families. There were small square tables and aluminum chairs, vending machines, a television tuned to a cartoon channel, and cameras conspicuously placed around the room.

Conklin bought a few candy bars, and a moment later Chris Manolo came through the door. His orange jumpsuit was loose on his bony frame, and his big eyes got bigger when he saw me.

"Goddamn. Sergeant Boxer?"

"Hey, Chris. How the heck are you?"

I introduced Conklin, saying, "He's the most trustworthy person I know."

Manolo said, "Nice to meetcha," and after dragging up a chair and accepting a Snickers bar, he brought me up to date on his last three years in San Quentin. He'd gotten his GED, found Jesus, and realized that he was gay.

"And you, Sergeant?"

I told him that I was still in Homicide, that life was good. But enough of the small talk.

"Chris, have you heard about the new gun law?"

"Sure. The pot is boiling," he said.

Conklin said, "Chris. There's a rumor of guns coming into the country from Mexico. Probably military weapons."

"Well, if that's true, the smugglers are going to run the table, put the small fry out of the game. I don't know if you can stop it."

Then Manolo gave us headlines that had been passed around the cell block, unverified, of course. Nevertheless, they were astounding.

"I hear some new gun gang is pooling resources. The way I heard it, they're going to move tractor-trailer loads of weaponry in from Mexico. Dark of night. The vehicles would be camouflaged with decals from big-box stores. I don't know if this caravan is going to go in one long train, or if it'll be single trucks taking back roads.

But again, if true, they're going to flood California and points east with military-grade weapons.

"Don't put my name in your report, please, Sergeant. If anyone spills details, like who or when, they're gonna pay."

I thought, *You talk, you die.* I wondered if Roy Abend had talked to the police, or if he was part of the gang. I asked Chris if he had ever heard Abend's name, and he said, "Wasn't he a narc?"

"Yep. For six months."

After thanking Chris, I told him there'd be a gift for him in the commissary and we said good-bye.

Outside, breathing free air, I said to Richie, "Well, we have confirmation that Donahue was making drug deals with Swanson. Buy it from him and sell it to others. Manolo thinks that Vega's gun cartel could be for real. Not a waste of time exactly."

"Worth two bills' worth of salty snacks, but that's about all," said Conklin.

"Right, Rich. We need facts."

I was still trying to shake off the smirking image of Ted Swanson as my partner and I boarded the ferry and headed home. And I heard myself call out in the tall-ceilinged open space below the tiers, *Swanson, the SFPD thanks you for your help.*

If he'd achieved any popularity in the last three years, he was about to lose it.

CHAPTER 23

ANDREA SAVINO STRUCK out for the car with her long stride, towing the blue Rollaboard, with Claire in her wake.

Her silver Honda SUV was parked in the short-term lot a hundred yards from the door. There was a medical examiner decal on her windshield and a larger one on the rear bumper. When Savino opened the rear hatch, Claire saw that, like herself, Andrea Savino was fully equipped for whatever she might need at a crime scene.

Her medical tool kit had her name and number written on a strip of tape across the lid. There was a stack of body bags and sheets, a blanket, and an encased digital SLR camera. A pair of green rubber boots were wedged in behind the spare tire, and what looked like a raincoat and a change of clothes were packed flat inside a Space Bag. A short crowbar, a folding ladder, and tackle boxes probably filled with gloves and test kits completed the portable lab.

Claire's carry-on wouldn't fit. Savino closed the hatch and made room for Claire's belongings in the back seat.

Savino said, "Dr. Washburn—"

"Please, call me Claire."

"Sure, Claire. We're about three miles out from Saint Barney's Hospital, which is where I work in the dungeon. Do you need anything before we get there?"

"Nope. Just lay it out for me. What's the plan?"

"Come to my lab and take a look at Katie," said the young ME. "I've photographed her both clothed and undressed. I sent her clothes to the lab. Externally, she appears severely dehydrated. I found no signs of abuse, sexual or otherwise. No bruises or abrasions. Soaking wet, body temp in the 30s. It looked like she'd been lying in that ditch on Route 253 for the whole time she was missing. The X-rays showed nothing remarkable. No breaks or prosthetics. She weighed 38.2 pounds, underweight for her age and size."

"What about the blood screen, fingernail scrapings? Rape kit?"

"I put six kinds of rush on it, but you know. It's Friday. I even told the lab manager I'd have dinner with him."

"Really?"

"Desperate times call for desperate measures."

She looked at Claire. "I crossed my fingers behind my back."

They both laughed and got into the car.

Savino started the engine and backed up, drove out of the lot.

She said, "Chief Pou is going to give you everything he's got. Both of us are hoping we can do the postmortem today."

Claire said, "I need to book a room for the night. Where do you suggest?"

CHAPTER **24**

THE CEMENT-BLOCK walls of Andrea Savino's basement office were painted white. The room was furnished with an old gray metal desk holding a Dell desktop computer and a *Dr. Quinn, Medicine Woman* coffee mug. The corkboard behind her desk was covered with overlapping memos and a picture of a spotted dog with a black band across one corner of the frame.

Chief Robert Pou sat with doctors Washburn and Savino at the ME's desk.

Dressed in jeans, a button-down shirt, and a tie under his Rosewater PD windbreaker, Pou was a dark-haired man in his early forties, now focused on the contents of his bulging briefcase. He smiled and said "There you are" when he laid hands on the Caruso file. He passed it to Claire, then moved his chair closer to the desk.

Claire said, "I'll read it all, but can you summarize the contents?"

Pou said, "Sure thing. Now. Regarding the man who found the girl's body. Brian Bolliger. Doesn't make a lot of sense that he would have killed Katie and then called the cops, but stranger things have happened.

"So we ran him through the database. No record. And I spoke to Bolliger's boss, Arthur Richards of AR Trucking, who not only vouched for him but had gone over his mileage log and authenticated it. Before Bolliger found the child's body, he hadn't been in Northern California in two months. We grilled him like we had Ted Bundy in lockup, and in our opinion, Bolliger is clean."

Claire leafed through the documents in the Caruso folder as Pou spoke.

Said Pou, "We canvassed the Carusos' neighbors and the two families who own farms within five miles of where Katie..." Pou choked up a little, then continued.

"We talked to the owners and their pickers and packers, a total of twelve workers. We terrified the hell out of them, and still none of them set off any alarms. No one knew anything about the Carusos, no one had seen the child."

The chief cleared his throat, pulled a handkerchief from his windbreaker pocket, and blew his nose.

"'Scuse me," he said. "Anyway, the Carusos have a hardware store in town. They welcomed us to park outside the store, and so we made ourselves available all morning to anyone who wanted to talk to us.

"Nobody saw or heard anything suspicious. No one saw Katie walking on the road. No flying saucer dropped her off. Dr. Washburn, behind the red tab in the folder are statements from all of the individuals who came forward while Katie was missing, including two men who were accused of hanging around our park and the lower-school playground. Got all alibis verified."

"I don't see Katie's medical records," Claire said.

"I know, I know," said the police chief. "Katie saw a pediatrician, Dr. Sven Wallace. That is, up until last year around this time, when Wallace died suddenly of a heart attack. He was smoking a cigarette and set fire to his office. Nothing remains of his records on Katie."

"Damned shame," Savino said, and shook her head. "Adding to your 'nothing,' nothing came from her sexual assault kit. There's always a chance, if she was killed, that her body was washed before it was dumped. We're waiting for the toxicology report."

Pou asked, "Could she have been drugged?"

"Possibly," said Claire. "But hell, she could have died from an aneurism or a brain tumor. Andrea and I will do the autopsy right away."

Pou said, "I'll leave you to it. Here's my number. Call anytime you want. I have personal interest. Katie goes—went—to school with my daughter, Carol Lee."

A half hour later Claire was gloved, gowned, capped, and mic'd up, standing at a stainless steel table. She looked down at the draped body of a six-year-old Caucasian female with strawberry-blond hair and a gap between her two front teeth. Claire had autopsied hundreds of children and it never got easier. By definition, all children were innocent.

Claire tugged at her gloves, then murmured, "We've got you, Katie. Tell us what happened."

CHAPTER 25

AT DAY'S END I called Joe from the car to tell him I was leaving work and coming home. Julie picked up my call.

"Daddy's in the baffroom," she said.

"Okay, sweetie, I'll be home real soon. Did you and Daddy have dinner?"

"Of course."

"Good. Kisses."

About fifteen minutes later I opened the door.

Martha, my shaggy old border collie, sat looking up at me, flapping her tail against the floor. After I stowed my gun, I scooched down and gave her a real good rub. Then Julie was in my arms. I carried her to the kitchen, saw that Martha's bowl was overflowing with kibble. There were flowers in a vase on the counter, and the dishwasher was winding down.

"Martha was walked?"

"Mom. You worry too much."

"I know it."

I called out, "Joe?"

"In here, Lindsay."

Joe was in his office in the spare room. He stood to hug me and flinched when I hugged him back.

"How're you feeling?" I asked him.

"On the upswing," he said. "I'll be done here in about ten minutes. Have to finish this report for Steinmetz."

Julie talked to me through the bathroom door as I showered and dressed in my pj's. She was telling me that she wanted to change the bedtime rules. That she was old enough to watch grown-up TV.

"Not yet," I shouted.

She switched seamlessly to the story of the Cheshire Cat, saying she didn't like his name and suggesting several alternatives. Chestnut because he was nutty. Chester because that was a real name.

I was laughing when I opened the door.

Julie looked up at me, stretched her arms out wide, saying, "And then, while he was up in a tree, he just disappeared—except for his smile."

"You are too funny. You know that?"

"I doooooo."

I tousled her hair, and together we went out to the living area. I took "Mom's chair," next to Joe's recliner, and Julie climbed up to my lap and watched a sitcom with us. I almost felt bad when it was time to put her to bed. There were whining protests, foot-dragging, grabbing me by the waist and begging me to let her stay up just a little longer.

"Daddy said I could stay up late."

Joe called out, "Blaabbbbbermouth."

"Joe?"

"Julie, I said you could stay up until Mom came home. Right?"

"But I'm not ready."

I said, "Come on, Bug. Sleep is good."

She was working up to a heartbreaking sob as I took her hand and led her into her room. I distracted her with the change from day clothes to a hand-me-down nightie with whales on it from her cousin Meredith.

Julie sniffed, then asked, "When's my birthday, Mom?"

"Pretty soon now."

"Can I have a party?"

"Well, sure. But the rest is a surprise. Come on, Jules. Climb aboard."

I tucked my little girl into her bed, arranged her stuffed toys, patted the bed so that Martha would jump up. When they were both in their places, I kissed Julie, Martha, and finally a stuffed cow named Mrs. Mooey Milkington good night.

Back in the living room, I took my chair, exhaled loudly as I organized my thoughts.

My phone rang from the far side of the apartment. It has a cheerful little ringtone, but I wasn't in the mood for chipper. When I didn't answer the call, my phone rang again. I walked back to the foyer, pulled my phone out of my jacket pocket, and saw Claire's name on the screen.

I pushed the green button and said, "Hey. Where are you?"

"I'm in Rosewood, in the morgue waiting for lab tests on that little girl, Katie Caruso. The parents were here earlier, sobbing over their daughter's dead body. Father's maybe thirty. Mom is twenty-five. It took three of us to keep them from falling all over Katie. It was awful to see without thinking about Rosie."

I pictured that sad scene and commiserated with my best friend.

"I wanted to call you before I start the autopsy," Claire said. "I think I know what killed this child."

"Tell me," I said.

I heard voices rising up around Claire.

"They're still here. I'll call you later," she said. "Oh, God. It's late. I'll call you tomorrow."

Claire left me hanging on a hook, yet another unsolved case.

Joe said, "You okay?"

"It was a long day's work."

"Tell me about it," he said. "Was Swanson glad to see you?"

"Only if you believe the words that come out of that criminal's mouth," I said.

"So therefore…"

"I'll tell you everything, Joe. But let's talk in bed."

Lights out, under the covers, Joe's arm around me, I told my very smart former G-man husband every last thing before he winked out. Turns out, I wasn't as tired as Joe. Images of Donahue and Abend circled inside my mind. Was their casual connection through Swanson meaningful?

Or were their deaths unconnected and I was fashioning a case out of coincidence? I don't remember falling asleep.

CHAPTER 26

CLAIRE FUMED AS she closed the Y section she'd made in Katie's chest. She spoke into her microphone, aware of Andrea listening intently to her conclusion.

She had not only determined that Katie had been dehydrated, as Savino had said—the little girl's tissues were dry, tacky to the touch—but she'd also discovered that Katie's pancreas was vestigial, all indicating that she'd had type 1 diabetes and had needed insulin injections in order to live. Both the autopsy and the results of the blood work confirmed that the child had died from ketoacidosis.

Claire stated her name, the date, and that Katie Caruso's proximate time of death had been less than a week before the autopsy.

Disgusted, Claire ended her report and stepped away from the autopsy table. She pushed up her mask and exhaled. A young life had been lost at great pain when the child could easily have been saved.

Why? Why hadn't Katie been receiving her medication on time, or at all?

Savino covered Katie's body with the sheet. She said, "So we agree. Ketoacidosis."

"This sucks, Andrea. The Carusos were so busy they forgot to manage her insulin? She was six. She needed them. Katie had to have been showing severe symptoms for days before she went missing."

Savino asked, "Are you comfortable calling it neglect? Or not?"

"Let's give Pou a chance to weigh in before we make it official," said Claire. "How long do you think it will take for him to get here?"

"I'll bet a buck he's sitting outside the hospital with the engine running, waiting for our call. Which I will now make."

Claire turned away from the table, threw her cap, gown, and mask into the trash. She was seized with a strong desire to call home and speak with Edmund. Tell him to double lock the door. And she wanted to hear Rosie's voice. But her family would be sleeping. And she needed to speak with Katie's family even more.

She wanted answers. Needed them.

Savino called Chief Pou and woke him. While they waited for him to arrive, Claire and Andrea discussed what Katie would have gone through in her last days: extreme thirst, flushing, headaches, confusion, and cramping. Merely drinking water would have caused her to vomit. Because she'd been in the most extreme stage of dehydration, her blood flow would have been minimal, unable to carry oxygen to her organs. Her heart and lungs would have failed. As they had.

"Her parents couldn't have missed seeing this," Claire said. "You agree, Andrea? And how did she get five miles from home?"

"Not on foot," Savino said. "Just not possible."

A half hour later Chief Pou hurried through the morgue doors. Once he'd heard the pathologists' explanation for the little girl's death, he said, "Let's go."

"Go where?" Savino said.

"Carusos' house," said Pou.

"I should call them," she said.

Andrea had grown up in Rosewater. She knew everyone in town, was friends with most of them.

"You have their number on your phone?" Pou asked Savino.

"I will in a minute."

"Okay. Do that. And then you ladies put on your jackets and let's pay them a visit. We'll call them right before I kick in the front door."

CHAPTER **27**

ANDREA SAVINO AND Claire Washburn followed Chief Pou's Ford 4 x 4 pickup north into farm country at the edge of Rosewater. His deputy, Will Christian, was in Pou's passenger seat, on the phone with dispatch requesting backup. When the chief took a right turn off the highway onto a rutted dirt road that curved through a grassy field, then cut his headlights, Savino did the same.

Peering into the darkness, Claire could just make out the Carusos' unpainted farmhouse, standing alone on a rise. There looked to be two rooms up, two down, a chimney to the left, and a porch rounding the front. Blue light blinked in a second-floor window.

"They're awake," she said to Savino.

Savino said, "You know, I really don't want Pou to go Rambo on them. We know how Katie died, but not why it happened."

Claire agreed up to a point.

"Andrea, I know you care about them. I'm a little more objective. I could even say that I'm on the fence, hoping there's a good explanation for this freakin' tragedy. But Pou's got to put pressure on them. If the Carusos feel cornered by the evidence…"

"They'll confess," said Savino.

"Right. Or they'll convince Pou that Katie was kidnapped or turn on each other—or run."

As the vehicles closed in on the house, Pou slowed, then he parked on the windowless side, near the base of the chimney. Savino pulled in beside him as the chief and Deputy Christian quietly exited the truck. Claire and Savino joined them in the side yard.

Pou pulled a folded paper from his shirt pocket. A search warrant, no doubt.

"Doctors, you stay out here," he said. "Will and I'll go in first. Caruso has a temper and guns."

The two uniformed men walked up the porch steps. Pou knocked on the front door, knocked again, and called out Bill Caruso's name. Caruso leaned out of his upstairs bedroom window.

"Robert? You have news for us? I'm coming right down."

Claire watched the front door open and the two cops enter the house. She had been working hard to quash the image of the Carusos sobbing over their dead child. It had almost killed her to watch. Now she wondered. Had the grief been real, or guilt confronting the truth?

Andrea Savino tapped Claire's arm as the front door opened again and Deputy Christian stepped out of the house, closing the door behind him. He walked over to Claire and Savino.

"The Carusos want to talk to you both. Chief says just keep it to the results of the autopsy. I'll walk you in."

CHAPTER 28

IT WAS AFTER eleven when Claire and Savino entered the Caruso house.

Claire noted that the low-ceilinged living room was about twenty feet long by a dozen feet wide. The furnishings were solid, nothing dainty. There was an antique mirror over the fireplace, framed photos on the walls—the family, the pie contest at the county fair.

A sofa under the front windows was covered with rumpled bedding. In front of the sofa was a long plank, stained and shellacked, serving as a coffee table. On the table was a plate of leftover dinner, a water glass, and a half-empty bottle of red wine.

Weeping, Karen Caruso bundled up the sheets, blanket, and pillow and tossed them to the floor of the hall closet. Crying softly, she tightened the sash on her robe, collected the remains of her dinner, and took them to the kitchen. Bill Caruso stood by the fireplace, peering down at the search warrant in his hands. Claire read his expression as both alarmed and lost.

Karen came back from the kitchen and dragged two dining chairs over to the coffee table.

Chief Pou said, "I'm fine on my feet. We won't be here long."

Claire and Savino took seats, and the Carusos sat at opposite ends of the sofa. Deputy Christian stood inside the doorway. All eyes were on Pou when he said, "It appears that Katie died because she was diabetic and didn't get her meds. What do you all know about that?"

"No," said the father. "Katie had the flu, right, Karrie? We kept her home for a day because she felt sick. She had a low fever. Karrie came home to give her lunch, and we made her dinner when we got home at around six."

Bill Caruso went on.

"Next day—you know. When we woke up, she wasn't in her bed—or anywhere. Robert, I called you to tell you that Katie was gone."

Pou said, "I hear you, Bill. And I want to believe you. And I want you to hear from Dr. Washburn. Claire, can you say a few words?"

Claire wondered if she could boil this horror story down to a few words. It seemed unlikely.

She said, "Mr. Caruso, you knew that Katie was diabetic?"

Karen answered, "Of course we knew. She was born that way. Type 1."

"So you knew she had to get insulin every day?"

"We did that, didn't we, Bill? She always fought us. She always cried. But we tried to entertain her. Make a game of it."

Andrea Savino spoke up. "What about the day you said she was sick? Did you skip her injection that day?"

Bill said, "We gave her the shot. I think so. We were worried. And she was crying something terrible."

Savino said, "You know that Dr. Washburn is a well-known pathologist. We had to get the best for Katie. We sent out blood and tissue samples to the lab, and the lab techs worked overtime."

Bill walked over to Karen and put his arm around her. The woman was fragile or a good actor. Claire still wasn't sure.

Savino said, "It pains me to have to say this, but Katie's body tells us that she died before you reported her missing, and she'd been without insulin for a full week before she died."

Karen shook off her husband's arm and got into Andrea Savino's face.

"Bullshit, Andrea. That's not true. You've made a mistake. A big one."

Claire said, "I'm getting a glass of water."

No one stopped her or even watched her go to the kitchen. There was a doorway but no door, and Claire heard Chief Pou say, "So that I'm clear, Dr. Savino. Katie was already dead the entire time her parents reported her missing."

"That's right," Savino said. "We can tell from the state of Katie's body how long she'd been deceased. And her organ damage could only have been caused by a chronic lack of insulin."

Katie's mother shouted over Savino, "You're saying that she died because she missed an injection? Noooooo. She was abducted. Starved. The bastard that took her didn't give her her insulin. There's your chronic lack. I'm telling you, Robert, and it's the truth. She was stolen from us. That's why she died. That's what happened."

CHAPTER 29

CLAIRE LOOKED AROUND the kitchen, pulled on blue latex gloves, and opened the refrigerator. She moved aside the carton of beer, the bag of lettuce, the packages of sandwich meat, the eggs. She opened the crisper and felt around the fruit, then checked the shelves again.

There were no preloaded insulin pens in the refrigerator. She checked the drawers under the counter and the cabinets, looking for unopened bottles of insulin that could be kept unrefrigerated for up to a month. She found nothing. She did it all over again, then she peeled off her gloves and stepped into the doorway to the living room.

She signaled to Chief Pou.

When he joined her, she said, "Chief, there's no insulin in the refrigerator or anywhere in the kitchen. Prefilled pens should be kept cold. Unopened bottles can be kept at room temperature. I found neither."

Pou thanked her, and they went back into the main room.

Whatever Bill Caruso saw in Pou's face unleashed him, and he made a rush for the back door.

Deputy Christian, younger, faster, stronger than Caruso, reached out, spun Caruso around, and threw him against the wall. Pictures of birthdays and prize pies crashed to the floor. The deputy pulled Caruso's right arm behind his back, cuffed the wrist, then wrenched Caruso's left arm back and cuffed that wrist to the first.

Karen went to her husband and pounded his back and shoulder with her fists.

"What did you do, Bill? What did you do?"

The fight drained out of Caruso and he stopped struggling.

Pou took Katie's mother by the shoulders and held her at arm's length. He said, "Karen, stop it. Your little girl died a painful death almost a week ago. She was lying in a ditch five miles from here. How did she get so far away? Lying there halfway between the Andrews and Sachet farms while you were telling me, telling the public, that someone took your daughter. There were no marks on her, Karen. No one tied her up or gagged her or hit her or raped her. So what happened, Mother? You gave up? You snapped?"

Karen croaked one word. "No." But it wasn't convincing.

Pou said, "You and Bill were both responsible for Katie's care and well-being—"

Bill turned to Pou, wrists behind him, the cords in his neck so distended, they threw shadows.

"What the hell are you saying, Robert? You and me. We've known each other for fifteen years—"

Pou interrupted him.

"Bill. Karen. This isn't personal. It's your last best chance

102

to tell the truth. Do that, I talk to the DA and he might cut you a deal."

Bill Caruso shouted, "We told the truth, damn you!"

Pou looked at his phone, read a text.

"Dr. Savino, the coroner is on his way to the morgue. You and Dr. Washburn should go now to meet him. Where's your coat, Karen?"

"Now?" Karen asked.

Pou said, "Put your hands behind your back, young lady. I'm not going to hurt you."

After Pou cuffed her, Christian took a denim jacket from the hall closet and arranged it around Karen Caruso's shaking shoulders. Pou's voice was loud and clear. "Bill Caruso, Karen Caruso, you're both under arrest for reckless endangerment resulting in homicide and for interfering with a police investigation. I'm going to read you your rights."

Claire and Savino left by the front door, found the car by touch, and headed back to Saint Barney's in the dark.

CHAPTER **30**

CLAIRE AND ANDREA Savino were in the windowless basement morgue, waiting for the coroner.

They had filled out forms, snacked on peanut butter crackers and coffee, Claire counting twenty-two hours since leaving home Friday morning. Savino had leaned back in her chair and closed her eyes when Ted Scislowski, the Mendocino County coroner, arrived.

Claire checked her watch. It was ten to three in the morning.

Scislowski had a heavy step and a firm handshake. He introduced himself to Claire, shook her hand and Andrea's. His white hair was half combed, his glasses were smudged, his shirt and hands were streaked with grease.

Scislowski said, "I'm very sorry I kept you waiting."

He explained that when he'd gotten the call from Chief Pou, he had driven from Boonville, east toward Rosewater. At mile eleven he'd blown a tire and had to change the flat.

"Please accept my apologies," he said to the pathologists. "I'm glad you stayed and waited for me."

He brought a chair over to the desk and sat down beside Claire and said, "You saw Rosewater as you came in from the airport, so you know that the whole town is about the size of a man's hand. This lost little girl is one of four thousand citizens of this place, and she's been the subject of a great deal of anxiety and press attention. People want to know what happened."

Andrea said, "We can answer that for you, Mr. Scislowski. In about six terrible words."

Without a hint of rebuke, Scislowski said, "I'm going to need more than six words, I'm afraid, but the quicker we can answer the questions—well, enough said. Andrea, Dr. Washburn, I need you to take me through all of what you know. Don't leave anything out."

Scislowski followed Savino to the tiled and stainless-steel-furnished cold room. Savino wheeled the gurney over to Scislowski and pulled down the draped cloth, exposing the stitched Y incision in Katie's chest, dark lines of thread cross-hatching the waxen body of the deceased child.

Scislowski said "Ah, shit" as he looked at Katie's small body and said it again as Savino taped autopsy photos to the wall. She described the X-rays and photographs, then asked Claire to talk about the condition of Katie's internal organs.

Claire summarized the results of insulin withdrawal on a diabetic: the dehydration, the loss of blood flow as the body tries to conserve moisture, the overall collapse of the system and imminent death.

Savino read from the CSI report of the criminalists who'd examined the scene where the body was found. Last, she handed Scislowski a clipboard with the lab results of Katie's blood.

While the coroner looked at the lab report, Savino said, "Katie wasn't beaten or constrained or sexually molested. Dr. Washburn and I agree that Katie Caruso's death was due to the complications of chronic untreated diabetes mellitus, type 1."

Scislowski looked again at the CSI photos of Katie's small body lying in muddy water in the irrigation ditch. She'd been wearing pajamas. Blue ones. A stuffed animal floated alongside the beer cans and the long strands of Katie's hair.

He shook his head, clucked his tongue, and finally said, "Pathetic. Awful. Beyond awful. Was God watching this?"

The coroner took a few deep breaths, then spoke again.

"Frankly, I don't know why the Carusos didn't hide her body. Maybe their attorney can spin something sympathetic out of that."

At just after four in the morning, Deputy Will Christian drove Claire to the Sundown Motel.

"Bill Caruso made a statement," the deputy said. "He says they skipped an injection a few times. Then they realized they were out of insulin. The wife forgot. Bill said it was her job. Then he admitted that they'd both messed up."

Claire asked, "Caruso said 'messed up'?"

"Right. When we talked to Karen, she blamed Bill. Then finally broke down and said it was unspoken that she was supposed to give Katie her shots and she got fed up. She told Bill it was his turn, and when he didn't do it, then she went to work with Bill and they agreed they'd catch Katie up the next morning. Still didn't pick up her insulin."

"Let me guess," Claire said. "In the morning, Katie was dead."

Deputy Christian nodded and said, "They laid her in the back seat and drove until they found a ditch. Put her in it with her stuffed toy, concocted a story, and when they got home, they called the police."

"They killed her," Claire said.

Deputy Christian nodded. His expression was grim.

"We're going to investigate Katie's death as a homicide. Could come down to 'reckless' or 'negligent.' Ditching her body isn't going to work in their favor."

Claire stood in the motel's shower for a long time, then dressed in her one clean set of clothes and repacked her Rollaboard. Then she sat on the bed and called to book a car to the airport and a seat on the 6:00 a.m. flight to San Francisco.

She took a chance and lay down. She put her head on the pillow and let herself feel everything she'd blocked while autopsying Katie's small body. She knew how much the child had suffered, as organ by organ her body shut down. She felt a resurgence of the rage that had come over her when she realized only minutes into the autopsy that Katie had died not just of diabetes but neglect.

Tears rolled down Claire's cheeks and she didn't try to stop them.

Her phone rang on the table next to the bed. Claire sat up, looked at the caller ID, and said "Washburn" to her hired driver.

"I'll be right there," she said.

She brushed her teeth, settled the motel bill over the phone, gathered up her things, and headed out into the predawn morning.

With luck, Edmund and Rosie would be waking up around the time she came through the door. She wanted Edmund to hold her while she told him everything. And she needed to hug Rosie, braid her little girl's hair, dress her, and take her to the park.

CHAPTER 31

MY CELL PHONE rang in the dark. I grabbed for it, fumbled, and finally palmed it. The screen read 6:05. Clapper was calling.

By the time I said, "Boxer," Joe's phone buzzed with its discordant *blat-blat-blat*.

We both sat up, put our feet on the floor. Clapper's voice was in my ear.

"Morning, Boxer. This is your wake-up call. A DB was just found inside his parked car on Washington Street. Name is Carl Barrows. Welder. Twenty-three. Unemployed. No record. No note of any kind with the body.

"Looks like a Donahue kind of thing because there was a vial of fentanyl on the seat beside him. Like Abend, his lips were stapled. And the words *You talk, you die* are written on his forehead in marker."

I gasped. "I know Barrows. He was picked up in a gun sweep on Tuesday. I was in arraignment court. The bail was fifty grand. He must've bonded out."

"He'd have been better off in jail."

I said, "Where's the crime scene? I'll go."

"Northern is catching. I'm putting together a task force," said Clapper. "Brady has been notified. I need you to call Conklin, Alvarez, McNeil, and Chi. My office, seven o'clock."

"Copy that."

But Clapper wasn't done talking. He said, "I've asked for the FBI to send a team."

I was wondering why he was bringing in the FBI when Clapper said, "See you at seven," and clicked off.

At the same moment Joe said, "Fine, Craig. I'm on the way." He put down his phone, stood up, and hiked up his pajama bottoms. He said, "Steinmetz wants me in Clapper's office for a seven o'clock meeting. Was that Clapper calling you?"

"Yep," I said. "What did Steinmetz say?"

"He said Clapper's rounding up a task force, his senior homicide squad—that would include you. And two from the FBI. That would be me and Wallenger. It's got to be about what Vega told me. Supersize gun convoy coming across the border. Maybe they've already crossed it."

I nodded. That made sense. I hooked a thumb over my shoulder, pointing to the bathroom. "You go first. I'll call Mrs. Rose."

I phoned our granny-nanny and asked her to please, please pick up the pieces of our morning.

"We both have to run out. Police emergency."

"No problem, Lindsay."

"Martha is going to need—"

Julie called out, "Mommyyyyyyy."

"Oh, no," I said.

"Got it," Mrs. Rose said. "I'll be there as soon as I throw something on and put my teeth in."

"Thanks, Gloria."

"Glad to do it."

I dressed in a hurry: clean shirt, yesterday's trousers and jacket, a clean pair of Joe's socks. Who had time to do laundry, anyway? Joe tended to Julie while I speed-dialed my colleagues and told them what little I knew.

Mrs. Rose, as good as her word, rang the bell and looked as fresh as if it were noon after a deep sleep and a good breakfast. She had "thrown on" a fetching aqua-blue, rose-dotted chenille robe over her nightgown. Her slippers were furry, with pointy ears and jiggly eyes. She grinned and tapped her front teeth with an index finger.

I laughed and gushed over her, and a few minutes later Julie was getting oatmeal, and Joe and I had geared up, found both sets of car keys, and jogged down the stairs.

Traffic was light. We were never out of the other's sight as we took Geary Boulevard and arrived at the Hall together. Joe parked his Mercedes in the All-Day lot, while I parked my humble Explorer on Harriet Street. I had a time advantage as I cleared the magnetometer in the lobby by flashing my badge at security, while Joe had to empty his pockets and remove his belt.

I waited for him at the elevator, and when he joined me, I pressed 5.

There was a coffee urn in Clapper's office, and I filled a cup for myself and one for Joe. The chief greeted the room and introduced the FBI members.

"Special Agent Mike Wallenger led the team in the Cow Palace arrest of an illegal-gun dealer. He was working with Joe Molinari. You all know Molinari is Boxer's husband and a veteran of several intelligence agencies, including the FBI, and is a consultant to them and us on this particular mission impossible."

There were nervous smiles in the room, even mine.

Clapper said, "Our job is to break the back of a two-headed snake."

He walked to the urn, filled a coffee cup, then rested his butt against the leading edge of his desk.

"Here's what you need to know about the job at hand."

CHAPTER **32**

CLAPPER FACED HIS task force of seven, his back to his desk, silhouetted by the pale morning light seeping in through the blinds.

He said, "I've diagrammed our assignment."

A whiteboard stood to the left of his desk, and he'd drawn a crisp black line from top to bottom along the left side of it. Morgue portraits of the three dead men were taped to the large open space to the right of the line.

Clapper had marked his timeline with points of relevance. First bullet was the day the restrictive gun law had gone into effect.

Next bullet was the Cow Palace gun show. Clapper drew an arrow and scrawled the name *Vega* next to it.

He picked up the pointer lying in the tray at the bottom of the board. He used it to tap the next three dates on his diagram: The day Brian Donahue's body was found. Two days later, the discovery of Roy Abend's body, mouth stapled. And finally, last night, Carl Barrows.

He brought the group's attention to the photo of Barrows's unlined face.

"You can't miss what's printed on Barrows's forehead with a marker pen. 'You talk, you die.' Talk about what? It wasn't spelled out. The same words were found on a scrap of paper found in Abend's pocket.

"Regardless of their former status as cops, or the fact that Barrows wasn't and had never been in law enforcement, this adds up to three probable homicides, very likely all related. Motive? Squealing about something that made someone extremely unhappy. Caused him to send a warning to others. Forensic evidence? Zip. No prints, no photos or video, no witnesses.

"Medical reports. Two deaths by overdose, very possibly delivered to the victims by a second party. Abend's death was by blunt-force trauma to the back of the head. The absence of evidence in all three deaths, the warning that there was a death penalty for talking, the time frame of the murders, lead me to a reasonable conclusion that the same person or group of persons killed these men. But what was the link?"

Alvarez raised her hand, and Clapper said, "Yes?"

"The bodies were discovered by different individuals in very different locations?"

"Yes," said Clapper. "That's right."

Alvarez said, "And the killer or killers left the discoveries to chance."

Clapper said, "What does that mean to you?"

She said, "The killings were done fast. The victims knew their killers, so that's why there was no evidence of struggles. The killers wore gloves, so there was no trace evidence to clean up."

"Good points, Alvarez. What are your thoughts about the notes?"

"Killer or killers having a good time, maybe. Mocking the victims. And if it was a real threat, figuring the warning would get out to the desired targets."

Clapper nodded his agreement and asked Wallenger to tell the group about Alejandro Vega.

Wallenger got to his feet and brought the task force into the takedown of Vega at the Cow Palace gun show.

"Vega had a forged license to sell guns, and 103 illegal weapons in his booth, plus about the same number in his vehicle," Wallenger said. "I think he would have sold them all if we hadn't arrested him in the first hour of the show."

Joe picked up where Wallenger left off, saying, "Vega told me that the news of his arrest would probably get him killed in jail. He asked me to try to protect his family. I said I'd do my best, and in exchange for that, Vega told me that he was part of a start-up gun and drug cartel. That the players were small-timers who'd banded together in force. His story matches the one from Boxer's CI. Vega let me know that a convoy would be coming from Mexico to California with a serious cargo of military-style weaponry and an unknown amount of street drugs. He mentioned fentanyl."

"Did he give you any other details?" Clapper asked.

"No time, names, buyers, or means of distribution," said Joe. "Mike and I handed him over to the Mexican police. We've followed up and were told we'd be notified if something useful came of the arrest."

"So, that's what we have," Clapper said. "Three very clean homicides. Notes indicating that two of them were killed for having leaked information. Might or might not be tied to this convoy of weapons.

"Second thing, maybe a lead, Donahue and Abend both knew Ted Swanson. Boxer and Conklin paid a call on Swanson yesterday. Boxer, you have something to add?"

I was about to give a short report on our meeting with Swanson when deafening bursts of gunshots sounded. Someone was firing an automatic rifle right outside Clapper's office.

CHAPTER 33

THE SOUND OF gunfire echoed in the air.

What the hell is this?

The eight men and women in Clapper's office pulled their guns and ran to the corridor. By the time I'd edged through the logjam of cops in the doorway, the tableau had frozen. Ten feet away, standing alone on a patch of marble floor, a heavy, fortyish white man with crazy eyes gripped an AR-15 with both hands. The gun was pointed at the ruined ceiling.

Cappy McNeil got the shooter's attention.

"Hey. Buddy. Drop the gun. You don't want to hurt anyone, right? You don't want to die, do you? So put it on the floor."

"Screw you," the shooter shouted angrily.

Maybe he *did* want to die. My mind sped forward a few seconds into the future when that wacko lowered his gun and cut down the homicide squad in three seconds. It would be a massacre, but it hadn't happened yet. Cappy had called out the shooter, and I knew Cappy would fire if the guy didn't put the gun down. Now.

Or the guy would fire first.

I was thirty degrees off-center from the shooter, behind other cops. I was lining up my shot so as not to hit Cappy or anyone with a badge when Brady broke from where he stood on the shooter's blind side and dove for his legs. The man went down with a loud *woof* as the air was knocked out of him. His gun skittered across the marble-tiled floor and spun slowly toward Conklin's feet.

Conklin holstered his nine and picked up the rifle by the shoulder strap.

The shooter screamed at Conklin from the floor.

"You can't take that."

"I think I can," Conklin said, carrying it back into Clapper's office. Paul Chi, Cappy's longtime partner, held the shooter down, pressing the muzzle of his nine to the back of the guy's neck while Cappy cuffed him.

"What's your name?" Chi shouted.

Cappy patted the man down, searching pockets for ID that he didn't find.

Cappy said to his partner, "Let's do it, Paul," and together they hauled the big man to his feet.

Chi said, "John Doe, you're under arrest for possession of an illegal weapon, for threatening the lives of eight police officers, for resisting arrest, and for damaging a public building."

Then he read John Doe his rights.

The situation was stabilized, but the shooter had terrified all of us. Then it came to me that I had seen him before. Who was he? Where had I seen him?

I called the desk sergeant at the seventh-floor jail.

"Bubbleen, we've disarmed a crazy outside the chief's office and he's in custody. Send two men for him. The bigger the better."

"On the way," she said.

Two prison guards got out of the elevator. They each took one of the shooter's arms, and as he yelled, "We will not comply," the guards manhandled him up the stairs to lockup.

And then I remembered who the shooter was, how he'd gotten into the building with his gun, and how he'd hidden it. He was Ben someone. He worked in custodial services at night. On weekends.

Clapper faced us in the corridor outside his office. We all looked shaken, high on adrenaline with no place to take it.

He said, "Anyone else have something to say?"

Cappy cracked, "You talk, you die."

Clapper tried to suppress a grin and waggled his finger at Cappy. Then said, "We meet every Friday at 7 a.m. until we've got suspects under arrest and we've stopped the runaway gun train. Homicide, report to Brady as usual. Wallenger and Molinari, you're with me.

"Everyone, work your street sources; squeeze them, threaten, pay them off, whatever it takes to get us the top dogs."

CHAPTER 34

AT FOUR THAT day Conklin and I were in an unmarked gray Chevy heading toward Chinatown. We had history with gangbangers in this neighborhood. One bust in particular had begun with a warrant and ended with SWAT battering down the door of an apartment off Jackson and engaging in a firefight with six Chinese gun merchants, who were shot to death along with one of ours as collateral damage.

Kenny Chen was part of this gang; a small fish but a fast swimmer who'd given us a bad tip, then evaded our net. Since that time he had rebuilt the Washington Street gang, not quite to its former glory, but the thirty-year-old had connections here and abroad, animal instincts, and big aspirations. Once he'd even had the balls to try and bribe me.

I'd studied him for a few years and knew that when he wasn't dealing or asleep in his Volvo, Kenny Chen hung out at the Li Po Lounge, a well-known dive bar named for a Chinese poet and popular with locals and tourists alike.

Conklin nosed our unmarked car into a no-parking zone and

slapped a police vehicle notice on the windshield, and we walked to the bar near the corner of Grant Avenue and Washington Street. From the street, Li Po looked festive: brightly colored and wrapped with neon-lit, come-hither signage. It was almost irresistible. My partner held the door and we stepped into Li Po's dim interior.

Entering this lounge was not just a change of scene. It was a change of culture and maybe a throwback to a different time. Paper lanterns and pennants hung from the ceiling. Music poured from unseen speakers and filled the large room. The bar itself was beautiful by any standard; serpentine, it dominated one side of the room, and a Buddha the size of a large child held a place of honor in a niche behind the bar.

The opposite side of the room was furnished in red leather booths, half of them occupied. I picked out Kenny Chen, sitting alone at the last table in the back, with a view of the front door. He was as pale as a vampire, dressed all in black, and finished with a long black ponytail and drooping mustache.

As we closed in, I saw that he was busy with his phone and didn't see us approaching. Chen started as I slid into the banquette beside him, and Conklin took a seat across from Chen, blocking the man's long view.

"Mind if we join you," I said. It wasn't a question.

Chen looked angry, puzzled, then he remembered me.

"Sergeant Boxer? You're not still busting my balls about that shooting years ago? Told you then, telling you now: I had nothing to do with it. As far as I'm concerned—"

"Something entirely different," Conklin said, and he smiled. "I'm Inspector Rich Conklin. I'm not sure we've met. Wonder if you can help us with a case we're working, not connected to you at all."

CHAPTER 35

CHEN TURNED OVER his phone and placed it down on the table, folded his hands, and gave us a look loaded with attitude.

"Let me guess. You have guns on your mind?"

No kidding?

What did Chen know? Was this rumored weapons convoy common news? Or had someone in particular told Chen? If so, had that person died?

"You have something to share?" I said.

"And if I tell you what I know?"

"I'll put a note in your jacket saying that you assisted the SFPD. That's like an IOU. You may need it one day."

Chen sniggered. "Oh, goody."

I said to Conklin, "Come on, Richie. We're wasting our time."

"Wait, wait," said Chen. "I might have something. Let me buy you drinks."

I sure didn't want what he was having. Chen's mai tai was a potent mixture of three rums and a secret "Chinese liqueur."

Conklin said, "Sorry, but we're on the job."

I reached into my back pant pocket, tugged out a slim wallet, and wiggled two fingers behind the plastic window. I produced a tightly folded hundred-dollar bill and placed it on the lacquered table, held it down with two fingers.

I said, "Kenny? You know something worth this?"

He sniggered for the second time.

"A hundred bucks and a note in my file? This day is turning out to be like winning a game show. Where's the confetti?"

I started to retract my offer, when Kenny Chen put his cold hand on top of mine.

"You want to know about Al Vega?" he asked me.

The look on my face said, *Damned right.*

Chen pulled back his hand and tapped on his phone. Then he turned it to face me. I saw a news story under the CNN banner headlined *Prison Break in Guadalajara.*

"His name is in the story here," said Chen.

"What are you saying? He escaped?" I said.

"Only saying, now you know everything I know."

Chen tapped the back of my hand. I retrieved the hundred, tore it in half, and gave him what I considered more than his share.

"I'll give you the rest in exchange for information regarding Vega's current whereabouts. Good information."

He muttered in Chinese and pocketed the half hundred-dollar bill. That's when I saw the gun in his waistband.

"Put both your palms flat on the table, Kenny."

"What?"

I nodded at Conklin, who pulled his gun.

Reaching beneath Chen's python-print jacket, I removed the gun from his belt and gave it a look. It was a Luger semiauto. Illegal since last week.

I slid out of the booth, told Chen to get up, put his hands on his head. And I pocketed his gun.

I spun him around and cuffed him while Conklin called for backup. I read Chen his rights, which he refused to acknowledge. Conklin slapped the back of his head, saying, "Do you understand your rights?"

Chen said, "You're a tool, you know that?"

Conklin read Chen his rights again, one line at a time, adding "Do you understand?" after each line. We walked Kenny Chen through the eerie wall of sound, past the customers and the Buddha and a couple of bartenders, who cast their eyes down.

The three of us were on the street when a cruiser pulled up to the curb. I identified myself, and Conklin folded Chen into the back seat.

Conklin smiled at me. I understood that smile to mean, *Some days I love my job.* I smiled back. Then I spoke to Officer Einhorn, who was at the wheel, telling him to take Chen to booking and that we'd meet him there.

My partner and I stood together outside Li Po and watched the squad car pull away. I asked Conklin for the keys.

I wanted to drive.

CHAPTER **36**

BRADY HELD A team meeting at seven that evening, and we stayed clumped around him at the front of the room for over an hour. Cappy and Chi had gone through Swanson's files and found Roy Abend's tipping point.

Chi said, "There was one word on Swanson's six-month performance review of Abend. 'Insubordinate.'"

Conklin said, "Wild guess, Abend wouldn't go along with Swanson's plot to rob and kill people and deal millions in drugs."

"Probably true," said Chi. "For whatever reason, Swanson disliked him. Abend quit before he got fired. Or killed."

We talked, kicked the Abend mystery around, then, with no suspects and no action plan for tonight, Brady sent us all home.

I stumbled through our apartment door at 8:20, so wrung out, I could only think about food.

Joe was on the phone in his office when I waved at him, patted our dog, and looked in on Julie, who was sound asleep. There was a pizza box on the kitchen counter, and I headed for it. I polished off a big, floppy slice of cold pizza right out of the box. While I was there, I guzzled down the remains of Joe's glass of Cabernet. I was thinking about a refill before I'd finished the dregs at the bottom of his glass.

Joe finished his call. He read my face and came over to my chair.

"You okay?"

"I think so. Claire autopsied that little girl and she sounds bad about it."

"How about I give you something else to think about," my husband said.

"Don't hold back. Make it good."

He laughed, then said, "I know this guy at the National Public Radio station in Sacramento."

I said "Uh-huh" to encourage Joe to keep talking.

"Bob Berman. He's a producer."

"Uh-huh."

"He asked to interview me about the Scientific-Tron case a couple of years ago. I couldn't. I was out of it for too long, as you know. Then I got busy. Then I said okay and penciled in a date. Forgot it's tomorrow."

"Tomorrow is Sunday, right? And it's in Sacramento?"

"Yep. Berman's show starts at one. So if we leave at ten, we can have a nice relaxing drive. I do the interview for an hour tops, then we stop for lunch and drive home."

"Oh. I'd love that, Joe. You've got a date."

CHAPTER 37

JULIE PUT UP a grade A fuss, crying, "No-no-no-no, I want to come with you." Again. And again. Lindsay almost gave in, but Joe didn't bend.

"Sweetie, we would love to bring you, but we can't do it. I have to work."

"No-no-no-nooooo."

The doorbell rang and Mrs. Rose knocked her two-beat knock.

Lindsay kissed Julie Bug on each cheek, gave her a good long hug, and grabbed her jacket from the hook in the foyer as she opened the door. By then, Martha was whining. The fuss was now grade A-plus.

Mrs. Rose stepped in, took a couple of mental snapshots, and decoded the situation. She said to Julie, "Guess who's going to the dog park?"

Joe and Lindsay said good-bye to Julie once more, promised to be home before she knew it, and left Julie and their shaggy dog with Mrs. Rose.

Joe's car was fully gassed and he started her up, then pulled out onto Lake Street and headed up through the Presidio and across the Golden Gate toward Sacramento.

During the drive Joe talked with Lindsay, going over the subject of his upcoming on-air interview about the last night of Sci-Tron. He wished he hadn't agreed to do it. Much of what had happened that night was hazy, but what he did remember was almost too vivid.

He and Lindsay had been celebrating their anniversary at a seafood restaurant on Pier 9, right off the Embarcadero. There was a rosy sunset that evening, and they had a direct view of the sky, the bay, and Scientific-Tron, a futuristic science museum made entirely of glass and metal tubing that took up most of the opposite pier.

They were toasting to happy days when there was a deafening boom, followed by an impossibly loud crack, as if the sky had split in half. A mushroomlike cloud rose above a heavy shower of splintered glass as Sci-Tron was bombed out of existence.

Joe knew that the museum was open that night and that at least a hundred visitors were inside when the bomb exploded. He and Lindsay immediately left the restaurant, and while Lindsay waited for police responders, Joe's training and instincts sent him into the shifting remains of the museum to look for survivors.

"I can still remember every step of my search through the wreckage," he said now to Lindsay.

It had been dead dark inside, but like a cat, he'd picked out obstacles and stepped around or over them: overturned exhibits, beams and panels faintly illuminated by broken lighting, hissing and sparking under the crumpled superstructure. And he remembered the woman, her arm poking out from under a pile of aluminum sheeting and shattered glass. She'd asked him to find her husband and tell him where she'd hidden the key to their safe-deposit box—and then a secondary explosion had grabbed him up and thrown him down.

Much later Joe had learned that his skull had been fractured, and recent memories had dribbled away. Even now, when trying to recall that night, he had only split-second flashes of images. But Lindsay was a reliable witness. She remembered clearly when the firefighters finally brought him out on a stretcher. She recalled exactly what the emergency doctors had told her. And she'd been with him in the ICU as long as the hospital had allowed.

As Joe prepared himself for his NPR interview, Lindsay filled in some of those facts that had been lost to him. The name of the woman under the wreckage, who'd died. Julie's visits to him in the hospital. His family flying out from New York to be with him. That his doctor hadn't known if he would live or die.

"Bob Berman should ask *you* to speak about the aftermath," said Joe of the show's producer.

"No, please don't suggest it to him. I'm a terrible public speaker."

"You'd be great."

"You'll be better."

Joe parked in the lot, ran his hand through his hair, his fingertips traveling the scar running a crooked path from the top of his head to the back of his neck. Could he really describe that night without losing track of the events?

Producer and interviewer Bob Berman met them at the front desk. Berman looked to be under forty, with a generous smile, a pink shirt, and an NPR bow tie. He welcomed them, grasping their hands with both of his. Then Berman walked them around the pie-shaped office space, designed so that the individual studios were wedges, the optimal shape to produce the pristine sound NPR required.

Berman said to Joe, "We get callers in to the show, and as you know, we're going out live. So if you need more time to answer a caller's question, you can say, 'Let me get back to you on that.'"

"That could happen," Joe said. "You've been warned."

CHAPTER 38

JOE FELT SELF-CONSCIOUS as he waited for the green light to flash *go*. He didn't like the spotlight. Never had. He wished again that he'd politely passed on this interview, but Bob Berman had been convincing. "Joe. You saved lives as a citizen. This is a feel-good story. Hey. You risked your life to save others. Take a bow," Berman had said.

Now he and Berman sat in facing armchairs inside one of the green-painted, wedge-shaped studios. The window at the narrow end of the room framed the control booth. Berman was making small talk with him about the history of the round CapRadio building, which was said to have been designed along the lines of the starship *Enterprise*.

While Berman loosened Joe up, sound tests were run, mics were adjusted, and Lindsay gave Joe a thumbs-up from her seat behind the glass. The engineer counted down with his fingers from five seconds to one. Then Bob Berman greeted his audience and introduced Joe Molinari as former deputy director of Homeland Security as well as a special agent with the FBI for decades.

Joe thanked Berman and, hoping he sounded somewhat natural, said that he was glad to be there. Berman spoke next, setting up the Sci-Tron event that had put Joe's face on TV news and national newspapers' front pages.

Berman said, "Deputy Director—"

"Joe is just fine."

"Okay, then. Joe. Please tell our audience about the last night in the life of San Francisco's world-famous Scientific-Tron."

With refreshed images in his mind, Joe spoke to Berman as if they were alone, about his decision to help, which made itself, the darkness of the interior, the twisted beams and jagged panes of glass.

Prompting Joe, Berman said, "And one of those beams came down on you."

"I only remember waking up a few days later in the hospital. My wife, Lindsay, was there, and I learned that the fire department had done a fantastic job of rescuing survivors."

Berman held up a finger. He was listening through his headset. He said, "Joe, we have a caller on the line. And what's your name, sir?"

"Walters," said the caller, his voice loud inside the studio. He said, "Agent Molinari, this museum is an old story. Why don't you talk about how you and a team of armed FBI muscle arrested and deported a vendor at the Cow Palace last week?"

Berman said, "Mr. Walters, you're off topic—"

Joe said, "I can't discuss the gun show...."

"I'll discuss it for you," said Walters. "You're an anti–Second Amendment deep-state spy. The man you arrested at the gun show was guilty of offering guns for sale. That's all. But you personally delivered him to the Mexican federal cops. Maybe you also know that Vega's family was just slaughtered in Guadalajara."

Shocked at what Walters had said, Joe stared at the control booth. He hadn't heard this about the Vega family. Was it even true?

Berman shook his arm, trying to get his attention.

Joe said into the mic, "Mr. Walters, I'll say it again. I won't and can't discuss FBI business—"

The man calling himself Walters talked over Joe.

"Look out, Molinari. I followed your cop wife yesterday. I'm staring at your car right now. Here's your license plate...."

Berman stood up and faced the engineer, ran a finger across his throat, signaling to close down the phone call. Lindsay had, by then, bolted out of her seat, pushed open the control room door, and run for the exit. Joe ripped off his headset, and he, too, fled the studio. He caught up with Lindsay at their car.

Panting, she said, "If he was here, he's gone now."

Joe punched numbers into his phone. He identified himself and asked for Sacramento's police chief, who got on the line.

"I received a death threat from a caller to a live radio show," said Joe. "This guy had eyes on my vehicle five minutes ago and was gunning for my wife, too. We're at the CapRadio parking lot. Black Mercedes sedan. Whoever made the call is gone, but I need to be sure....Yes. We'll be waiting for the bomb squad."

CHAPTER 39

JOE AND I stood in the parking lot and watched the robot roll back up the ramp into the rear of the armored vehicle. The bomb squad slammed and locked the doors, and Hank Clooney, the expert in charge, told us, "No problem. You're good to go. Good-bye and good luck."

We eyed Joe's middle-aged Mercedes with lingering suspicion. There had been no bomb attached to the undercarriage, no explosive charge wired to the ignition. The car was certified safe. We strapped in, and when Joe started the engine, she purred like the old panther we knew her to be.

I was still in a state of high anxiety as we headed south down I-80, back toward San Francisco. I listened for ticking sounds, watched passing cars for a rolled-down window and a gun aimed at us. There was no such car.

I called Clapper and was put straight through.

"Boxer, is Molinari with you? Put me on speaker," he said.

I did it.

Clapper wasted few words, asking, "Has that Walters guy called you again?"

Joe and I said "No" in unison.

Clapper said, "We've got the number. He used a goddamn burner phone, of course."

"I'm starting to wonder if he was really out at the car," Joe said. "He could have gotten my tag numbers anytime. If he had access to a DMV database, or saw my car parked outside our apartment…"

"True," Clapper said. "He could be a crank. Or he could have you in his sights right now."

I told Clapper where we were and that we were going home. While Joe spoke to FBI section chief Steinmetz, I called Mrs. Rose.

"Everything okay?"

"Sure, sure," she said. "Ms. Cutie-Pie, Martha, and I are at Koret. We're about to have lunch. I brought sandwiches."

I said, "We'll be home in an hour at the most."

Joe drove at maximum legal speed and then some. We didn't stop for a delightful lunch as originally planned, but food had been an idea in a different mood and time.

"What you said to Clapper. You think Walters was putting us on," I said.

Joe said, "The more I think about it…I'm picturing the guy standing next to me at Vega's booth when I asked Vega to show me a semiauto. This guy saw my badge and yelled 'Fed' to warn Vega. And ATF moved in, Vega fired on Wallenger, you know. It all went down."

"So that caller could be the guy you saw or someone he knows."

Joe said, "We'll watch our butts. What else can we do?"

"I'll watch yours," I said. "You watch mine."

"I always do," said Joe.

I was laughing at his joke when my phone jangled. I didn't recognize the number, but I clicked on it and said, "Hello."

A man's voice said, "I'm keeping an eye on you, Sergeant Boxer. You carry a gun for protection. Me, too."

Was he the radio-show caller? I couldn't tell. I said, "Who are you? What do you want?"

"I want to put my gun in your mouth."

There was a buzz, a click, and even though the caller had hung up, I still yelled at the phone. "Coward. Bastard."

Joe pulled off the road and turned off the engine. He asked me what had happened. I told him. We made a few more calls.

CHAPTER 40

I CALLED MRS. Rose again from the car.

"Slight change of plans, Gloria," I said. "Joe's dropping me off at the park, okay? We're about ten minutes out. Where are you exactly?"

"On a bench near the carousel. Not far from the stairs."

"Got it," I said. I heard Julie shouting to Martha, who barked back. They sounded joyful. I said good-bye to Mrs. Rose and watched traffic as Joe phoned Steinmetz. It was a quick call.

Joe said, "Steinmetz wants me to meet him at the office as soon as I can get there. He's calling Clapper."

I said, "Clapper is going to put me under protection."

"Fine with me," said Joe.

Was I fine with being housebound? I had a job to do. Cases to close. And if I was a target, I'd rather be a moving target. While Joe called Wallenger and told him the story, I scanned my phone for missed calls and texts. There were two calls from Claire. None from the nameless terrorist who'd just threatened me. Had my secret terrorist watched us leave the radio station?

My gut said he had.

There was a clear inside lane ahead of us. Joe took it with a vengeance, going over the speed limit, slowing at intersections, gunning the car again. I saw no one following us, but I still had a creepy feeling that we were being watched.

We were nearing the Koret Children's Quarter in Golden Gate Park, where our daughter was laughing and shouting and having a good time. Koret is an extraordinary playground, a dream of a place for parents and kids. The centerpiece is a century-old carousel with old-timey music and over sixty menagerie animals, colorfully painted, with gilded hooves and horns.

Joe took the lightly traveled ring road past the dog run and wave-shaped climbing wall. When we were within shouting distance of the carousel, he pulled over and we both got out of the car.

Julie was expecting us and called out. I ran toward her while Joe cast his trained G-man eyes around the park.

"I went on the camel," Julie said.

"The camel? For real?"

Mrs. Rose confirmed that this was true.

"And before that," said Julie, "I rode the dragon."

Mrs. Rose said, "I took pictures. Talk about a natural-born dragon rider, this kid's got it."

"Can't wait to see them," I said. "But for now, how about we take Julie and Martha and give you a lift to your car?"

We were in separate cars but we stayed close and arrived at Lake Street together. We parked, waited for Mrs. Rose, and crowded into the elevator, then disembarked in a gaggle on our shared floor.

Seven hours after beginning our harrowing getaway, we were

safely home. I exhaled loudly, shaking off my tension like a wet dog. Joe opened our front door and Mrs. Rose opened hers, but she made a hand motion, signaling that there was something she wanted to tell me.

"Joe, I'll be right there."

I crossed the hall and entered Gloria's apartment, which was sunnier than ours and furnished with eclectic furniture from her marriage and her parents' home.

She closed the door and said, "Lindsay, I can't be sure. I want to underscore, not sure. But I thought someone was watching me when I left with Julie. The car was dark, black or maybe midnight blue. The sun was glancing off it and I didn't want to stare. But I did see that he pulled out and stayed behind me. Made all the lights, and when I got to the parking lot, I locked all the doors. He drove past me without stopping and then disappeared."

I asked, "Did you see his face?"

"I wish," she said. "It all happened too fast. He was white, if that helps. And he wore a cap."

"Did you take a picture of the car?"

"I didn't want to take my hands off the wheel."

My fear was back and instantly overtaken by fury.

We were targets, all of us.

CHAPTER 41

MRS. ROSE AND I stood together inside her living room, worrying out loud. I told her that Joe had gotten a call from a listener who'd said he'd been following Joe's "cop wife." And that a sicko had called my cell phone and had offered to put his gun in my mouth.

I'm sure my face showed just how scared I was.

"What is this about, Lindsay? Why is all this coming at you and Joe?"

"It's about guns, the kind that can kill fifty people with a clip. Did you hear about the new law that makes those guns illegal? Some people really don't like that."

Mrs. Rose said, "Oh, my God. And I thought I was overreacting."

"I just don't know. But if anything alarming happens again, and you can't reach me, call 911. No. Don't cry. I'll check into this with my chief, okay? The car that followed you could have been undercover cops assigned to protect my family."

"You think so?" Mrs. Rose said. "That would be a…a tremendous relief."

"If not," I said, "I'll be getting police protection and it will extend to you. You think if you looked at mug shots you could identify the driver?"

"Doubtful. I'm sorry."

My phone rang from inside my handbag. It was Joe's ring. I answered, saying, "Honey, I'll be right there."

"I have to go, Linds. Julie needs you."

Mrs. Rose told me she had a few chores to do, and after we'd hugged, I crossed the hall.

"Sorry," Joe said, "Steinmetz is waiting for me."

"Joe. Gloria thinks she was followed to the park this morning by a midnight-blue or black sedan. She wasn't close enough to see the driver's face. She didn't get the car's make or tag number."

"Was she threatened?"

"Just unnerved. Me, too."

"I'll tell Steinmetz. Lock the door when I leave."

"Of course."

"If someone calls and you don't recognize the number, don't answer the phone."

I kissed Joe good-bye, watched through the front windows as he crossed the street and got into his car. I saw nothing unusual. No parked dark sedans. No diabolical trolls loitering on our street.

I unleashed Martha and filled her water bowl. Julie had eaten a sandwich, but I was anxious and hungry. Scrambled eggs would do the trick. I cooked up a batch and made toast. Julie joined me at the counter with a glass of chocolate milk, and after I'd cleaned up the kitchen, I did another security check.

Our front windows have a wide view of Lake Street. I looked down and watched the regular stream of light Sunday-afternoon traffic. Everything looked normal.

And then it didn't.

Parked a block and a half down on Lake, across the street from our apartment building, was a dark BMW sedan. At that distance and from fifty feet above the street, I could only make out movement in the front seat. Two men, maybe three. Damn it. My binoculars were in my car.

I didn't like this at all.

CHAPTER 42

I TOLD JULIE, "I'm going to see Mrs. Rose. I'll be right back."

I knocked my three-two tattoo on Gloria's door. When she didn't answer, I pushed the bell. She came to the door with wet hair and a towel in her hand.

"What happened?" she said.

"I think that car is out there. I need to check it out."

"Yes, I'll watch Julie," she said. "But, Lindsay, be very, very careful."

"I'll be quick. And careful."

Back inside the apartment with Mrs. Rose, I told my little kiddo, "I'm going downstairs, but I'll be back in a couple of minutes."

"Whyyyyy?"

"I'll be right back, honey. Mrs. Rose will keep you company."

I ruffled Julie's curls while thinking out my game plan. I would just walk west on our side of the street, pass the car, then double back on the opposite side so that I could approach the BMW from the rear. Snap the tags and maybe get a sidelong look at the occupants. Then I'd call it in.

What could possibly go wrong?

I didn't wait for the elevator, just trotted downstairs, took a right outside the building's front door, and kept my eyes down. No one looking at me would think I was surveilling the BMW. Nobody.

Eyes straight ahead, I walked west past the intersection at Twelfth. When I was clear of the BMW, I cut behind it as planned and took a photo of the California tags. Then I took to the sidewalk, speeding toward the storefronts. Looking as inconspicuous as a five-foot-ten blonde with a long stride can look. I kept striding and cleared the front of the car.

The windows of our eleventh-floor apartment were in view, and my phone was in my hand. I waited for the green light to change and was checking my shot of the BMWs plates when I heard a shout that would have turned boiling water to ice.

"Hey, Boxer," a masculine voice yelled from the BMW, now three or four car lengths behind me. "Good luck shutting down our guns."

I turned to see the man's face, but the windshield was tinted and I was too far away. I crossed Lake to my side of the block and used a parked FedEx truck for cover. I called dispatch and got May Hess, shift supervisor and longtime friend. I briefed her on the morning's incidents in short, sharp strokes, ending with the shout-out from the BMW.

I said, "It looks like two or three occupants inside the car, possibly armed. They need to be detained, forthwith."

My next call was to Clapper. I hoped I'd get lucky, that the chief would pick up. That he'd tell me he had me covered. But I got his voice mail instead.

I left a brief message. "Urgent. Call me."

CHAPTER 43

I HAD NO emotional distance from that car across the street. If my theory was right, the occupants had waited for Gloria to get into her car with Julie Anne, my baby, and tailed her to the park. My theory grew by the second. They could have been watching me and Joe when we got to Koret and followed all of us home. They knew where we lived.

I had to fight with myself. I wanted to but could not draw my gun, go to that car, deal with three men without a partner, without backup, without solid footing for an arrest.

Where was my backup? Where?

The FedEx driver came out of the building next to ours and got into his truck. He started the motor. Why hadn't Clapper called me back by now? The BMW was still parked where I could see it. For how long? Was I going to make a dash for my front door? Or was I going to walk into what could be my last minutes on earth?

I pulled my gun from my waistband, walked out from behind the truck, and set a course for the passenger side of the Beemer.

Just then I heard my new favorite sound in the world: sirens coming from opposite directions. Two squad cars converged on the BMW, blocking it in against the curb. A third car passed me and blocked off the eastbound lane. A pair of uniforms got out to direct traffic.

I turned back to the BMW and saw Sergeant Robert Nardone and his partner, Officer Martin Einhorn, asking the driver for license and registration. With gun in hand, I crossed over to where cops were on the Job.

Nardone and I have known each other for ten years. The last time I'd seen Bob, he'd been pushed down a flight of stairs by a psycho killer. I was glad to see him, and as for Bob, it took less than a second for him to read the emotions in my eyes, all of the fear and fury I couldn't quite suppress.

So I told him the story.

"Lindsay," he said. "We got it. Stand down. Please."

Nardone ordered the Beemer's occupants out of the car.

There were three young adult males, decently dressed and of diverse ethnicities. None looked older than late twenties.

They were aware that several cops had loaded guns pointed at them, and put their hands on the Beemer's roof as ordered. They obeyed, but at the same time they were laughing. Like this was a great joke.

I couldn't just stand there and watch.

The smartass who'd been in the front passenger seat, the one who'd called out to me, was leaning over the car.

I stepped in and frisked him.

The bulge in his jacket pocket was a wallet, not a gun. I opened it. His name was Anderson. John D. He lived in Cow Hollow. The picture on his license matched his face. Handing off the wallet to

Einhorn, I reached under Anderson's arms. He laughed, saying that he was ticklish, which was close to incendiary given that I felt murderous.

I ran my hands down his legs and didn't find a weapon. Not even a toothpick.

He started to take his hands down, turn around.

"Stay where you are," I said. "We're not done yet."

CHAPTER 44

NARDONE AND EINHORN patted down the two others, who were making demands.

"What is this about, Officer?"

"What are we supposed to have done?"

"Isn't this what's called police harassment?"

Nardone said, "Shut up, you."

The pat-down produced wallets, phones, keys, and cigarettes—nothing illegal.

While Officer Einhorn collected IDs and ran the names through the cruiser's computer, Nardone and I questioned the driver, a handsome twenty-six-year-old with dirty-blond hair, good teeth, and no fear of law enforcement. His name was Anthony Ruffo.

"Did you drive to Koret playground this morning?"

"Not that I remember."

"Why are you parked here?"

"Why not?"

Ruffo volunteered that he could park where he wanted. That

this was a free country—and he offered many variations on that theme.

I said, "Free country, yes. Harassment, no. Stalking. No."

While I kept an eye on the three men, Einhorn and Nardone turned their backs and had a powwow at their cruiser. Then Nardone came over to me.

He said, "Boxer, the car is registered to Anthony Ruffo Sr. Junior's license is valid, registration up to date. No priors. Not wanted for anything we could find. The car is in a no-parking zone. That's it."

"They knew my name, Nardone. They called me by name."

"You've been in the news, Boxer. You're almost famous. What do you want to do with them?"

"I need their names. We'll do a thorough background check and the FBI will do the same. I don't see how we can hold them."

"Let them go," Nardone agreed.

Einhorn gave back the wallets and other items, and the three punks got back into their sixty-thousand-dollar car. I leaned into the driver's-side window and said to Ruffo, "Don't let me catch you loitering in this neighborhood. For any reason."

He said, "Any reason is not a crime. Sergeant."

"Smile, Ruffo."

I snapped a picture, but I could feel my face coloring. I'd phoned in a three-alarm fire for a parking violation. The joke was on me. And I didn't get it.

Ruffo started up the car and headed toward the Bay Bridge. After thanking the uniforms, I turned tail and went home.

CHAPTER 45

CINDY WAS TAKING up her outside third of the bed and Richie had the rest of the mattress, sprawled out and snoring.

She couldn't sleep and it was too early to get up, so she gave free rein to her thoughts. They started with Richie. He'd come home last night at just after midnight. He'd showered, sat on the edge of the bed, and just fallen into it.

She'd asked, "You okay, hon? Talk to me."

Lying on his back in the dark, he'd said two words, "Civic Center," but he'd been too fatigued to produce more than the two words, let alone string five or six into a sentence.

Cindy had pulled the blankets over them both and filled in what he hadn't told her. Richie had done a double shift and called her after 6 p.m. as he and Alvarez drove to City Hall. He'd told her that the Second Amendment faithful were protesting and that they were armed.

"I love you," he'd said. "I'll call you later."

But he hadn't. Cindy had turned on Eye on the Sky News and watched the swarm of protesters, all chanting, "We will not comply," and brandishing their automatic long guns. Some fired into the air. Others took out storefronts and streetlights. Cops from all stations had flooded in and arrests had followed. Looked like a dozen of them.

Cindy knew Rich well. He was a steady guy who thought things through. His winning manner defused nearly all explosive situations. But the automatic-gun revolt was exceptional. He wasn't even trained in mob control. The deliberate provocation by this loose band of armed citizens had been activated by righteous anger and had its own unpredictable life.

As she'd heard on her police scanner, the opposition—the no-guns protesters—were out, too, and many had brought their children to see this historic moment.

While the riots in the street were on camera, and the mainstream news covered the demonstration, they hadn't yet homed in on the undercurrent in the halls of law enforcement. That a massive but unspecified load of military-style weaponry was en route from Mexico to the City by the Bay.

That mysterious gun run and the three unsolved homicides—Donahue, Abend, and Barrows—seemed connected, and the stress of it all was affecting Richie as never before.

And Cindy was barely coping with stress of her own.

Her mind switched over to the trove of scrapbooks the psycho killer Evan Burke had gifted to her so that she would write his revolting life story. And Cindy knew it had all the makings of a bestseller. The scrapbooks were filled with photos and Burke's notes about his female victims, and those young dead women haunted her. They even had body types like hers: size 8, five four to five six.

Cindy was Burke's type.

She felt sick whenever she focused on Burke's victims, but she had to do it. That was what it would take to elevate a set of scrap-books into a blockbuster true-crime book that would make her name as a writer, attract a movie deal, and in any case, provide the financial foundation for the rest of her life.

The rest of her life included Richie.

CHAPTER 46

AT SEVEN O' something Cindy slid carefully out of bed and went to the kitchenette. She made instant coffee with heavy cream, grabbed a banana from the fruit bowl on the counter, and took her breakfast to her office table in the living room.

After opening her laptop, she scrolled to the second chapter of her book-to-be. The facts were there. Even the writing was good. But she saw that she'd shied away from the grittier stuff. The chapter needed a shock to get readers' hearts racing without grossing them out so badly they'd slam the book closed and write a one-star review on Amazon.

It was a thin line to walk.

Cindy wasn't ready to face the chapter about the schoolgirl Burke had killed in the parking lot of her Sunset District prep school. Not just yet. Possibly a little light procrastination would put her in the right mood.

She clicked on her browser's news page and was scrolling down past the riot at City Hall when she saw a Katie Caruso headline. The little girl had lived a hundred miles north of San Francisco, in a rural town called Rosewater. Claire had gone to Rosewater Friday morning to help a friend's niece do the autopsy.

The twenty-point type read *Arrests Made in Caruso Case* and the byline was a writer at the *Rosewater Daily News*. But the story was a tease. The writer didn't name the suspects or enlighten the reader with facts or quotes from the police chief because the case was in progress. No quote from the district attorney's office, either. Hell. It was Sunday and the DA's office was closed.

Cindy had about a hundred questions about the Caruso case and she had an inside source. Claire could answer all of the questions—if she was awake and willing. The last was the tough one, but Cindy took a chance. She texted Claire at seven fifteen, typing, *Claire. U awake?* and tapped Send. A second later a little bubble of text blooped onto her screen.

Claire: *You okay?*

Cindy: *Yes. Fine. Where are you?*

Claire: *Home. Kicking off my shoes.*

Cindy: *Can you spare a few words? What's the verdict on Caruso?*

Claire: *The parents confessed.*

Cindy: *OMG. They killed their daughter?*

Claire: *I'm out of bounds here, sweetie. You should contact Chief Pou in Rosewater.*

Cindy thanked her friend for the tip, and after they'd said good-bye, she put her coffee in the microwave. Two minutes later she was back in her desk chair with a view through the living room window. It was seven twenty. Lindsay would be awake, walking the dog or feeding Julie. She texted a message and hoped for the rare possibility that Lindsay was not only up but in a good mood.

Lindsay didn't reply to Cindy's text.

But a moment later she phoned. She didn't say "Hello" or "Cindy, are you crazy?" She said, "Do you have time to talk?"

"I do," Cindy said. "Of course I do."

"Between us, Cindy."

"We're friends, Linds. Just trust me, will you?"

"Joe and I are being stalked," said Lindsay. "Threatened."

"By who? And why?"

"I'm going by hunch and a trail of bread crumbs," Lindsay said. "It's got to be people who want to get the law repealed on automatic weapons. They threatened Joe. They threatened Mrs. Rose. They threatened me."

CHAPTER 47

I CALLED IN late Monday morning.

I had some work to do before going to the Hall. First, I looked out the window and identified the patrol cars making sure the Molinari family was covered against stalkers or worse.

I heard the sound of an automatic staple gun in my mind. I called dispatch to make sure the three cars were really there for us, then fed Julie and Martha, called Mrs. Rose, and asked her to take Julie to the school bus.

My own mother couldn't have done better caring for us than that dear woman who'd become a family member, despite all the drudgery and danger that doing so entailed for her.

I didn't wake Joe, just drove in thick Monday-morning traffic to the Hall of Justice. I took the stairs to the fourth floor and said hello to Bobby.

He said, "You're not getting enough sleep."

"Don't I know it."

The bullpen was busy, and I saw that Brady was in his office. He looked up as I came toward his open door, and I just walked in.

"Boxer. Sit your butt down."

I did it and said to Lieutenant Blond-and-Blue, "You spoke with Clapper?"

"He called me, yeah. You notice the cars outside your place?"

"I did."

"Good. Well, they're there—24/7 security detail until you and your family are safe."

"What are your thoughts?" I asked, expecting a theory on the threats.

Instead he said, "Another man with stapled lips has shown up dead. He was on the last ferry Sunday night, crossing back to San Francisco from Larkspur."

"Tell me that you're kidding."

Brady said, "When the ferry docked, a guard coming off duty from San Quentin found him sleeping on a bench seat with a newspaper blanket. Attempts to wake him failed, and the stapled lips gave him away as dead before anyone felt for a pulse."

"Do we know his name?"

"Arthur Guthrie. Chi knew him. Guthrie was a prison guard. A cop wannabe. Has a wife. No kids. Dollar bill in his pocket with the usual message. 'You talk, you die.' But no drugs. He was shot in the back of the head. One and done."

I said, "Shot? Not bludgeoned or drugged to death? These murders are clearly part of a pattern—but so random."

Brady nodded his agreement.

He said, "Whoever killed Guthrie did it their way. Doesn't look personal. I'm thinking multiple killers with one motive."

"Who's catching the case?" I asked.

"Alvarez and Conklin are working it now," said Brady. "ATF wants in, and maybe they know something we need to know."

"That Guthrie died on the Larkspur ferry makes me want to question Swanson," I said. "Maybe the dead man stopped by to say hello. Or get instructions."

"I'm waiting for the warden to call me back."

It was already half past nine, so I headed up the bullpen's center aisle, said good morning to Conklin and Alvarez, edged between Conklin and the wall, and dropped into my chair.

Conklin looked severely sleep-deprived, and while Alvarez still had the dewy skin of youth, she also looked beat.

"We were working the protest at City Hall," Conklin said. Alvarez filled in the details: the indignation of the rioters, the weapons, the chants, the assault on the government seat.

"Then came the protest against the protest," said Alvarez. "It was like standing in the middle of a two-way cattle stampede."

Conklin said, "And in today's news…"

He passed me his notes from Claire's backup pathologist, Dr. Dugan, as well as morgue photos of the unfortunate deceased, Arthur Guthrie.

I read the memo.

It said, "This is a preliminary report on the victim identified as Arthur Guthrie based on the ID on his person. Well-nourished Caucasian male, late twenties, stomach contents attached. Blood screen pending. No skin under the nails. No bruising on the body. No identifying tattoos. Old scar across the left scapula. No other marks on the body. Wedding ring on left ring finger, inscribed 'Art and Mary forever.' Approximate time of death between ten and twelve Saturday night. Cause of death, gunshot wound to the back of the head. Manner of death, homicide. Lips stapled together postmortem."

"The 'You talk' note from Guthrie's killer is at the lab," Alvarez told me. "I just got off the phone with Hallows," she said of our Forensics director. "Optimist that he is, he said that 'there might be sixty thousand prints on the ferry.'"

"Probably an understatement."

I opened my pencil drawer, took out a few Kind bars. Chocolate with nuts. I offered them around, got no takers, so I opened one for myself. I said, "No gun was found, I'm betting. No witnesses to the shooting?"

Conklin said, "Just the guard coming off duty from the prison. Richard Darby. He found the body."

Conklin texted me Darby's contact info and said what he was thinking. "These murders are so meticulous, Linds. So freaking clean. Nothing adds up to a lead or in any way points to a doer."

I asked, "Why was Guthrie returning from the Q?"

Alvarez said, "So far we don't know. The guard, Darby, didn't know anything about him. He's checking for us. Going through the visitors log, but we should do that again."

I said, "Brady and I are going to the Q today. We want to talk to Swanson and let him bullshit us for a half hour. Maybe he'll show some pity and give us a break."

Conklin said, "And then the skies are going to open and all our prayers will be answered."

I punched his arm and he pretended that I'd knocked him silly. That's when Brady came up the aisle. He had a word with Bobby, read a message slip. He looked up at the ceiling for a moment, then walked a dozen feet over to where Conklin, Alvarez, and I were following him with our eyes.

"What news?" I said.

"Swanson. He hanged himself in his cell. He's dead."

I didn't believe it. I stared, openmouthed, until Conklin spoke:

"Ted Swanson killed himself? Come on, Brady. He'd never."

Brady said, "Warden Hauser is faxing me his suicide note."

Brenda liked to say it was so '90s of us to still have a fax machine, but the warden and our squad room both had one. Ours was on the shelf behind Bobby's desk, and it had started to chug.

Bobby pulled the fax from the machine and brought it over to me. I focused my eyes on Ted Swanson's farewell to his wife. I didn't know his wife. But unless her heart was made of steel, when she read this, she'd cry.

CHAPTER 48

THREE HOURS LATER Lieutenant Jackson Brady and I were with Warden Hauser in his standard-issue civil service office at San Quentin.

There was a window with a watery view and that was it. No framed certificates or family photos, no cheesy shots with a government bigwig. Hauser was as efficient as his office. He made direct eye contact and handed Brady a few papers, saying that he should review them now and sign them after he'd seen the body.

Brady looked at the papers, then asked the warden, "How was Swanson acting before his death?"

"He seemed well adjusted," Hauser said. "He didn't cause trouble. Earned the privilege to eat in the dining hall at his own table. The way the inmates talked about him, I'd say he had a cult following."

"Meaning?" Brady said.

"Mystery man. A high-profile, dirty, rotten ex-cop."

I found it too easy to get lost in memories of Swanson's regrettable, unalterable past. Conklin, Brady, and I had been there for the bloody finale of his multimillion-dollar crime spree. I remembered identifying dead members of the SFPD. I'd searched for the body of the cartel's kingpin, known as Kingfisher. He wasn't there.

When Brady said my name, I snapped out of it and returned to the present. I asked the warden, "Did anyone notice that he was suicidal?"

Hauser said, "When you saw him last week, did *you* think he was depressed?"

"No. I'd say opposite of depressed. What changed?"

"We saw nothing. No apparent illness. No apparent threats. If your next question is why we didn't have him watched, he was on the short list of inmates at risk. A guard went by and checked on him every hour," the warden said. "Swanson knew when a guard was due, and he used the opportunity to make his last move. I just spoke to his wife. She had no idea this was coming. Never. She thought he was content."

"She visited him?" Brady asked.

"Recently. Friday afternoon. She was here at least a couple times a month. Sometimes she brought a toddler with her. A boy maybe two years old. Swanson looked normal. You can't always judge a man's insides by his outsides," Warden Hauser said. "You saw his suicide note?"

We had.

"Here's the original."

It had been written in block letters with a pencil on the inside of a cardboard Cup Noodles package. It read, "I'm very sorry, Kim. I love you too much to ask you to share my life sentence. Now you are free. I know you'll understand. All my love, Ted."

Fuck. If I hadn't known Swanson, I would have felt sorry for him, but it would have been a waste of pity on the sociopath who had worn a badge.

"Did anyone here threaten to kill him?" I said.

"If so, we didn't know about it."

"Between cell checks, did anyone have access to his cell?"

Hauser said, "Don't see how. A prisoner on the block or one of a dozen guards would have seen and reported a break-in. He used ripped sheeting for a noose. Dr. Abel Tor cut him down. You ready to see the body?"

I nodded. Brady said simply, "Yep."

It was a long walk through the block and down a flight to the basement level. I had time to prepare myself, but it was still shocking to see the snake charmer with the looks of a movie star lying faceup under the lights, dead cold. The violence he'd done to himself had left wide bruises around his neck, and his eyes were blackened, like he'd been punched.

Dr. Tor was waiting for us. He was lanky and soft-spoken, pushing sixty.

Tor said, "I x-rayed his body. His neck was broken. Hyoid bone intact, so 90 percent certainty that he wasn't strangled by another person. The knot was under his jaw, right here. That broke his neck. Only signs of a struggle were injuries to his ankles from kicking at the wall and scrapes on his wrists, last-second attempt to pull himself up. I saw no defensive wounds. I'm calling it suicide."

Looked that way to me, too.

Ted Swanson's signature charm was gone for good.

I wasn't sorry that he'd killed himself, but my conscience was kicking me in the ribs. I'd put a jailhouse target on him. I did it out of pique. Out of long-held anger. Out of revenge.

CHAPTER 49

WARDEN HAUSER OFFERED Brady and me an office two doors down from his, and we used it to question guards and inmates who'd been within shouting distance of Swanson's cage between midnight and four this morning.

The guard who'd found Swanson's body and blown the whistle was Dan Harris, a guard with twelve years at San Quentin and several years at Grand Rapids PD. He was disgusted with himself for not finding Swanson before it was too late.

"I flashed my light on his bed when I come by at two. He was sleeping. Same at three. At four, he'd hung himself. Still warm but no pulse."

Swanson's closest neighbor on the tier had heard nothing.

"I sleep really tight," said fellow inmate John Capuana. "Always been a deep sleeper."

More of the same from six others. Heard nothing. Knew nothing. Felt bad.

We left the prison none the wiser, and I was angrier leaving than I'd been when we arrived. Fucking Swanson had had the last word.

Brady and I followed the mile-long pedestrian path, reaching the ferry stop under the slanting rays of the late-afternoon sun. I would have thought that we'd both seen enough death in our work to get past the sight of Ted Swanson's corpse without emotion.

Swanson had been a bad cop and a criminal. The worst. But we'd known him, worked with him, and for a long time we'd trusted him, too.

I was reeling from all things Swanson, and it would take the length of that walk for me to tell Brady what was hurting me the most. Even confiding in the man who was my boss, partner, and good friend was frustrating.

Other people were walking along the path. Some were coming from the ferry, others going toward it. Small groups passed us, chatting, railing, laughing, crying, and I didn't want to be overheard.

So the conversation between myself and Brady was choppy.

In a lull between pedestrians, I asked him, "Do you think he killed himself or that someone got to him?"

"What do you think?"

"Didn't I ask first? Okay. I think anyone could have written that suicide note," I said. "Block letters in pencil, pressed hard on soft cardboard?"

"I'll give you that, but Swanson was in the SHU. How does another soul get into his cell and string him up without being seen?"

"It's been done, Brady. Guards turn their backs. Guards get paid off. Bad guy gets the key to the cell. I don't know. Maybe they make skeleton keys in the shop. We don't know that no one got into the cell. We only know that no one is saying so."

We stepped off to one side to let people pass us. I had to tell Brady what had happened when I was here before.

"Listen, Brady. I didn't tell you this earlier, but after Conklin and I met with Swanson, we were going through that wide-open recreation area to meet with my former CI, Chris Manolo."

"Okay. And?"

"The ceiling is open all the way up to the fourth tier," I said. "And while walking through, I yelled out, 'Swanson, thanks for helping out the SFPD.' Something like that."

Brady looked at me. I couldn't meet his gaze, but I said, "I shouldn't have done that. But I have a real hate on for Swanson."

"Don't we all?"

I said to Brady, "Now, if he was killed, or even if he killed himself, that makes me ask if Swanson wasn't part of this whole guns and drug operation. Maybe he was a boss, directing the operation from his cell. He could have sent messages in and out through his wife. Other visitors. Screws."

We were walking again. Ramps were being hooked from the ferry to the dock. We picked up our pace and I kept talking.

"Brady. Former cops who knew Swanson have been murdered. Donahue. Abend. In some cases, their murders involved drugs. Swanson stole millions in fentanyl that has never been recovered. Is this a coincidence?"

Brady said, "So you're thinking, 'You talk, you die'? And if Swanson talked to you…"

"I said so to hundreds of people in one shout. Anyone who heard me could have found it believable. That Swanson talked to me. And so he talked, he died."

We stepped down to the ferry dock and got into the line to board.

"Am I paranoid? Or am I making sense?"

Brady said, "If you and Joe hadn't been harassed, Boxer, I might think you're reaching. Now I like it as a theory. Let's meet with the chief. Talk it over."

CHAPTER 50

RETIRED BAILIFF ROBERT Nussbaum was at the reception desk when the call came in for Lieutenant Brady.

"I'm sorry, he's out. I can take a message....No. I don't know when he's expected." Bobby paused while the caller got so overheated, his voice carried out of the phone, into the front of the squad room.

Bobby let him go on about how this was important, how the caller was a former cop and to please patch the call through to the lieutenant's phone.

Bob held the phone a few inches from his ear and finally said, "Mister. Stop what you're doing."

Apparently the caller stopped yelling, and Bobby said, "I will certainly pass—no. No. Just give me your name and number and tell me what this is about, and the lieutenant will get your message....Spell that for me?" Then Bobby repeated it.

"Ransom. R-a-n-s-o-m. And your first name?...Got it. And what number is the best one to reach you?...Let me read it back."

Bob read it back, assured the caller that he would speak personally to the lieutenant. "You take care, too."

When he'd finished writing down the message, Bobby swiveled his chair around to face Rich Conklin, who'd been trying not to eavesdrop across the distance of about twelve feet.

Bobby called over to Conklin and Alvarez, "Can you two spare a few minutes in the break room? I need a coffee."

Conklin called back, "Bob. Let's go."

Alvarez said, "Did I hear something about coffee?"

"Why, yes. Yes, you did," said Bobby.

The three of them went to the break room, which had recently been painted a cheery yellow to cover five years of people writing notes to themselves on the walls. They took mugs down from the cabinets and found the fixings on a tray near the Mr. Coffee. Bobby poured, and then all three brought their coffee back to the squad room.

Bobby called over to Conklin.

He said, "That James Ransom who just called says he has information about Swanson."

Alvarez smiled and said, "So did Mr. Ransom say what he wants?"

Bobby stirred his coffee with a thin wooden stick and said, "Ransom said that he's a former cop, that he just heard that Ted Swanson died, and that he has to talk to the lieutenant. I did a quick check in the personnel files and he came up," said Bobby. "He transferred here from Chicago PD fifteen years ago. He worked our patrol unit for five years. Teddy Swanson was his partner."

"Let me have his number," Conklin said. "I think he'll talk to me."

CHAPTER 51

SIX MONTHS AFTER transferring from Las Vegas PD, Sonia Alvarez was still finding her way around San Francisco. But North Beach she kinda knew; it was central to Chinatown, the Financial District, and Russian Hill. Plus, North Beach was one of San Francisco's main nightlife areas. Former cop James Ransom now owned a bar called North Beach on the Rocks in the thick of it.

Rich Conklin met Alvarez at the car, handed her the keys, and tapped the bar's address into the GPS. During the drive Conklin repeated to Alvarez what Ransom had told him over the phone.

"Ransom said he knew Swanson like a brother, that Teddy was out for number one only. That he would never kill himself. I buy that," Rich said. "Swanson was a self-centered, dangerous bastard, but he's dead. I wonder why Ransom's call was so urgent."

"He's grieving, maybe. And frantic to get to the truth."

"Yeah. Could be right."

North Beach on the Rocks was hidden away in a lane off Columbus Avenue.

Conklin said to Alvarez, "Put her right there."

She double-parked without blocking the street. "Perfect," Conklin said. He put the cherry light on the roof, laid a card reading SFPD on the dash, and got out of the squad car.

A large fortysomething man with a beer belly and a full head of black hair had seen them coming and opened the door, making sure that the CLOSED sign faced the street.

Conklin made introductions just outside the open door to the bar. "I'm Jimmy Ransom," the man in the doorway said. "Barkeep and owner of this little dive. Thanks for coming, thanks very much," he said. "Come in, please."

Ransom led them lengthwise through the nice and clean drinking establishment. He introduced the barmaid setting up the bar, the young man taking chairs off the tables. There were oil paintings of sailing ships, large TVs on the walls, a high shelf of beer steins, two life-size plaster mermaids sitting on a pair of barstools; displayed nearby were photos of customers posing with them: grinning, leering, making rabbit ears.

Alvarez smiled when she saw the figures. "They have names?"

"Cleo and Marisol," Ransom replied. "Where are my manners? Can I get you guys a drink?"

Alvarez answered, "A bit early for us, thanks, but I'll be back when I'm off duty."

"Anytime," said the Rocks' proprietor, leading the way. "My office is right back here."

The corridor skirted the bathrooms and emptied into a cozy office at the rear. The desk was in a back corner, and the rest of the room was furnished with comfortable upholstered furniture and a coffee table made of a boat's hatch cover. Other nautical details adorned the wood-paneled walls.

Alvarez knew that Conklin had no interest in the decor. He was observing Ransom. In the short while she'd worked with Richie, she'd found him to be a beguiling interrogator, unthreatening but sharp.

And there was Ransom, eager to talk.

Leaning forward in his chair, arms crossed with his elbows on his knees, Conklin said, "Jimmy, how did you find out that Swanson died? It only happened last night. Late last night."

Ransom said, "Ted's wife called me. Do you know Kim?"

"I knew Nancy, his first wife," said Conklin. "Ted remarried after he was incarcerated?"

"Kim had a child from her previous relationship, and the whole setup appeals—appealed—to him."

Conklin asked, "What did Kim tell you?"

"She said that Ted was murdered."

Conklin sat back in his chair and Alvarez took over.

"Jimmy, at present there's no indication of murder. Ted left a suicide note for his wife. But his death is being investigated."

"Good," said Ransom. "I feel better. Not great but better. You sure I can't get you anything? Mind if I...?"

Alvarez said, "Not at all."

Ransom produced a bottle of J&B from the file cabinet and a glass from the windowsill. He poured a few fingers for himself, returned to his chair.

Alvarez continued. "When did you speak with Ted last?"

"Day before yesterday, I think. Every month or so I'd pay him a call. You understand, we were partners for five years. He moved up and I moved out, but we stayed in touch. I heard about his sideline ops from friends in common. And of course I heard about, you know. The shoot-out with that Mexican gang..."

Conklin sighed. "It was a war zone."

"I read about it, Inspector. I don't have the right words to say how shocked I am that my old partner is dead...."

"But?"

"But he was greedy. And he liked himself a little too much. That's why I say I don't think his ego would let him kill himself. But whatever, I'll help you in any way I can."

Conklin asked, "Did Swanson ever say anything to you about a gun racket? Running military weapons in from Mexico?"

"Guns? No. Nothing."

"What about enemies? Did he mention any names?"

"Not a word," Ransom said, "but sure, plenty of cops, their friends and family, hate him. That Mexican drug cartel doesn't like him much. All Ted complained about was the bad food and that he was alone so much.

"Look here," Ransom went on. He plucked a pen and a pad from his desk and wrote on it as he spoke.

"This is Kim Swanson's number. Maybe she'll help you. I'll call her and tell her you're okay."

Ransom put down the pen, and Alvarez picked it up by the pocket clip. When Ransom wasn't looking, she slipped the pen into her pocket. On the way out Alvarez took a photo of Ransom with Cleo and Marisol, the mermaids. He mugged for the camera as Alvarez said, "These are great."

She and Conklin thanked Ransom for his time, he said to call anytime, and cards were exchanged.

Back on the road, Conklin driving, he commented on the snapshots of Ransom with the mermaids. "Clever, Sonia. You're gonna run Ransom's mug through facial rec?"

"Oh, I thought I'd run the mermaids."

"Smarty-pants."

Alvarez laughed and said, "I snatched his pen, too. Tried not to smudge his prints."

Conklin smiled and told her, "You're good."

And then he said that he didn't give a crap about Swanson or how he died, or that he had old friends who believed in him.

"This case is all about the guns."

"Wherever they are," said Alvarez. "I think we should talk to the widow first. If he was passing information through her, maybe she'll drop a clue."

CHAPTER 52

LATE FOR WORK again, I stopped at the front desk to see if Brenda's uncle had anything for me.

Bobby put down the phone and asked, "Did the lieutenant get hold of you? He said that Clapper's Friday meeting has been moved up to today at nine. What's going on?"

I was hoping, praying, that Clapper had gotten a break in the see-nothing, hear-nothing rumored gun run from Mexico. Or that a big fat lead in one of our open homicides had come to light. Better yet, a confession to the Abend murder. That would send me to the moon. I'd liked Abend, and I just hated that we were still in nowhere-land. Same was true with Donahue, Barrows, and now Guthrie.

Bob said, "It's ATF's meeting. They're with Clapper now."

"ATF? Thanks, Bobby."

I checked my watch. It was ten to nine.

Edging past Alvarez to my desk, I greeted her and Conklin. "Morning, Rich, Sonia. What do you guys know about this ATF meeting?"

Conklin said, "Your husband would know."

I said, "Joe knows about this? He was asleep when I left."

"Brady told us ten minutes ago."

"Huh," I said. "Something's up."

I looked down the aisle to the office at the far end. Lights were on in Brady's office, but he wasn't there. ATF. What was up with that? I called Joe. Got his voice mail. Left a two-word message. "Call me."

Alvarez said, "We met with James Ransom in his bar yesterday."

"Oh, right. What did he have to say?"

"Said Swanson was a real sweetie pie," Alvarez said.

"He did not say that."

She grinned and I grinned back. Swanson was nothing if not a traitor, a thief, and a killer. She said, "Ransom's making a call for us to Swanson's widow."

Conklin added, "The way Ransom put it was that Ted loved himself too much to end it with a knotted sheet."

"Ha! I think he's right. So what are you thinking?"

"We ran Ransom through all available databases and he's clean."

"So nothing on Ransom?" I asked.

"What's less than nothing?" said Alvarez. "Ransom is who he says he is. Swanson's former partner for about five years. His prints and photo match his file. Ransom has no record."

Conklin said, "After the meeting we're going to pay the second Mrs. Swanson a call."

"Can't wait to hear about that," I said.

Together, Alvarez, Conklin, and I trudged upstairs to Clapper's office. We weren't the first to arrive, but the sofa was unoccupied and we took it. I saw Joe and Wallenger sitting on the other side of the room. Joe saw the question on my face and mouthed, "I didn't know."

I looked around and took mental roll call of the attendees. Sitting in the side chair next to Clapper was a muscular man in a dark ATF uniform. He had a dimpled chin and big brown eyes, and he looked irked. Like he was pissed to be here.

Brady was half sitting, half leaning against the window ledge between the sofa and Clapper's desk. When all the seats were filled by the task force, Clapper said, "Everyone, this is local ATF division chief Fred Braun. I believe you FBI agents are already acquainted with him, so to save time, if you ask a question of Chief Braun, state your name.

"First, he has something to say. Chief?"

I imagined Braun saying, *We've got the guns and the men who brought them in. Cross that off your list.*

Oh, man. When I'm wrong, I'm really wrong.

CHAPTER 53

BRAUN STOOD, TOOK off his jacket, and hung it over the back of his chair.

He clasped his hands in front of him and took the floor. "Thanks, Charlie, and hello, everyone. I don't know you all, but we're all working the same case and from the same starting point.

"As you all know, FBI special agents Mike Wallenger and Joe Molinari were at the Cow Palace gun show last week and had a low-rent mutt named Alejandro Vega under their guns before ATF put down the melee. I witnessed that myself."

Braun went on. "As you also know, Vega recently escaped Mexican custody. But the rumor that surrounds him about a small-beans cartel and a shitload of military weaponry—well, let me just say this: ATF has devoted countless man-hours and resources to this pile-of-crap story. And it's bull."

Cappy said, "What? That can't be right. Dead men have turned up, probably connected to this gun deal—"

Braun sharply interrupted him. "You are?"

"McNeil. Sergeant," Cappy snarled.

"Well, McNeil," said Braun, "we know about the corpses with the stapled lips, the fentanyl, the 'You talk, you die' slogan. I'm here to tell you that there's a guy in or around Mexico City putting out hits on losers in our area and making the hits look like some very enormous deal.

"It's not," Braun said. "It's a scam. I can't tell you this scum hit boss's name, because he uses aliases and he's what they used to call a master of disguise. But this ghost is somewhere in Mexico, and our authority does not extend across the border. Yours, neither."

Braun continued with his air of protest, saying, "As I told Chief Clapper, this whole murder by proxy is just some psychopath's idea of a good time. There may even be a different killer for each of your cases. I have it from a highly placed US government official, a reliable source. There is no wagon train loaded with guns. No stash of drugs. We've been played. What you do after this is up to you."

Braun said to Clapper, "Okay, Charlie. I've said my piece, so I'll get out of your way."

Clapper said, "Okay, we heard you. You made your point. But you know what? We're not frigging buying it. We have sources, too. And have good reason to suspect what your source says is bull. But thanks, Fred, for stopping by."

The head of the San Francisco Bureau of Alcohol, Tobacco, Firearms, and Explosives hung his jacket over his arm and headed for the door. Clapper followed behind him. After the ding of the elevator sounded, Clapper returned. He closed his door and addressed the task force.

"Keep working on the homicides on our patch. Abend. Donahue," he said. "The guns are primary. Keep working our CIs, turning over rocks, working our way up the ladder until we get to the big dicks leading the charge."

He exhorted us to double down on background checks, interview subjects and know-nothing witnesses, and get search warrants for victims' homes and vehicles.

Clapper smoothed back his hair, perched on the edge of his desk, and continued.

"As Boxer and Molinari will tell you, they were both threatened over the weekend, and the guns were mentioned."

McNeil said, "Lindsay?"

"I'll tell you after the meeting."

Clapper went on. "I know we're coming up dry, but as some poetic brainiac once said, 'It's always darkest before the dawn.'"

Alvarez said, "Chief?"

"Yes, Inspector?"

"Are you buying Chief Braun's story of an incognito hit boss? Or is ATF trying to shake us off, then swoop in and grab the glory?"

"I vote for that," said Wallenger.

"And I second it," Joe said.

Clapper added, "I wouldn't put it past him, but I don't care. We don't report to ATF. They do their job. We do ours."

I raised my hand. Chief said, "Boxer."

I said, "As you said, Chief. We've got no tips, no forensics, and our best lead hanged himself in his cell."

"You left out a word, Boxer."

"Sir?"

"The word is 'yet.' No leads yet. No evidence yet. Everyone who is in has to be all in. Anyone want out?"

He gave us about a minute of silence. I thought about the

on-air threat to Joe. I thought about the dirtbag wanting to put his gun in my mouth. I thought about those mutts in the BMW following Gloria Rose and my little girl. I was seething, but I bit down on the feeling. If there was one thing for sure, it was that I wouldn't stop before the killers were nailed down, the gun deal wrapped up, the perps in jail.

I wasn't a quitter. I knew everyone in the room as well as if we'd grown up together. I knew none of us would raise our hand, walk out the door. We kept our eyes on our chief.

The moment of silence ended, and Clapper spoke.

"All right, then. Be sharp. And be careful. Meeting adjourned until Friday morning."

CHAPTER 54

SONIA ALVAREZ AND I jogged down the stairs to Homicide, swapping snark about ATF chief Fred Braun basically telling us, "Nothing to see here."

She said, "Sounds to me like he's worried. Like we're getting in his way."

"Ha," I said. "If only."

"You mean, if only he'd tell us what we don't know."

"Exactly."

We grinned, then stormed the bullpen, got coffee in the break room, and joined Conklin at our triangulated desks. A moment later Brady entered the squad room and took the floor, saying, "Let's go over the whole deal."

Standing between us and Bobby, Brady asked for progress reports since yesterday. We all sounded off. After that our boss prepared us to be called up at oh dark hundred if we were needed to break up a gun-packing mob of protesters.

Having accounted for "alla that," Brady turned to the three of us who were landlocked at our desks.

"Conklin. That Jimmy Ransom dude. Did he make the call to Swanson's wife?"

"She's expecting us at eleven o'clock."

Brady said, "Conklin, you and Boxer go talk to the widow. Alvarez, the hotline got jammed with calls while we were in with Clapper. I need you to pick through them, see what's actionable. Everyone, I'll be in my office, running point. I need reports from alla y'all before you punch out for the day."

Conklin and I signed out an unmarked gray Chevy and headed north. The second Mrs. Swanson lived in San Rafael, an upper-middle-class town close to San Quentin. We easily found the Swanson house, a wood-shingled home situated some twenty feet above the road, facing a woodland. Similar forest-type homes were at the same elevation along Picnic Avenue.

SWANSON was on the mailbox. A driveway cut around it and up the hill from road to garage. A dusty blue Sienna minivan sat at the top of the drive.

Conklin parked next to the Sienna. The GPS robo voice said, "You have reached your destination. You have—" Conklin shut off the engine and we both unfastened our seat belts.

From the driveway I saw a wide black ribbon crisscrossing the front door. It said as plain as words that there had been a death in the family.

CHAPTER 55

CONKLIN AND I were early for our meeting with Mrs. Ted Swanson, born Kim Wong. She was expecting us, but would she welcome us or tell us this was a bad time and to get the hell off her front step?

Curtains parted inside the plate glass window at the front of the house, and we were watched coming up the gravel and railroad tie walkway.

The door opened and Ted's widow said, "Come in. I'm Kim."

Kim Swanson was Asian, looked to be in her early forties, and was dressed in black pants and a crisp white shirt. Her hair was pulled back into a short pony tail. She wore no makeup. I noted the plain diamond engagement ring and matching wedding band on her left ring finger. A small boy of about two was clinging to her right hand and staring up at us with his light-colored eyes.

"Come in. This is Tommy," Mrs. Swanson said as we followed her into her neat-as-a pin living room. "I haven't told him. I don't know how."

She called out, "Lily, Lily," and a preteen girl, dark-haired like her mother, came out of one of the bedrooms. Kim asked her to take her brother into the TV room so she could talk to us privately.

Kim offered us upholstered chairs and took a seat on the sofa across from us. I looked around. Saw baby-safe furnishings, plugs over the electric sockets, a small blue horse on wheels near the sliders to the back deck.

A simply framed photo of Ted and Kim stood on the lamp table. I assumed it was their wedding photo: Kim in a fawn-colored shift, Ted with a tan sports coat over his orange prison jumpsuit.

Kim picked up the picture and held it in her lap with both hands.

This woman had just suffered a heavy blow, but I wanted to get right into our questions for her before we lost our opportunity.

I told Kim that Conklin and I were sorry for her loss, that we'd both known Ted at Southern Station. She nodded. But this information meant less than nothing to her.

"I was at his trial," she said. "I watched both of you testify against him."

I nodded, and Richie looked at his hands, but we made no excuses. Kim had no questions for us. Pretty good bet that she wanted us gone.

I asked, "How long had you and Ted known one another—"

"Before we got married? About five years," she said. "His old partner, Jim Ransom, and I...well, it doesn't matter. I knew Ted's ex-wife, Nancy....It's all inconsequential, isn't it? You must have questions about Teddy's death."

Conklin said, "We have one or two. Sergeant Boxer and I saw Ted last week. We hoped he might help us with a pending case. He had nothing for us but seemed to be in a good mood."

"He was, wasn't he?" said Kim. "What day did you see him?"

"Friday morning."

"I saw him Friday afternoon," she said. "That was the last time. I guess it's better that I didn't know what he was thinking. The warden sent me the note Ted left for me."

"You recognized Ted's handwriting?" I asked.

"Yes. And what he wrote, that he worried about me being imprisoned because he was locked up. He'd expressed this thought before. Listen, Officers, I didn't think he was telling me good-bye. He didn't show me anything that made me think he was going to do what he did. But I know he wanted Tommy to have a life, not to have to tell his friends that his father was behind the walls of San Quentin."

Kim's voice caught in her throat. She excused herself and went to the bathroom down the hallway. I could hear her crying, then the sound of running water, and when she returned to the living room a few minutes later, her face was pink and she held a wad of tissues in her hand.

Kim Swanson sat down hard and leaned back in the love seat.

A long moment later she said, "Ted mentioned that he'd gotten threats. But his delivery was as if he were telling a good story. Not like he was afraid. I can't stop thinking about that. I can't stop. I should have told the warden, but I didn't."

I asked, "Did he say who made the threats or why?"

"No. No. He never told me his business. He was sparing me. Maybe he could have been transferred to another prison. I would have moved the family. But Nancy also has kids. It was too much."

"I'm so sorry, Kim," I said. "Did he say what the threats were?"

She nodded and her tears dropped to her blouse. She dabbed

at her eyes, her nose, and cleared her throat. "He said that he was told to either kill himself or I'd be a dead mom walking."

Ted's widow lifted her head to look at me.

"He was a better man than you thought, wasn't he?"

I nodded yes, but I was thinking no. Maybe Swanson had sacrificed his life for his wife and children, but it was because of him, and *only* him, that other family men had died. My next unspoken thought followed on the heels of that one. Conklin and I had seen Ted on Friday morning. Kim saw him that afternoon, after I'd shouted up into the tiers that Ted was helping the SFPD.

I flashed on the notes in the pockets of dead men. *You talk, you die.*

Was his suicide on me?

Conklin asked, "Why did you tell Ransom that Ted was murdered?"

She sighed. "Because I was shocked, furious that Ted could have killed himself without someone knowing. In a way, it is true. Whoever threatened us essentially murdered him."

Conklin gave Mrs. Swanson his card and said "If we learn anything…" in the kind way he has. Although I knew he was being sincere, Kim's expression had turned to stone.

She walked us to the foyer and saw us out. Then she closed the black-bannered door without saying good-bye.

CHAPTER 56

I GOT BEHIND the wheel of our unmarked Chevy, backed down the driveway, then headed north.

Shouting at the windshield, I vented to Conklin during our return drive from San Rafael. I told him how furious I'd been the last time we saw Swanson—as if he didn't know. That I'd been frustrated by Swanson's breezy manner, his obstinacy, his rejection of a chance to make amends. And to punish him, I'd slapped a target on him with my shout-out, "Swanson, the SFPD thanks you for your help."

I hadn't planned to say that, but it was no excuse. I'd known I was misinforming the residents of the C Block that Swanson had talked. Within hours Swanson was given notice. If he didn't take himself out, his wife was a dead mom walking.

I told Conklin that I felt sorry for Kim Swanson, who was only guilty of having the appalling judgment to marry a cop so dirty there wasn't a suitable word to describe him. Not to mention a man doing a lifetime stretch in maximum security with no possibility of parole.

Now he was dead.

I said, "Kim was left with a suicide note penciled on a scrap of cardboard."

"And a little boy. And maybe the house."

"Right," I said, "no thanks to me. I might as well have knotted the sheet around Ted's neck myself."

Conklin did his best to console me, good friend that he is. He was so logical and clear spoken, his words stayed with me verbatim.

"Swanson was a stone killer, Linds. First, second, and third. You didn't kill him. You didn't threaten his wife. You blurted about seven words—and that's all. So take it easy on yourself, okay?"

"Look," I said to Rich. "I'm not making myself crazy because I liked him. I'm kicking myself because he probably had information that could have saved I don't know how many lives. He may have been the fucking mob boss. And now we'll never get that information."

"Lindsay. You and I both know Swanson wasn't going to tell us anything."

Right.

While Conklin checked the car back in, I crossed Bryant to MacBain's and got sandwiches to go. I carried lunch back to the bullpen and shared it around.

Alvarez said, "I've called back all sixteen people who left messages on the hotline. Not one had a verifiable tip, or even an interesting hunch. The hotline is now officially the complaint line—"

She was interrupted by Bobby approaching me. "Sergeant, I was transcribing a message for you."

"Who called?"

My mind leapt to the worst. Had something happened at home? Was Julie okay? Joe? Gloria Rose?

Bob dropped off a printout. "I wrote it out exactly as he said, and I read it back to him."

"Thanks, Bob."

The message was from my CI Kenny Chen. He'd stayed in jail for a night or two, then bonded out.

Chen had dictated to Bobby: "I still have that torn hundred-dollar bill. Now I need you to make it a hundred thousand. Half down when I deliver the information you want about the guns. The other half after the bust. You know where to find me tonight at 8. Don't be late. Come alone."

CHAPTER 57

KENNY CHEN PICKED up my call on the first ring.

I said, "I know you have great respect for me, Kenny, but I can't get you 50K on my say-so. Not on yours, either."

"Listen, Sergeant. I'm putting my life at risk and handing you the biggest bust of your life."

"Put your mouth near the speaker. I can't hear you."

He shouted, "I'm giving you everything! Drugs, M4s, AKs, and the grunts who are bringing the stuff in. As a bonus, you also get to pick up the potential buyers. This is going to be the hottest deal of your life. For cheap. Bring the money, Sarge, unmarked bills, no tracking device. You don't like what I tell you, say no and I'll sell the intel to ATF."

I said, "I'm bringing my partner."

"I said to come alone."

"You've met Conklin. He plays fair."

Chen hung up. I didn't know if that was *Okay* or *Drop dead.*

Between eleven that morning and half past seven p.m., Clapper and Brady commandeered three vehicles from repo: a van with a roof rack; an old, recently souped-up silver Camaro; and a black Lincoln sedan.

By 8:00 p.m. Grant Avenue between Washington and Jackson was swarming with tourists and bar hoppers. It was more traffic than I'd expected on a Tuesday night, and Li Po was the star of the show. Blazing with neon signage, lanterns, and brightly colored flags as it had been when Conklin and I met with Chen over the weekend, the place just drew a person in. I stood on the sidewalk with Conklin. My phone was pressed to my ear as I scoped the street for our vehicles.

Brady was in the van, watching us from across the street. His voice was in my ear, and my mic was in the breast pocket of my jacket, disguised as a pack of gum. Kenny Chen was a sneak by definition, and although he had scored points with us over the years, he'd lost his cred with me when a tip from him had become a fatality.

I carried a canvas bag with the requested bounty inside. As suspicious as I was of Kenny Chen, I wanted him to be for real. If he had solid information, the payout was worth it. If he was lying or if he got aggressive, I had backup to spare.

I asked Conklin if he was ready.

"Remind me, Boxer. I wanted to be in Homicide, right?"

I grinned at him. "More than anything in the world."

"Just checking," he said. "Let's do it."

He held the door and we walked into the watering hole from another world. The serpentine bar crawled along one long side of the room. The Buddha was in its niche in the backbar. Eerie music came from ceiling speakers, and the lighting was barely there. A waitress asked us if we were having dinner with them tonight, and I said, "We're meeting a friend who usually sits at the back."

"Oh. Oh, Mr. Chen is expecting you."

We told the young lady that we could find our way. Chen was sitting at the back table talking to a man with his back to us. I spoke to Brady while talking to Conklin.

"Looks like we'll be a foursome."

"Copy that," said Brady. "I'm sending Chi into the bar. He'll be another set of eyes."

That was good. Not only was Chi one of the smartest cops I knew, he spoke Mandarin. Knowing that he had our backs, we approached Chen and said hello. The man sitting across from him got up and went to the bar, too far in the noisy dive for him to overhear our conversation.

Chen said, "Let's make it quick. You two look like actors on cop TV."

CHAPTER 58

I PUT THE satchel on the table, unzipped it, showed my CI the banded packets of used twenties and fifties. Kenny Chen stood up, looked inside the bag, stirred the packets with one hand, then, satisfied, sat back down. He gulped his drink to the bottom and slammed the glass down on the table. He was apparently ready to give me fifty thousand dollars' worth of information.

He said, "There's a tunnel that runs under the border between Tijuana and the Otay section of San Diego. Two Mexican guys will come out of the manhole on our side with sixty-five pounds of fentanyl. When pressed, they will give up the name of who's behind the operation in exchange for a deal."

The waitress came over and refreshed Chen's drink. Conklin and I said no thanks, and when she moved away, Kenny continued telling us the details.

He said, "Three box trucks are carrying the weapons. All three have logos on the sides saying, 'Fresh to You.' They will be moving toward Pennsylvania Avenue at the same time. The buyers will take the trucks and go to points unknown—get me?

So you have to have all the manpower you can get and make sure you're on time. After the transaction is finished, the mules and the drivers will take off. Don't know where. Only thing that matters is be on time. This is all going to happen fast."

"Coordinates and time of this operation," said Conklin.

Chen took a folded piece of paper out of his breast pocket, placed it on the table, his fingers holding it down.

"It's all here. When, where, and my mobile number. It's a burner, so it's only good for the next forty-eight hours and then I ditch it."

I took the paper. Now that I had it, I wanted to drag Chen off his ass, throw him against the wall, toss him into the van with Brady, and return the money to the mayor.

I pushed the canvas bag over to my CI and took the other half of the torn hundred-dollar bill out of my hip pocket. I gave him that, too.

His eyes smiled. "I knew you were good for it. Meet me back here tomorrow night with the other 50K and a big wide thank-you. I'll be waiting."

I said, "You'd better be on the level, Ken."

"Don't insult me, Sarge."

Conklin got out of his chair, covered me from the rear as we passed Chi at the bar, and headed out to the street. I didn't know if Chen was full of crap or if we were headed for the Medal of Freedom. But we had a lot to do.

I spoke to Brady through my mic disguised as a pack of spearmint, and he said, "Good job, you two. Chi, hang around for a while. Watch what happens."

CHAPTER **59**

CLAPPER WANTED TO see the team. After we'd crowded into his office, he closed his door and passed me on the way to his desk, saying, "Boxer, let's have it."

He was in a dark mood. Understandably, given the rumors of a gun payload on the way to California floating around the net, but from our side of the net, we were grateful that there were no new "You talk, you die" murders. Clapper had told the press not to buy the rumors. He would let them know if or when there was news.

Now Clapper scowled as he looked at me. I knew he wanted something good, something bulletproof and worth the fifty thousand he'd wrung out of our scant account for payoffs. I felt for Charlie, who'd been chief for only about six months. I remembered when he was head of the forensics lab, a job he'd loved. Or as Conklin said, Clapper had been promoted into hell.

Also, the mayor was facing an election in just a few months. Unsolved homicides would work against him. Capture of illegal guns and kingpins could get him another term.

I said, "Chief, my CI is a crafty little creep, but what he told me about the arms and drug-smuggling scheme seems credible."

"You've worked with him before?"

"Yes. Four out of five times he was right. Once he was wrong. SWAT saved the day, but we still lost an FBI agent."

"You trust him now? Why?"

"I get the feeling he's ready to cash out of the CI business. The plan he described seems believable, and he only gets the rest of the money if we're satisfied. He called the meeting. I was tough on him. He persuaded me without selling. And I bought it."

"Conklin, you agree?"

"The way I see it, Chief, it's something. With all the man-hours we've put into this case, we have nothing. If Lindsay's CI screws us over, we're back where we started. Zero. If he's right and we pull this off, it's heroic—until the next headline."

Clapper walked to his windows facing Bryant. He watched headlights on the street below for a few seconds, and we waited him out.

When he swung around, he said, "Okay, Boxer. You've couched it as a fifty-fifty deal, and I've half committed to rolling the dice. Spell out the plan."

Chen had given me a folded sheet of paper. I took it out of my jacket's breast pocket and looked at his hand-drawn map of the seediest side of Potrero Hill. He'd drawn an *X* on Pennsylvania Avenue and a star on the empty crash house the smugglers would use while waiting. The drop-dead transfer time to exchange contraband for cash was ten o'clock tomorrow night. The time and date were penned at the top of the diagram, along with a crude four-pointed star indicating north, south, east, west. I brought the diagram to Clapper. He looked at it and handed it off to Inspector Chi, who was standing closest to him.

"Pass it around. Last person makes copies for the rest of us."

"Okay, then," I said, organizing my thoughts. "My CI only knows some of the background on this deal. He was told that the guns would be coming over the border in big box trucks disguised as produce vehicles. The drugs would be transported underground through tunnels. Start point is somewhere in Tijuana to San Diego, to the drop-point in Potrero Hill."

"Cold Morning," Chi's partner, Inspector McNeil, said, referencing a similar guns-and-drugs deal from a few years back.

Alvarez said, "I'm new here. What's Cold Morning?"

McNeil said, "The biggest takedown in my young life. A thousand cops. Hundreds of pounds of drugs were sent on small electric carts through this half-mile-long, thirty-foot-high tunnel. Not just drugs, but a ton of guns and about a hundred vehicles. As I recall, it took two years to put that plan together."

I said, "Exactly. We have a day—or we have nothing."

CHAPTER 60

I LET THE phrase "or we have nothing" hang in the air.

Nothing—versus a huge bust, getting guns off the street, taking drugs out of the hands of conscienceless street pharmacists. Pride in job. Pride in self.

"Nothing" didn't stand a chance.

"Right, right," said McNeil. "Cold Morning was on a multistate scale."

Clapper sighed. He was stretched to the breaking point, as were we all. I looked at Brady. He had bags under his eyes. He winked at me.

He said, "Go on, Boxer. We're following you."

Clapper said, "Could you give your CI a name?"

"Uh. Let's call him Snoopy."

Clapper cracked a thin-lipped smile.

I carried on. "Snoopy tells me that apart from the drugs, there will be three trucks carrying the military-style weapons. The drivers are American, California tags on the trucks, familiar logos on the sides. The magnetic type that can be peeled off.

"Their destination is a transfer point on the wrong side of the tracks in Potrero Hill. Trucks can come and go there without raising a fuss. All along Pennsylvania Avenue are abandoned buildings, including a vacant warehouse, which will be the base of operations."

"Keep going," Cappy said. "I like it so far.

"Thanks, Cappy. I try. Now, before 10 p.m. tomorrow, we"—I pointed a finger around the room—"are discreetly slumped down in parked unmarked cars or otherwise in hiding. Here come the trucks, sagging from the weight of weapons. Drivers pull over and open their cargo doors. Drug mules appear from the empty warehouse and load keys of drugs into the trucks. Buyers appear in ordinary vehicles. Snoopy described them as 'used, family-type cars.' Buyers inspect the load, test the drugs, I suppose, and the cash transactions are made.

"The keys to the trucks are handed off to the buyers. The mules and the original truck drivers take the family-style rides and go off to wherever. The trucks are now a depot, and the buyers take them to a distribution point, site unknown."

"But before that happens," Brady said, "we break up the party with a surprise attack and overwhelming force. Lights. Guns. Gas. Flashbangs. Bullhorns. We're geared up and use our cars as shields. Chief, we could use some air coverage, too. And of course, the help of God."

Clapper had a few questions for Brady. "And what if they have surprises, too? What if Snoopy reports in both directions? What if you're outgunned, outmaneuvered?"

Brady said, "If I don't like it, we sit tight, then follow the trucks. If we can do it, we follow one or more of the other cars, but the payload is primary. Chief. Should we bring in the FBI?"

"Yes to Molinari and Wallenger."

I shot back, "It's either Joe or me. One of us has to stay to protect our home and child."

"Then Wallenger can pick another partner," said Clapper. "Boxer, Conklin, Alvarez, go to Potrero Hill and take pictures. When you get back, work with Brady and identify where our task force digs in. Do that tonight."

Inspector Conklin was holding Snoopy's diagram.

As the meeting broke up, he said, "If anyone needs me, I'll be at the copy machine."

There was some much-needed laughter. A few minutes later I was on the phone with Joe. We had a little problem.

She was three feet tall and turning four years old. Tomorrow.

CHAPTER 61

THE TIMING COULDN'T have been worse, but Joe and I couldn't bear to disappoint Julie. We had reservations for four at the Tonga Room in the Fairmont Hotel in Nob Hill. This was a big deal for a little birthday girl, and ours was up to the challenge. She had seen a commercial for the Tonga Room and was mesmerized by the Polynesian everything. The restaurant was lined with tiki huts thatched with palm fronds, one table under each, and water flowed between the huts.

Julie had seen the commercial and was transfixed by all thirty seconds of it: the huts, the dance floor adjacent to the restaurant where lithe millennials swung their hips to Hawaiian music, and the cherry on top—seeing a birthday cake brought to a tiki table, and all the diners clapping as a birthday boy of about seven shrieked with joy.

"Look!" Julie had shouted. *"Look at that."*

We murmured our appreciation and watched the news, and later that night Joe and I talked it over in bed.

"They serve alcohol, you know," Joe said.

"So do we. Hey, they do have a kids' menu," I heard myself say.

Julie has a fantastical imagination. We agreed that a birthday dinner at the Tonga Room would become a lifelong memory. Joe made a reservation the next day, and then the week went over the top. We were told by CIs that an enormous, illegal drug and gun deal was scheduled by unknown gangsters. Ted Swanson hanged himself. Unsolved homicides piled up.

But Julie was turning four. As Joe and I got dressed for her party, I was inside my head, running through the operation again as if it were already happening.

Clapper was our number one at the Hall. Brady was in charge on the ground and would be wired into the rest of the team. We had all cased the location, Pennsylvania Avenue in Potrero Hill, and had identified hidden parking areas, alcoves between buildings and other hidey-holes. The FBI had volunteered three other senior agents. Highway patrol was on standby to close off the roads once the perps were doing their deal. We had air cover on notice. We couldn't be more prepared, but still…

Julie broke into my thoughts.

"Mom. Let's goooooo."

"You mind if I put on some shoes?"

Joe drove Julie and Mrs. Rose in his roomy sedan, and I followed behind in my junk-filled Explorer. It was a short drive to the Fairmont Hotel, and once inside the Tonga Room, Julie jumped up and down and clasped her hands as though this was all for her—and it was. A fantasy coming true. I tried to get with her mood, but despite the festive ambiance and Julie's delight, I was not in a tiki-hut frame of mind.

Julie, however, was giddy but sat still long enough to share a pupu platter with Mrs. Rose. She posed for pictures in the dress

Mrs. Rose had made for her, red and flouncy with a sequined appliqué on the bodice that read *Guess Who's Four?*

Watching Julie's face, I could say with confidence that the Tonga Room did not disappoint. As for me, I turned down the sunrise-colored drink, and Joe did the same.

"You okay?" he asked me.

"Sure. Sure," I lied.

Joe took Julie over to the lagoon, right there in the Tonga Room, and then escorted her to the dance floor. While Julie Bug twirled and sang made-up lyrics, I checked the time. Seven fifteen. Almost time to go. Then, from inside my jacket pocket, my phone buzzed.

Brady was texting me, saying that he and Cappy were loading up the van and would be leaving the Hall in five. I copied that, and when Joe brought Julie back to our table, I put my arm around my daughter. I trusted Brady. I trusted the task force and I trusted myself.

Still. Shit happens.

CHAPTER 62

MRS. ROSE SPOKE to me from behind her hand, "She's going to sleep well tonight."

I signaled to our waiter.

"Let me guess," he said. "Cake?"

Moments later three or four young men in staff shirts approached with a chocolate cake. They sang the happy birthday song and handed me a long wooden match. I lit each of the four blue candles, standing for the four years of our precious girl's life.

Mrs. Rose drew a fish on her napkin and passed it to the birthday girl.

She said, "Jules. Kiss the fish and make a wish. And don't tell anyone what you wished for."

Julie said, "Like this?"

She kissed the napkin, giggled, and blew out each of the candles while making her private wish. My phone buzzed again. I pulled it from my pocket and viewed the number. I hoped it was Brady checking in again, but it was Kenny Chen.

I stood up from the table and answered his call. I said, "Kenny. Deal or no deal?"

"There's been a change of plans," he said.

"What? What kind of change?"

"The transaction is going on now. Right now."

"That can't be."

"And the location has also changed."

He stuttered when he said that. Nervous, I guessed, as well he should be. He gave me a new location on Carroll Avenue, a wide thoroughfare in an industrial section of Bayview. I knew the area well. I'd be able to find a place to hide the Explorer in one of the factory parking lots.

But executing the takedown with a new time, in a new location, and with dozens of moving parts was logistically impossible. Scores of people and vehicles were either on their way to or already secreted in positions near Carroll Avenue.

Chen interrupted the silence. "Are you gonna ditch?"

I said to Chen, "Keep your phone on." I hung up.

CHAPTER 63

I THOUGHT IT through. It would be impossible to reorganize in time without blowing our cover. There would be confusion and chaos and people could die.

But. One person, one vehicle, could wait and watch. Run tag numbers. Shadow a box truck.

I went back to our table and looked at Joe. He read my face.

"Go," he said. "Go."

"Sweetie," I said to my little one. "I'm sorry I have to leave. I told you. Remember?"

She nodded vigorously. Her curls bounced. Her eyes squinched up.

"Give me a big hug," I said.

I took her into my arms, wished her a happy birthday, and told her I would be home later to say good night again. "Bring home some cake for me," I said.

I kissed Joe, blew one to Mrs. Rose, and got out while I could. I texted Brady from my car. He didn't reply. I shed the dressy silk jacket I'd worn over my tac gear, buckled on my vest and shoulder holster. I checked my gun out of its safe under the dash and slipped it into its leather sleeve. Spare clips went into my pocket.

I was as ready as I could be.

I started up the car, turned on the headlights, and texted Brady again. *Call me. Urgent.*

My phone buzzed. I clicked on. Brady asked, "Where are you, Boxer?"

I told him, "Leaving Nob Hill. And you?"

Brady was at Potrero Hill. I told him what Snoopy had told me, that the location had changed, that the deal was due to come down a half hour ago.

I was driving toward Bayview while the two of us considered our options. Call the whole thing off or arrive late but still, maybe, see something, ID something, nab someone.

Brady made the decision. "Stand down, Lindsay. Hear me?"

I heard him. But my adrenaline streamed. And yet a split decision was duking it out in my mind. Convince Brady to go with me to watch armed gangsters divvying up millions in illegal guns and drugs? Or say, "Yes, boss. I hear you," then take a U-turn and return to the Tonga Room, kiss a fish, and have a piece of cake?

I said, "You and me, Brady. We can be eyes on the scene. That's all I'm suggesting."

"You kill me, Boxer. I hope that's a figure of speech."

I said to Brady, "Odds are, the party is over."

An open straightaway ran ahead of me.

I mashed the gas pedal and hit the sirens, speeding toward what my CI had called "the biggest bust" of my life.

I was burning adrenaline as if it were gasoline and I were on the road alone.

CHAPTER 64

I KEPT MY phone on and dispatch in the loop. My GPS showed that I was fifteen minutes from Bayview, which could be enough time for the transaction to take place and for the bad guys to get out of town. If they were on schedule. If. Questions surfaced in my mind.

Could we crash the party on the fly? Sneak a peek? Or were we going to be made as cops? Nerves are always involved when we strap on our guns. It keeps us smart, wary, ready. But in this case—I didn't want to think of how that would go down.

Would I get home tonight?

I turned my thoughts back to the road. Traffic was light. I tore through the sharp turns, none more than a few hundred feet from the next; Powell to O'Farrell in three minutes flat.

Cars peeled off the road as I came up fast behind them with my siren screaming, my flashers strobing. I was making great time, but I had to pull up short behind a line of traffic at a light, blocking the on-ramp to Highway 101 South.

I speed-dialed Brady and asked, "Where are you?"

"I'm in Potrero Hill," he said. "Pennsylvania Avenue is dead as a graveyard. No convoy. No mugs looking to offload guns. The stash shack is empty. A half dozen of our team will dig in near Carroll in case we need them. Where are you?"

"On the highway now. I'll be in Bayview in twelve, maybe fifteen minutes."

"When you exit 101, pull off the road. I'll meet you there."

I copied that as the light went green, traffic streamed onto the highway. I got out ahead of the pack and was closing in on Bayview. I wished Kenny Chen were sitting next to me, cuffed at ankles and wrists with just his sly mouth free to answer my questions.

Where did you get your information, Kenny? Are you in someone's pocket? Are you having fun yet?

Four miles of highway flashed by before I took the 430A exit, made a looping turn, and pulled onto the verge on the feeder road as directed. I texted Brady my location, buzzed down my window, and watched traffic rolling off the highway. A few minutes later Brady pulled up behind me in a squad SUV marked TO PROTECT AND SERVE on the sides.

Brady's expression perfectly mirrored mine. It was like we were stepping out onto a tightrope a hundred feet in the air, no net. I was confident in our forty years of combined experience dealing with murderers—but the tightrope had been made with unreliable information.

Still, I was committed for two reasons. Brady was the best cop I'd ever worked with. And I wanted to see this big-time crime-in-progress. I thought Brady and I would find a way to take this whole deal down.

CHAPTER 65

BRADY EXITED THE SUV with his bullhorn and climbed up into the Explorer. He bunched up the odd papers and whatnot I'd left on the passenger seat, tucked it all into the door pocket. Once he'd strapped in, I drove and we talked, making sure we had the same plan in mind.

I kept my speed below fifty, arriving on Carroll Avenue in Bayview within a few minutes. Carroll was wide, running past the rear yards of small factories and warehouses, tailing off to a section of modestly priced housing toward the bay.

Now, in the midst of this small industrial section, even in the pale light of a sliver moon, we could see cement mixers, cranes, wrecked autos, flatbed trucks, mountains of parts, pallets of marble, heaps and piles of this and that. I cut my headlights from high to park, and we drove down Carroll toward Arelious Walker Drive, checking out loading docks and lots filled with rows of delivery vehicles behind chain-link fencing. Brady pointed to an auto repair shop and a neat little pocket about halfway along

Carroll where we could back in between two old tow trucks and watch the street.

"This looks good," he said.

True, though not in the normal sense of the word *good*. The area was dark, forbidding, and quiet. I saw points of light deep beyond the open rear doors of the buildings: night-shift workers with caged bulbs hanging from overhead pipes, welding torches sparking, and faint sounds of oldies coming from car radios. But there were no men moving drugs into family-style vehicles from long trucks labeled with big-box store logos. There was nothing moving at all.

Brady got out of my car and guided me with hand motions as I backed the Explorer into that narrow space. With the vehicle hidden, Brady climbed back in and radioed our position to dispatch, while I texted Kenny Chen for possible updates. There was no answer from fricking Snoopy. I texted him again. Same result.

I'd just clicked off when a black Jeep Commander drove out of the dark across our field of vision, stopped, then backed up, blocking our only exit from this chop-shop cul-de-sac.

I said, "Brady, I could swear that that Jeep passed me at the exit. Just before you showed up."

A flashlight beam carved a tunnel through the darkness from the Jeep to our windshield. A male voice could be heard saying, "Yeah. That's her."

"Her" could only be me.

CHAPTER 66

BRADY MUTTERED, GRABBED the mic, requested immediate backup, all cars, and gave the location.

Within minutes every cop for miles would be going through walls to get to Carroll Avenue. But we couldn't wait. We pulled our guns. I flipped on the headlights, illuminating the Jeep that had braked at a right angle to us. Brady grabbed his megaphone, buzzed down the window, and, after a sharp feedback squeal, announced, "This is the SFPD. Get out of your vehicle. Slowly. Hands in the air."

I saw the red beam of a laser sight coming from the Jeep's driver side. And I saw the silhouette of an AK.

I yelled, *"Gun!"*

Brady and I ducked under the dash as bullets flew. First shots blew out the windshield. Shattered glass fell around us. And then our headlights popped. One. The other. The side-view mirror splintered. A shard of metal burned across my left cheek. Bullets pocked into the chassis. I dared not lift my head.

I heard laughter from the Jeep. "We got 'em."

Brady showed me his fist and unfolded his fingers: *One. Two. Three.*

My heart was thudding, but we'd been partners before and I trusted him with my life. On three, without raising my head, I turned on the ignition. With my foot on the brake, I put the car in drive.

Another fusillade of bullets sprayed the Explorer's chassis, the tires, every pane of glass. We kept low as shots whizzed through the space where the windshield had been. I heard a sucking sound as the rounds thwacked through the seat backs and out the rear window.

We didn't fire back. And for a very long moment there was silence.

Brady said, "Now."

I stamped on the accelerator, my head still down, and braced for impact. Thank God for the weight of the engine block. We T-boned the Jeep. I heard the crunch of metal crushing metal. I kept my foot on the gas until the Jeep was up against a wall of the shop on the opposite side of the street and could move no farther.

Brady said, "Ready?"

I scoffed from sheer nerves. "Yes, Lieutenant."

"Now."

I swung my door open and—using the doorframe with the busted-out window as a gun brace—started firing. Brady did the same.

Dispatch crackled over the radio. Clapper's voice.

"Cars en route. Speak to me, Lieutenant."

"Do we have air cover?"

"On the way."

I knocked my spent clip out of my gun and reloaded. I heard the Jeep's rear door, the one farthest from us, creak open.

A voice called out, "Don't shoot."

A thin, young-looking male got out of the car. His dark clothes made him featureless, but I focused on his AK. He was holding it out like a peace offering.

I yelled, *"Drop the gun! Drop it now."*

"You *killed* them!" he shouted. Then, still holding the AK, he turned and began to run.

Brady fired into the air and yelled, "Stop where you are. Throw your gun down."

The man-boy kept running with his automatic long gun, deeper into the dark of Carroll in the general direction of the highway.

When Warren Jacobi was chief, he'd told our squad, "When a suspect has a gun, they're shootable at any point, even if they're running away. Shoot front, back, whatever. Bring them down."

He was speaking of an incident we'd shared and never forgotten: a fifteen-year-old girl had reached into her jacket for her driver's license, pulled out a gun, and shot us both. We'd nearly bled out in an alley in the Tenderloin.

Now, here, this suspect had been warned and was still running. I fired. So did Brady, who was standing to my left, so close I could hear him grunt when he pulled the trigger.

The runner cried out and dropped against a pile of car parts.

Brady went to the fallen suspect and called out to me.

"He's not breathing."

He returned with the dead man's AK and threw it into the wreck of our car. With our own guns drawn, we approached the Jeep. Just then the squeal of tires and the looping din of sirens announced the half dozen police cruisers suddenly filling the street.

Once again I shouted into the Jeep, *"Hands up! Show us your hands."*

There was no movement, no call for help, no shots, nothing.

Then, as the sirens cut out, a weak voice came from inside the Jeep, saying, "I can't. Reach it."

CHAPTER 67

THE POLICE CHOPPER dropped a bright circle of light over the street, illuminating the cruisers pulling in, the crumpled mass of Jeep, my bullet-riddled Explorer, as well as the scrapyards in high relief and the scramble of cops.

Brady held his gun with both hands, and again I ordered the Jeep's occupants to put their hands up. To throw their guns out of the car. None of that happened. When we were much closer to the Jeep than felt comfortable, I peered in through the shot-out windows.

Two motionless people, a man and a woman, were sprawled in front, slumped against their seat backs.

I yanked open the driver's-side door and got a good look at the driver. It was Kenny Chen, wearing his python-print jacket, covered with blood. He'd taken shots to his right arm. His gun was half on his lap, half on the floor. His eyes were closed. As I reached in and disarmed him, he awoke, saw me, and tried to move his arm. He screamed, then passed out again. He was losing too much blood from his wounds. I didn't like him, but I didn't want him to die. He had a lot of 'splaining to do.

"Kenny," I said loudly, "Kenny, you're in bad shape. An ambulance is on the way. Talk to me. Who are you working for?"

No answer, but his right hand was crabbing along the front seat, seeking something.

I put my gun to his head. "I said, hands up."

Chen cried out in pain as he held them in the air.

Brady reached past me into the Jeep, draped Chen's good arm over his shoulder, and pulled him onto the road. Then he rolled Chen onto his stomach, frisked and cuffed him.

I said to Brady, "Meet CI 7990, a.k.a. Snoopy, a.k.a. Kenny Chen."

Brady said, "Mr. Chen, you're under arrest for attempted murder of a police officer. Add possession of an illegal weapon. And that'll hold you until we tote up the rest of the charges."

Brady was reading Snoopy his rights when the first ambulance arrived. Chen's eyelids fluttered open and he focused on me.

"You. Killed. My gir'frenn."

"I returned fire," I said.

He closed his eyes, so I called his name. Called it louder.

"Kenny. Stay awake. Stay with me."

He looked me in the eye and said, "Did you. Bring it?"

EMTs lifted Kenny onto a gurney and rolled it to the ambulance at the top of the road.

Had Kenny said, "Did you bring it?"

Had that idiot come here to get the money I'd left at home in the safe? Had he made up this meeting of the guns-for-cash exchange in order to get his hands on the 50K?

I hoped Kenny lived long enough to tell.

CHAPTER 68

I EDGED AROUND to the passenger side of the ruined Jeep and looked down at the slack body in the front seat. Blood covered her from chin to waist, and she was bleeding from a neck wound. Her face was turned toward the driver's side, but even in the gloom I recognized Ted Swanson's widow.

I shouted, *"Kim. Can you hear me?"*

She didn't answer. I called dispatch. Shouting over the sirens, I stated my name, my badge number, and our situation.

"Officer-involved shooting. Three offenders down, one showing no sign of life. Roll more buses to 1420 Carroll in Bayview. We need the ME and CSI."

I hadn't taken my eyes off Kim Swanson. She hadn't moved. I reached in again, this time finding a pulse in her wrist. It was faint, but she still had one. Her gun had slipped from her hand and had fallen to the floor near her feet. I gloved up, took it out of her reach, and bagged it with the kit from my thoroughly punctured car.

CSI would identify her gun, but I knew it well. It was a Glock .45, the make and model used by the SFPD a few years back. It made a cracked kind of sense.

Kim had tried to kill us with Ted Swanson's gun.

CHAPTER 69

THE HELICOPTER MOVED off. Radios squawked and chattered, but the sirens were still. Auto mechanics, marble cutters, welders, came out of the warehouses and factories asking questions, getting no answers. Instead they received directions to stand back and touch nothing as barrier tape was stretched from point to point, outlining a rectangular section of the road that was the primary crime scene.

Our task force arrived. I saw them all plus a handful of FBI agents I didn't know. Cappy, Chi, Conklin, and Alvarez checked in to see that Brady and I were okay, then started questioning possible witnesses to the shootings. Asking for information, any video of the event, if they knew the victims.

Now that the noise had dropped fifty percent and no one was shooting, I put my hand to my cheek. It was sticky.

Brady said, "Lindsay?"

"It's nothing," I said.

"You're lucky, my friend."

"True for both of us."

Clapper called Brady, who filled him in. I walked in circles, noting the arrival of the coroner's van, the activities within the tape, the arrival of Forensics director Gene Hallows and his CSIs, who set up lights and began to process the scene. The rest of us gathered beyond the tape, but I stood apart.

Brady clicked off his call with Clapper.

I asked, "What did Clapper say?"

"You know. We're benched. Chi is in charge. We're gonna turn over our guns and badges to him. Then we need a lift. We're both going home."

I nodded. There was still so much adrenaline in my system, I felt raw. I'd shot a guy and he'd died. I'd been betrayed by Kenny Chen and by Kim Swanson. I wondered if the gun deal had gone down elsewhere unimpeded. Was it still waiting in the wings? Or had Kenny fabricated the whole thing?

There was nothing left for us to do here, and it was likely that the investigation would be turned over to the state police so there'd be no question of our guys showing favoritism. We'd be required to see the department shrink. Until Brady and I were cleared of wrongdoing, we'd be at home.

I forced myself to feel good about wearing sweats all day. Grocery shopping. Walking our dog. Spending quality time with my husband and child.

Provided we were cleared, we'd be back on the Job in a few days. Or we could be on ice for months.

Brady called out to Sergeant Paul Chi. We both handed him our guns and badges, told him we were okay.

"We'll have reports to you and Clapper tomorrow," Brady said.

That's when the press arrived. First a sound truck from WACD. Cameras rolled. Then network reporters, local reporters—

including Cindy. She hadn't seen me yet, but she would in seconds. Maybe Conklin would answer her questions, but if she asked me what had happened, I would have to say, "Sorry, I can't discuss a case in progress."

Cindy offered me and Brady a ride to his car and we accepted. She said, "Brady. Don't make me beg."

He told her he couldn't discuss the case, and she said, "You know, my dear friend, I'd love to be surprised sometime. Like, 'Cindy. How would you like an exclusive?'"

He grinned at her. "If I could, I would."

Conklin came over, touched my cheek, said, "Peroxide, okay? I'll call you in a couple of hours."

"Good. Don't forget."

Brady's SFPD vehicle was still at the base of the highway's off-ramp. We thanked Cindy for the lift. I hugged her good-bye and got into the squad's SUV with Brady. He asked me something as he started it up, but I didn't hear him. I leaned my head back and fell asleep as he drove me home.

CHAPTER 70

I WAS IN my car with Brady to my right, my car wedged between two tow trucks, taking heavy fire from an unidentified black Jeep, when someone shook my shoulder.

The blankets were on the floor. "Joe? What time is it?"

"Seven fifteen," he told me. "You were flopping around like a beached tuna."

"Whoa."

And the whole violent dream came back—but it wasn't a dream. It was a memory. Vivid. Almost real. I nodded and covered my eyes with my hands.

Joe said, "There was a video of the shooting on the news this morning. It'll be on YouTube by now."

"Did you tape it?" I asked Joe.

"Sure. Come watch while I get Julie ready."

"I have to get ready, too."

"No, you don't. Clapper said you're not going to work."

Oh, right. My gun and badge were locked up in Clapper's office. Same for Brady's official accoutrements. I swung my legs over the side of the bed and held the edge of the mattress until I felt steady enough to get to my feet. I followed Joe to the living room and dropped into my chair.

Julie was playing with her cereal at the kitchen table, sorting out the little marshmallows from the whole-grain Os.

"Jules, finish your breakfast," Joe told her. "You'll miss the bus."

"Booo," she said. "Hi, Mom." She shoveled cereal into her mouth.

"Hi, kiddo. Don't eat too fast. Chew. Swallow. Repeat."

Joe pressed the TV clicker and the tape rolled. I dialed down the volume. I knew what was coming from the first frame. The video had been shot from the corner of Carroll and Ingalls and had captured twenty-two of the scariest seconds of my life.

Now I watched the images shot from a distance of forty feet. Muzzle flares sparked on both sides of Carroll. Flashing and laser beams were coming nonstop from the Jeep, pounding into the front end of my Explorer.

And we were giving as good as we got.

I crossed my arms over my chest and held on tight. I still felt the broken glass cascading around me. The headlights popping, left, then right. The side-view mirror splintering.

Joe said, "Enough?" and made a move to turn off the TV.

"No. No, I want to see."

He sat back down. The angle of the video slipped and blurred as if the cameraman thought it was all over. There were several seconds of silence, then static. In my mind I was watching Brady's fist, his fingers counting off three seconds, his soft voice saying, "Now."

The camera hadn't captured that. Hadn't caught me standing on the gas pedal as I ducked below the dash and prayed. But now the picture was back. I saw the Explorer shoot off the mark, crash into the Jeep's midsection. My radiator sent up a plume of steam.

Joe said, "Cheese and rice, Blondie," cleaning up some mild swearing for Julie's benefit. On the TV, morning anchor Boris Neiman spoke. I read the closed captions: *Civilians and police mixed it up last night in Bayview. Injuries and death ensued....*I asked Joe, "Was my name mentioned? Brady's?"

"No. Anonymous video."

Julie was making her way over to my chair. I picked up the remote and turned off the TV.

"Who's Snoopy?" Julie asked.

I pulled her into my lap and said, "What do you know about Snoopy?"

"You said his name before."

"I was sleeping, right, Jules? I was dreaming. He's someone I used to know through work."

Joe said, "Lindsay. Go back to bed. I'll take Bug to the bus."

"Is it too early to call Brady?" I asked.

"I'd let him sleep."

I said, "Okay," and went back to bed. A minute later I grabbed my phone off the night table and called Brady.

He said, "How you doing, Lindsay?"

"Fantastic," I joked. "You?"

"Never better," he said, returning the ball over the net. Then he got serious. "Listen up. Kim Swanson passed away in the ambulance without regaining consciousness. CPS has her kids. Your dirtbag CI is in the ICU. Unconscious."

"What do you think?" I said. "Flowers or balloons?"

"I'd say a card. Instead of *Get Well*, how about *Go to Hell?*"

I had to laugh. Then I asked, "What do we know about the guy we shot?"

"His ID reads Roger Chen. He could be Snoop's family, but Chen is a common name. So nothing there. He'd just turned twenty-eight. Unemployed. No record. Samuels and Lemke are going through his apartment now. We have no idea who to notify unless Snoopy wakes up."

"Did the Chen guy fire on us?" I asked Brady.

Brady said, "Chi's waiting for a report from the lab. Either way, he was armed and refused to drop his weapon. Boxer, Clapper wants to see us today at two. Write up your report. I'll see you there."

I lay back and put Joe's pillow over my face. But I couldn't sleep. I couldn't get the pictures out of my head. I got up, made coffee. While it dripped into the pot, I opened my laptop and began typing my report, putting down what I remembered, picturing it all again.

CHAPTER 71

CLAIRE WASHBURN HAD begun Kim Swanson's autopsy at 6:00 a.m. and now at 9:55 was wrapping up. As always, she'd been meticulous and had taken great care to record every step, every observation.

She'd photographed the body clothed, then unclothed. She'd weighed her "patient" and noted every wound, every mole, plus the small tattoo—of a heart and the word *Ted*—on her right ankle. Even Kim's expensive mani-pedi was documented.

After the exterior exam, blood was drawn, labeled, and put aside for the crime lab.

Then Claire began the interior exam. Every organ was weighed and described for the record. She documented the location of the three slugs she'd found in the body. She bagged and labeled them. Six others had grazed Kim or were through-and-through. She made a note for the record.

Claire returned the organs to their cavities and stitched up the incisions while Bunny Ellis, Claire's assistant, cleaned instruments and prepared to put Mrs. Swanson's body away.

"Bunny, please call the lab. Tell them that Kim Swanson's clothes and belongings are ready for them. Also, the slugs I removed from her body."

Bunny said, "Sure thing, Doctor. I'm ready for a little break."

"Call the lab, we'll clean up and take a half hour."

Claire emailed the digital recording of her notes to a transcriber at the Hall, after which she and Bunny hefted Kim Swanson's body onto a stretcher, moved her into the cold room, and transferred her to a drawer. Bunny wrote out a toe tag and a label for the drawer, then slid it shut.

Claire went to her office and phoned Lindsay.

Lindsay said, "I can't talk for long. I have a meeting later with Clapper. Anything you can tell me that I should know?"

"Uh. Let's see. Mrs. Swanson was a well-nourished Asian woman, five foot five, 130 pounds, died between eight and ten last night. Cause of death, multiple gunshot wounds. Of the three bullets I took out, two were kill shots. Plus one that went through her left carotid artery. Another tore through her left ventricle. No stomach contents. We'll wait for her blood to come back from the lab, but she died from gunshot wounds, no question."

"Thanks, Claire."

"Linds, what was she doing there?"

"I'll tell you when I know."

Claire said good-bye to Lindsay as her office door opened. She looked up to see a thin Asian girl of about twelve wearing a T-shirt over tights, ballet flats. Her eyes were puffy with tears. She stood in the doorway and, looking hard at Claire, said, "I want to see my mother."

"Your mother?"

"Kim Swanson. I'm Lily Wong. Her daughter."

"Lily, I'm sorry about your mother. Who brought you here?"

"Mrs. Velshi. She's in the waiting room."

"Who is Mrs. Velshi?"

A woman in her fifties appeared in the doorway behind Lily. She had a soft face and gold-and-silver hair, and looked distraught.

She said, "Oh, Dr. Washburn, I'm sorry. Someone left the door open and Lily slipped through."

Lily said to Claire, "Mrs. Velshi is for children like me. Kids with dead mothers and dead families."

CHAPTER 72

PLEASE STAY HERE, Lily," Claire said, offering the child her desk chair after collecting the files on her desk and locking them in a cabinet. "I need to speak with Mrs. Velshi."

Claire walked Mrs. Velshi from her office out to the reception room. The front desk faced the door to the ME offices and was a dozen feet from the door that led to the interior of the morgue.

The reception room was lined with extruded plastic chairs in a soothing blue gray. A patrolman was sitting in one of those chairs, a crocheted handbag in the seat beside him. No one else was waiting. The pretty young woman behind the reception desk showed by her expression and agitated hand movements that she wanted badly to speak with Claire.

Claire said, "It's under control, Amy. We'll talk later."

Claire turned back to Mrs. Velshi.

"Mrs. Velshi, the morgue is off limits to children, period," she said. "Who are you to this child?"

"I'm Nora Velshi, caseworker with Child Protective Services. But this poor little girl. Her mother didn't come home last night.

Her stepfather killed himself a few days ago. Lily's little brother is in a crib downtown crying nonstop. And I've taken Lily away from her home. She can't go back. She wanted to see her mother, and I had to try. Officer Seldon here said it would be okay to ask. Dr. Washburn, Lily is heartbroken."

The police officer stepped forward and said, "If there's anyone to blame, Dr. Washburn, it's on me. I thought it was worth…"

"Okay. Okay. Give me a minute."

Claire collected Lily from her office and returned her to her guardian in reception.

She found Bunny in the washroom and told her about Lily and Mrs. Velshi. "We have to do this. You have a spare set of scrubs?"

Bunny was close to Kim Swanson's size. They dressed Kim's remains in coarse blue cotton pants and tunic. Brushed her hair. Taped a gauze bandage over the gunshot wound in her neck. Got her wedding and enagement rings from the bag of her effects. Once the dead woman was properly dressed, Bunny covered her up to her underarms with a drape. Last, Claire and Bunny folded Kim's hands over the cover.

Kim Swanson looked bloodless and was cold to the touch, but she appeared to be asleep.

Claire went to the doorway to reception and called Mrs. Velshi and Lily.

"We're ready for you now. Five minutes only. Okay?"

Lily nodded. "Yes." Tears dropped from her face to her shirt. "Yes, yes, yes!"

Claire understood the child's anger and why Officer Seldon had brought her here. Claire led Lily and Mrs. Velshi to the autopsy suite and held open the swinging door. Lily didn't hesitate. As soon as she saw her mother lying on the gurney, she threw herself across Kim's chest and sobbed.

Claire said, "I'll wait with you."

Lily whipped her head around and said to Claire, "He got her killed, you know? *He* did it."

"Who is 'he'?" Claire asked.

"You know," said the young girl.

Claire said, "I really don't. Please tell me."

Lily didn't speak again. Claire stood off to the side, and after five minutes Mrs. Velshi gently disengaged Lily from her mother's body.

"Tommy is waiting," Mrs. Velshi said.

Lily allowed herself to be shepherded out of the autopsy suite. Claire followed them out to the waiting room. The police officer stood up and gave Mrs. Velshi her handbag, and all three walked out of the medical examiner's office.

Claire watched them go.

Whom had Lily meant when she'd said "he" got her mother killed? Claire went back to her office and called Lindsay.

PART TWO

CHAPTER 73

WHEN CINDY OPENED her eyes, she was lying faceup on the ground, confused and nauseated. She rolled onto her side and spit up on the sidewalk, then tried to get to her feet—and failed. She fell back, weak, disoriented. She felt a blinding pain, like an electric charge, radiating out from her nose across her face, her head, and her shoulders, out to her fingertips.

She touched her face and yelped. When she pulled her hand away from her nose, she saw the blood on her fingers.

What had happened? Had she been in a fight? Gotten hit by a car?

A shadow fell across her.

She shielded her eyes and looked through the slats of her fingers. A man loomed over her. Late twenties, white, with sandy-colored hair. His smug smile offset his good looks. Did she know him?

"Need a hand?" he asked her.

The sun was too bright. She closed her eyes and turned away. She sensed, more than knew, that he wanted to hurt her. She whispered, "I. Need to lie. Still."

His shadow bled away, and now the events of the morning came back to her in bursts. Lindsay had been benched. Cindy had gone to get…she pictured pastries dusted in chocolate, the walk to Sweets. Then what? She'd texted for an Uber. *Meet me at Sweets. I need a ride to Lake Street.*

The car had crawled behind her. The driver, half leaning through his open window, had hassled her. He didn't get it. She had to go to the shop before going to Lindsay's. He'd called her a bitch. She'd said something. Like 'Get away from me." And when she'd turned—he'd gotten out of the car.

Now she remembered. God. *He had a gun.* She'd looked into his eyes and his face had hardened. She didn't remember after that. He must have punched her.

The sun was red through Cindy's eyelids. Blood slid across her cheeks, dripped into her blouse and onto the sidewalk. Her nose was throbbing, and her lips were cut, but she was thinking straight. She lifted her eyes but only as high as the man's waist. His right hand was cradling the fist of his left. If there'd been any doubt that he had struck her, it was gone. But he wasn't holding his gun.

Still, he could have jammed it into his waistband. *He could shoot her.*

Think, Cindy. If she wanted to live, she had to become very small. Helpless. No threat to him. As if she'd never seen him. That she didn't see him now.

She had to retrieve her backpack. If she didn't get her bag, he could find out where she lived.

There. Her black leather backpack was just out of reach. She stretched her arm as far as she could and clutched the strap, pulled the bag to her side. Still looking down, she pressed her palms to the sidewalk, leaned forward, and somehow got her legs under her. Now, she thought, if she ignored the pain, she could stand.

With tremendous effort Cindy lurched to her feet. She pulled the bag's strap over her shoulder and had taken a couple of steps toward the street when he called out to her.

"Cindy? You're Sergeant Boxer's friend, right? I have a message for her. You have to tell her."

He *knew* her. Knew her *name*. That she was close to Lindsay.

Cindy mumbled, "I have to go home."

The man kept speaking.

"Ready? Here's the message. Tell Lindsay, 'It's not over yet.' You get that, Cindy? 'It's not over yet.'"

Cindy crossed the street at the green light and kept walking. The man who'd assaulted her shouted after her, "Cindy! You heard about the dead men with their lips stapled together?"

Cindy kept walking, more steadily now, faster. She knew what he meant. That message had been written with a marker pen on one of those dead men's foreheads: *You talk, you die.*

This was a death threat.

Cindy heard car doors slam. She turned her head and saw the man who'd flattened her get back into the black car's driver's seat. Was this really happening? Oh, thank God he was leaving.

Cindy wanted to see the license plate, but her eyes were swollen almost shut, filled with tears and the glare of the sun. She pulled her phone from her pocket and pointed the lens toward the diminishing rear end of the car. She pressed the camera button again and again, taking pictures until the car turned a corner and was gone.

CHAPTER 74

I WAITED IN Clapper's anteroom, scrolling through a news feed on my phone, my canvas bag at my side. Brady left the chief's office, flipping a hand in a wave to me on his way out. Clapper came to his doorway and greeted me warmly. He seemed almost like the man I'd worked with when he was head of the crime lab.

"Sit, sit," he said. "How're you feeling?"

"Like I've been sleeping at a shooting range," I said. "I keep hearing gunfire. My hands shake."

"Understandable, Lindsay."

He reached out a hand to take my report. He ripped open the envelope flap, leafed through all two pages. In fact, he already knew what had happened last night. He'd been on the other end of the phone throughout the shoot-out.

He'd heard it from me and Brady between breaks of gunfire. At the same time, he'd had an open switch to dispatch on his office line. He'd handed the torch to Chi and relieved Brady of his rank pending investigation—protocol in cop-involved homicides.

Now he said to me, "Is there anything you want to tell me that's not in your report?"

"Between you and me, Charlie, I feel like a sucker, a rookie, a dumb-ass. Brady and I could have gotten killed. I feel stupid calling out the whole squad on Kenny Chen's wet dream, and for some reason I feel bad about Kim Swanson...."

"She went there for her own reasons, none of them good," Clapper said. "We'll never know for sure what they were."

"What I think? She blamed me for Ted. For my testimony at his trial. His sentence. His suicide."

"Don't carry this, Boxer. You didn't know her. You didn't arm her. Swanson's sentence was deserved. It's not on you. You want to hand me that?"

I gave Clapper the satchel full of banded twenties and fifties amounting to fifty thousand bucks that Kenny Chen had never touched.

I said, "Brady tells me that if Chen lives, he'll never walk again. Has he made a statement?"

"Yep. One word."

"Let me guess. 'Lawyer.'"

"Lindsay, you're going to have to see a shrink. It's mandatory. I think you'll be glad you did."

He dealt me a business card from a stack on his desk. This one had the name *Ari Greene, Psychiatrist* centered above the phone number.

I took it, said, "Thanks," and asked, "Brady's going to the review board, but not me?"

"He was the officer in charge. If they have any questions, you'll get your turn in the barrel. Tell you what. Stick around out there with Katie."

Katie Branch was Clapper's assistant, and Chief Warren Jacobi's before him. Clapper stood and I did the same. He said, "One more thing, Boxer. There's going to be a press conference. It's likely to be great for TV ratings but not for the SFPD."

"Cops shooting innocent people."

"If I were you, I'd keep the TV off tonight."

CHAPTER 75

KATIE WAS POKING the buttons on Clapper's blinking phone console. Her repeated "May I take your name and number?" was the soundtrack under the looping images in my mind. Me. Broken glass in my hair and on my shoulders. Stepping on the gas pedal, the jarring crash, shooting the guy who wouldn't put down his gun.

I was startled when Clapper called my name.

"They want to see you. Have you and Brady compared notes? I'll answer that," he said. "No. You didn't, right? You don't want to come off as getting your stories straight."

"Barely, Charlie. We spoke a few words at the scene. Anyone would have done that. There were no points of disagreement," I said.

Clapper shrugged. "Whatever you think."

"Do I need my rep? Did Brady have a rep?"

"It's not like that. The board needs to know about your CI so they can put the best face on this PR nightmare. Okay, Boxer?"

Not really, Clapper.

Back in chief mode, he led me down the hall to the conference room. He showed me in, pointed to an empty seat on one side of the oaken table, and took another for himself several feet away. I was flanked on all sides by top cops wearing dress blues and stern expressions. No one spoke, let alone said, "High marks for surviving Bayview meets the Wild West."

I was wearing my best jeans, button-front shirt, blue twill jacket. I felt underdressed, and whatever they called it, this was a review board and they were looking at me.

Adjudication of the Carroll Avenue incident had been shifted to the state police while the smell of gunpowder was still in the air. Captain Clint Wysocki was head of that body and, as such, head of this board. Because gunshots had been ricocheting inside my skull all night, I hadn't thought to research him.

I looked at Wysocki now. His face was lined. He had a receding hairline and a restrained but sympathetic smile. He also had ribbons on his jacket. A lot of them. He seemed okay. But that meant nothing. All that counted was what he did.

My guilt and self-indictment leached away, replaced by simmering anger at Kenny Chen's filthy assault and being judged by my superiors. I kept it below the surface, but it was there. My badge was at stake. If these officials were looking for a sacrificial lamb, I wasn't going to serve myself up, with or without the mint jelly.

Clapper introduced me to the room. "This is Sergeant Boxer. I've worked with her for fifteen years and can vouch for her a hundred percent. I was in touch with her and Lieutenant Brady before, during, and after the incident, and I ran point from my office throughout."

Captain Wysocki said to Clapper, "Chief, am I correct that you do not know, and have never met, the CI known as Kenny Chen?"

"Correct."

Wysocki said, "Sergeant Boxer, thanks for coming. Neither Lieutenant Brady nor Chief Clapper had met Chen. Tell us what you know about this man, what happened, so we're not surprised by his dying declaration or his upcoming book on police brutality. Tell us about your CI."

I figured I'd know what to say when I said it, so I started talking. I gave a brief overview of Chen's history with the SFPD, then went straight to the meetings at Li Po. I clearly sketched out the shell game Chen had played with me over the time and place of the guns-for-money exchange.

"So why would he do this?" I said. "We had offered him a substantial payment for his information on the gun convoy from Mexico. As he was bleeding out in his vehicle, with no gun convoy in sight, he asked me, 'Did you bring it?' He still wanted the money."

I admitted to being duped and concluded by saying, "Despite this disaster, we have four open homicides and strong reason to believe that they *are* connected to the truckloads of guns and drugs from Mexico that may still be on the way to California."

Katie came into the conference room, handed her boss a note, and departed.

Clapper read the note to himself, then said, "Mr. Chen woke up at Metro Hospital and posted a statement on the Blotter, an amateur crime sniffer's website. Here's what he wrote: 'I report to Sergeant Lindsay Boxer as a confidential informant. She had fifty thousand dollars for me for services rendered. So Boxer lured me to an out-of-the-way site and went to war. I guess she decided to keep the money. Too bad for her, I know what she did.'"

CHAPTER 76

LISTENING TO CLAPPER read Chen's "Boxer screwed me" defense made me rigid with fury. Chen was a rattlesnake, and more. He was out for revenge over what he'd lost on Carroll Avenue. Which was significant.

The note went on.

"'Boxer baited me. She and her partner killed my girlfriend and my cousin, and crippled me for life. Don't let Sergeant Lindsay Boxer get away with what she's done.'"

Hands went up around the table. Clapper didn't look at me during the onslaught of largely unanswerable questions, but he answered the last one.

"Boxer turned the 50K over to me this morning. She didn't have to be asked."

Moments later I was thanked and dismissed. Clapper walked me out to the hallway, where Conklin was waiting.

Clapper said, "Lindsay, like most snitches, Chen is a skell. His online statement wasn't sworn. He's putting out his version,

244

probably hoping to poison a jury or get a movie deal. Ignore him. Take some time off. Get out of town. I'll work on getting you a car. You have a preference?"

"Ford Explorer. And my badge?"

"Soon. Pending investigation. But I'll say it again. You did nothing wrong. You were played. Conklin, take it from here." And then he walked toward his office.

My partner smiled at me, but he looked worried. There was no hiding from the pain in his eyes.

"Cindy was attacked a few hours ago and wants to tell you about it," he said as we walked to the elevator.

"She was *physically* attacked?"

"Yes. She's got a hairline fracture of her nose, a puffy mouth, two awful-looking black eyes. But she's tough."

I checked my phone as we went down in the elevator, finding four messages from Cindy. I listened to the first one.

"Lindsay. Call me back. Call me back now."

The next three calls from her were hang-ups.

Conklin's antique Bronco was parked on Harriet Street. I saw from a distance that Cindy was in the passenger seat, so I got in the back.

She swung her head around to talk to me, and I got a look at her sweet face, now swollen and bruised. Her blue eyes were slits in the centers of two big purple circles.

"Oh, my God," I said several times. Then, "What happened?"

"Walked into a door," she said. She tried to smile, but before she could pull it off, she clapped her hand over her swollen mouth. "Ow, ow, ow."

"Cindy, can you tell me without moving your lips?"

"No staple gun, okay?"

"Promise."

As Conklin drove us along a well-traveled route to Lake Street, Cindy told me about her confrontation with the men in the black car and detailed what she remembered about the one who'd punched her.

"He had a gun, I think. Memory's been shaken some. Before he hit me, he had a gun. Afterward I didn't see it anymore. But he was holding his fist like it hurt, so I'm pretty sure he's the one who socked me."

I put my hand on her shoulder, commiserated, and bet a buck that his car was a black BMW.

"I've got a dozen out-of-focus shots of his rear plates," she said. "But there's gotta be something."

"AirDrop them to me."

She did, and I thanked her. And then my friend Cindy Thomas made a confession.

"Linds, I posted about the shoot-out on my crime blog."

Rich said, "Oh, no. You know not to do that."

She said, "I do. I do. But I didn't use names, no names at all. I wrote one paragraph saying there'd been police action in Bayview," she said, her words muffled by her swollen mouth. "I said that there'd been some casualties."

I said, "It's okay, Rich. Video was on YouTube this morning. Cindy, would you recognize that guy who punched you?"

"Maybe. But, Lindsay, he knows who you are. He said to tell you that it isn't over yet."

I slumped against the seat back. If these three guys in a black sedan were the same who'd shadowed Mrs. Rose to the park, and then set up where they could watch our apartments, Nardone and Einhorn had fed their ID into the database.

I leaned forward and asked Cindy, "When can you look at some mug shots?"

"Whenever you say. I can do it now."

"Rich, I can't work on this. Talk to Nardone and Einhorn. If these are the same three guys who've been tailing and harassing me and my family, we may already have their names, photo IDs, and maybe a lot more."

CHAPTER 77

I WAS WRUNG out and still steaming when I opened the front door to our apartment. Kenny Chen's statement on the Blotter was vicious. Lying bastard that he was, his story would appeal to half the people in the city. Cops had lured him. Then shot him to pieces. Bad cops.

Hey. Kenny Chen had tried to kill us.

I needed a new, bigger, better word for *infuriating*.

I found Joe at the kitchen island, his laptop in front of him, his hand wrapped around a mug of coffee. I hugged my dear husband, then bent to greet Martha, who half licked my face off.

Joe said, "Did you see my car?"

"No, what about it?"

He pulled his phone from his hip pocket and showed me a snapshot of his windshield and side windows. All of the glass was completely pasted over with pro-gun stickers reading WE WILL NOT COMPLY.

"I can scrape them off, but I didn't want to take the kiddo downstairs, and I couldn't leave her. I have an idea. Call Cat."

I got it. It was close to dinnertime, but I called my sister, Catherine. I knew she wouldn't mind.

First thing out of her mouth, "How are you, sis?"

"It's a long story. Can Joe and I take you and the girls out to dinner?"

"I'll make dinner," she said. "I've already shopped."

"Even better," I said to my younger—and only—sib. "And also, I need a favor."

"Whatever you need, it's yes."

I laughed, thinking of her sitting cross-legged on a yoga mat, offering me wishes like a genie in a bottle.

"Can you keep Julie for a week or so? We've got a situation here that could get dangerous."

"I saw that shoot-out on the news, Linds. I was about to call you."

"What did you think?"

"Ahhh, it doesn't matter."

"It does to me," I said.

"Okay. Us two? Same parents. Same house. And I like to grow tomatoes and make cheesecake. And you. You're the good side of our bad-cop dad. You really have guts, Lindsay."

I sighed.

"You okay?" Cat asked me.

"It's not over yet," I said.

I told her I was waiting to hear if I was even still a cop, that my car was junkyard trash. Oh, and that the guns-for-all coalition had just covered Joe's windshield with pro-gun stickers.

I said, "I want to get the little one out of here."

"Good, 'cause we all miss her," Cat said. "What's your ETA?"

"Six thirty or so, barring the usual potholes and logjams."

"I can't wait," she said.

While Joe was scraping his windows, I called Mrs. Rose and told her we were out for the night and that Julie would be out for the week.

"Lindsay. My daughter has been begging me to spend a night at her place. Good timing."

"Beautiful," I said. "Have fun."

I kissed the phone, then knocked on Julie's bedroom. She said to come in and I did, saw that she was staging a talk show with her dolls and toys. I marveled at her cuteness for a long minute, then asked, "How would you like to spend a few days with Aunt Cat and your cousins?"

She gasped. "Really?"

"Really. Let's pack."

"You're staying, too?"

"Dad and I are just going for dinner, coming home tonight. You lucky girl. You get to stay a week."

"Martha, too?"

"Definitely."

She danced around, chattered to her bedroom friends, then signed off her "broadcast," "This is Julie Anne wishing everyone a good dinner and sweet dreams."

CHAPTER 78

JOE AND I packed snacks and a bag for Julie, another for Martha. We locked up and headed downstairs. Once on the street, Joe and I moved Julie and Martha swiftly to the car, watching everything that moved on Lake Street between Eleventh and Twelfth.

I found our protective-custody squad car and asked the two uniforms to follow us for a while, make sure we weren't being tailed.

"No problem."

I said, "After that, take the night off, why don't you?"

Hurrahs from the protection team.

Once we'd cleared Fulton Street and were crossing Golden Gate Park, I buzzed down my window. Martha sat beside Julie's car seat behind me. The air blew back our doggy's ears, and I undid my pony and let the breeze play with my hair.

Joe dialed up his bluesy playlist, and my tension evaporated as the scenery flew by. Forty-five minutes after leaving Lake Street, we pulled up to Cat's cozy cottage by the ocean.

My sister and her two girls, Brigid and Meredith, were waiting in the driveway. Julie and her cousins squealed and hugged, then scampered off to play on the swing set in the backyard. Joe and Martha went for a run on the beach, and I caught up with Cat as we cooked and plated dinner in the kitchen.

Soon afterward we were at the dining table with its ocean view. Cat served her famous crab cakes and a freshly picked garden salad, then finished the meal with warm chocolate chip cookies and hot chocolate on the porch as we watched the sun leave the sky.

I was in love with my family.

All of this—the love, the togetherness, the sea breeze—made me want to stay at Casa Cat for another month. I wanted to meet Cat's boyfriend, Henry. I wanted to build sand castles with three young girls. I wanted to lie in the hammock with my sister and talk about the past, present, and future. And I wanted to sleep late and wake up with Joe to the sound of seagulls.

But I couldn't do that.

I needed to be home so I could watch my back. Table cleared, Joe and I hugged and kissed our kith and kin good-bye. Julie said, "Be good," which we found hilarious. After we pulled out of the drive Joe tooted the horn as we headed toward the highway north.

"Back to the real world," I said to Joe.

"I think we can be in bed by nine. Nine thirty at the latest."

We flashed smiles at each other in the dark.

"Sounds perfect," I said.

Once again I would prove to be wrong.

CHAPTER 79

JOE AND I heard the sirens as we approached Lake Street. There were so many sirens coming from all directions, magnified by the canyons of buildings and valleys of cross streets, that it was impossible to reason where the law enforcement vehicles were going—but this we knew: our address was inside this storm.

The streets from Park Presidio to Twelfth were clogged, but within three blocks of our front door, we could see the squads with flashers filling Lake Street from Funston Avenue all the way down Lake. From the lack of traffic, I knew that barrier tape had closed off that stretch of the street at both ends.

A uniform met us at Funston Avenue, vouched for us, and let our car under the tape. Joe parked across from our building, and immediately I saw a familiar white SFPD SUV parked in front of our door.

Brady and Conklin.

Brady was in the driver's seat. I approached, and my "What's wrong?" crossed the bow of his "Why don't you answer your phone, Boxer?"

I asked, "Why didn't you call me?"

"Check your phone," he said.

I slapped the pocket of my windbreaker. Crossed Lake and looked into Joe's car. No phone on the seat or the dash or the floor. And then it hit me. It was in the pocket of the blue blazer I'd worn to the review board hearing—a million years ago—this afternoon. I'd left the jacket at home.

I shouldn't have to explain to Brady that I was still rattled. Last night at this time we were pulling glass out of our hair and turning our jobs over to Sergeant Chi. Still, I couldn't bear to say that I'd left my phone at home, so I asked again, "What happened, Brady?"

"Guns on parade," he said. "Marching and shooting and about three hours of chanting."

"Come on upstairs," I said. "Julie is downstate."

Brady and Conklin were visibly agitated when they got into the small lift with me and Joe. Brady was inhaling through his nose, exhaling hard through his mouth. Like me, he was on leave without just cause, and Conklin looked like hell.

We all did.

It was weird being inside our big apartment without Julie and Martha, but it was quiet. I took drink orders. Brady and Conklin asked for hard liquor. Joe had wine, and I had herbal tea.

When we were all settled around the coffee table, I said, "Who's on first?"

Brady pointed at Conklin and my heart literally clenched, realizing I hadn't thought about Cindy since this afternoon. "How's Cindy?"

Conklin said, "She's okay. She recognized the dirtbag who punched her from his DMV photo. Name is Anthony Ruffo,

254

whose father owns that BMW. Turns out Ruffo gave Cindy a hairline nose fracture."

I swore and Brady held up a hand and waved me back down. "Go ahead, Rich."

"We picked up Ruffo, who travels all the time with his buddies. They're being held for assault and accessories to assault, which is enough to cage them tonight. Ruffo is going to law school. His father is a lawyer. Luckily, Cindy was threatened with a gun. Not that that's lucky—but you know what I mean."

Brady said, "They're soft little punks, and all we have to do is threaten them with a blemish on their spotless records and they'll spill. At least one will. Maybe they'll fight for the honor."

CHAPTER 80

JOE REFILLED GLASSES but just a touch. We were all out of gas, and Rich and Brady had to drive. I sat back in the lounge chair as Joe asked Rich about the man who'd punched Cindy.

"What did Ruffo say for himself?"

"He said, 'Cindy who?'" Richie replied. "But he knew she could ID him and he was going to have to give me something, so he told me that there was going to be a march down Lake Street and that it was all about the shooting last night."

I said, "I don't get it."

"Blowing away those shooters last night made you guys members of their team. Enemies of the anti-gun league. And Alvarez picked news from the police officers' grapevine. Another dead body. San Diego patrol cop. Fifteen years on the Job."

Richie showed us his phone with the picture of a dead man, his lips stapled together, the initials *YTYD* in black marker pen inked on the back of his hand.

You talk, you die.

Brady said, "I've never seen division like this in this city. This is the home of flower power, right? And that brings me to why I tried to call you, Boxer."

"I'm here now, Brady."

"Get ready for the unexpected. The plate glass window shop on Carroll has a motion-detector camera on the second floor with a wide view of the street. Cappy got their video, and I've seen it all from the moment we pulled in and parked on Carroll. It also captured the moment that Jeep rolled up and let us have it. Voices were captured. Not so clear, but I could hear 'That's her.' And 'We got 'em.'"

"That's amazing," I said. "And the car crash?"

"In full, grainy black-and-white," Brady said.

I started clapping. Couldn't help myself. Brady and Rich started laughing, and Joe joined in.

I said, "And, and, and?"

Brady said, "And Clapper emailed a copy to Wysocki, who said, 'The occupants of the Jeep were the initial aggressors. Without doubt.' That's self-defense, Lindsay. That camera even shows the guy refusing to put down his gun."

"So, what now?"

Brady reached under his jacket and pulled a gun. My gun. He handed it over, butt first. Then he unpinned a badge from inside his shirt. My badge. He handed it to me, his eyes not leaving my face.

I looked at him and asked, "We're back on the Job?"

Brady said, "Boxer. In my official capacity as lieutenant, Southern Station SFPD, I'm informing you that you are reinstated as sergeant of the Homicide Division. Since I'm your commanding officer, this is an order: go to bed and get some sleep. Arraignment court for those three pricks in the BMW is tomorrow morning at the Hall. Courtroom 2F. Yuki will pick you up here at seven. She's prosecuting."

I heard myself say, "Oh man, oh man, oh man."

It had taken twenty-four hellacious hours—and two delicious ones with Cat—to turn my upside-down world right side up again. Maybe. I remembered Cindy's message from Ruffo. *It's not over yet.*

Rich said, "Cindy and I will be there, too. Cindy will give Yuki the blow-by-blow of the assault."

Brady said, "Yuki might want to hear more about that car stop outside your apartment. It's documented. It might be critical."

"Joe?" I asked.

"I'm coming with you. Don't anyone try to stop me," he answered.

More laughter. Joe is a big, fit dude.

Everyone stood up. Conklin and Brady took turns hugging me, Rich saying, "Thank God you're back."

The men shook hands, and Conklin and Brady made for the front door.

As Brady left the apartment, the last thing he said to me was, "Boxer. Keep your phone on."

I slapped my empty jacket pocket and said, "Copy that."

CHAPTER **81**

CLAIRE AND LILY Wong, Kim Swanson's daughter, sat across from each another in a small booth at a diner four blocks from Child Protective Services. Dishes clattered in the kitchen. A man argued with his wife at the counter. Claire and Lily's waitress set down plates of eggs and toast in front of them, plus orange juice for Lily, coffee for Claire.

Claire shot a look at the clock over the cash register. It was eight fifteen. She didn't want to jump up from the table when Lily wanted to talk to her, but she was expected at her office no later than nine. There was that, and Claire thought the child might want to explain what she'd said to her after seeing her mother's body: "He got her killed."

Lily was in motion, crossing then uncrossing her legs, winding and yanking her hair, fiddling with the buttons on her blouse. It was clear that she didn't know how to talk about her grief and anger. Claire understood. If Lily had family, she might not have to go into the system. That went for Tommy, too. But caseworker Nora Velshi had told her they had not located family members.

As soon as end of day, the children would be going into foster care. Lily was especially distraught about that.

Claire peeled the lid from the small container of cream and poured it into her coffee. She said, "Lily, tell me what you're thinking. I want to help you."

"Uh-huh."

The child forked her eggs around. She tasted the orange juice. Looked dubiously at the toast. Pushed her plate across the table toward Claire, offering her whatever she might like.

Claire said, "Thanks, no. Take a few bites, Lily. Give your stomach something to work on."

Lily threw down her fork and left her plate in the middle of the table. Then she flung herself back against the vinyl-covered banquette while keeping her eyes on Claire.

"When I saw you yesterday," said Claire, "you said something like '*He* did it.' You didn't say who '*he*' is, but the police would really like to find him. You, too, right?"

Lily sighed. Covered her eyes with her hands. "I thought it was obvious."

Claire said, "Not to me."

"My *father*, of course," Lily said. "He convinced my mom to go someplace where there was going to be a payday. I told her not to go, but she said, 'It'll be all right.' And then she was packing a gun and saying, 'See you in a couple of hours. Please watch Tommy.' But it's not all right. It's the worst thing that could've happened. She has kids! How could she get into a gunfight? With the police?"

"I wish I knew," Claire said softly.

Lily looked at Claire with sad eyes. The kid was twelve, and without warning, her world had upended. Gone from TikTok and girlfriends teasing one another about boys to no mother, no home, no understanding. Nothing less than a tragedy.

Wait a minute.

"Kenny?" Claire asked. "Kenny Chen is your father?"

"Very good," Lily said. "Sleazy, no-good Kenny Chen."

Claire had gotten information early this morning from Metro Hospital that Kenny Chen had died in surgery. Claire did her level best not to let her face show her shock and surprise.

Lily said, "He's no kind of actual father. He's my mother's used-to-be sleepover boyfriend, that's all. If it had been up to him, she would have gotten rid of me."

That was Lily's melting point. There was room on the table for her to put her head down on her arms and sob. But there wasn't enough room for Claire to go over and sit next to her. She said, "Sorry, Lily. I'm so sorry this has happened to you."

She reached over and put her hand on Lily's shaking shoulders and let her cry it out. She didn't want to say that Kenny Chen was dead, in fact, on his way over to her office wrapped in sheets.

After a few minutes Lily stopped crying, grabbed napkins from the dispenser, and dried her eyes.

"I'm sorry," she said. "I don't usually do that."

Claire said, "You didn't do anything wrong. Do you feel up to answering a few questions?"

"I guess."

Claire guessed Lily was not up to that, but she had to try. "Lily? Was Ted Swanson Tommy's father?"

Lily scoffed. "I mean, that's what Mom said, but how would it be possible? Ted was in prison."

"Here's why I have to ask," Claire said. "Tommy's father, if it wasn't Ted Swanson, may have parental rights, and we should know that."

"So Kenny has rights to me?"

"Well. If he didn't waive them. But…"

Lily flashed her eyes across Claire's face and saw what she wasn't saying. "Did he die? Tell me he died."

Claire nodded. Lily started to laugh. "For real. He died? When?"

"In surgery last night."

The child became still, no doubt absorbing this news. Then she came back to the moment.

"Dr. Washburn, I only met Tommy's father a couple of times. Usually he came over past our bedtime. He was nice, but tell you the truth, I really didn't care. Mom was married to Ted!"

They left the diner together, and Nora Velshi was waiting outside. It was then that Lily said, "Jim, I think. That's Tommy's father's name."

"Thanks, Lily."

Lily said, "I might want to talk to you sometimes. Is that okay?"

"Definitely," Claire said. She opened her arms to the young girl, who came in for a big, tight hug, and Claire hugged Lily back. Kissed the top of the child's head. "I'm on your side, Lily."

Claire held on to the orphaned child and thought of the many little girls, alive and dead, who so often came into her life. Even when this confluence was painful, Claire knew that it was a blessing.

CHAPTER 82

ARRAIGNMENT COURT REMINDED Yuki of a large, sprawling bus depot. The room was ten times the size of a standard courtroom, and the dozen rows of long benches were packed with attorneys, their clients, the clients' families, witnesses, and kids who were crying, fighting, and crawling over people and the floor. Voices, cries, and coughs echoed. The people assembled here were already stressed out, and the stress ratcheted up as the back doors opened again and again, with more and more people squeezing in.

Judge Brookman demanded order but didn't get it. He banged the gavel nearly through the strike plate, and now he'd had enough.

Lindsay, sitting behind Yuki, whispered, "What's he doing?"

"Um. His thing."

The judge had gotten to his feet, stretched his arm in front of him, and pointed at a woman six rows back with three small, noisy kids. Brookman said with a slight Texas twang, "Madam, yes, you. Please take your family outside right now. Wait in the hallway."

"But, Judge," said the woman, "we're here for—"

"Tell the guard at the door to notify you when your case is called." Brookman swung his arm to the left and gave similar "Get out" orders to a couple and their restless brood. Brookman continued directing courtroom traffic until he was satisfied that his court was orderly.

Yuki was surrounded by her people, too. Quiet, intense ones. Rich and Cindy sat to her left, Brady on her right. Joe and Lindsay were behind her. Yuki'd dressed in red this morning. Red said, *Watch out. I mean business.*

Across the center aisle, halfway down a long bench, sat personal injury lawyer Anthony Ruffo Sr., wedged between his son and the son's two road buddies. The buddies may or may not have participated in major crimes, but Yuki had nothing on them.

Ruffo Jr. was another story. Unprovoked, the violent twenty-six-year-old had threatened Cindy with a gun. He'd hit her in the face with his big boy fist, his way of sending a message to Lindsay. If Yuki was half as good as Ruffo was bad, he'd be in lockup before court adjourned for lunch.

Yuki's attention was drawn to the bailiff, reading out their case number. She tapped Cindy's shoulder and they stood, edged past others in the third row until they were standing before Judge Brookman. Yuki knew the judge to be smart, no-nonsense, decisive. And yeah, eccentric. She liked him.

Mid center in the gallery, attorney Anthony Ruffo Sr. and his son bumped knees, stepped on toes, and finally took their positions beside each other, facing Judge Brookman. The judge read the charges against Ruffo Jr. and said, "ADA Castellano, let's hear it."

"I've got a lot to say, Your Honor."

"This is arraignment court, Ms. Castellano. You know how it goes. I read the charges. You give a brief summary of the reasons for those charges. I ask the defendant, 'How do you plead?'"

"It's complicated, Your Honor."

Judge Brookman poured water from a pitcher into a sixteen-ounce glass. He lifted it and said, "You've got until I put this glass down. On your mark. Get set."

He began to gulp down the water.

CHAPTER **83**

SONIA ALVAREZ WAS alone at the three-desk horseshoe at the front of the bullpen. Brady, Conklin, and Boxer were all in court, but retired bailiff Bobby Nussbaum had gotten a judge to sign a warrant, so for the last two hours Alvarez had been working her way through Kim Wong Swanson's financial records.

She'd been focused, shutting out the sounds of ringing phones and voices in the squad room. She had learned more about Kim in those two hours than she knew about her own sister—from Kim's first job as the administrative aide to a real-estate lawyer, through her two children's births, her jailhouse marriage to Swanson, and her rent- and mortgage-free house in San Rafael. But where was her will? Who was her next of kin? Had Kim made any plans in the event of her death?

Alvarez made her first call, to Sam LoPriore, the lawyer who had employed Kim Wong fifteen years earlier. It was a long shot, but when it came to cracking cases, Alvarez was a sharpshooter. LoPriore answered his own phone. Of course he remembered Kim. He was so sorry to hear that she had died. No, LoPriore knew of no relatives other than the children, but yes, he had drawn up her current will a few years before. In fact, he'd drawn up that new will because a friend of Kim's had bought the house where she had been living until—well, until she died.

"And the name of the friend?"

Alvarez held her breath. If she had any expectations, it was that she was about to learn the name of a new boyfriend or one of Kim's relatives. LoPriore knew of no relatives, but he did know the name of Kim's friend. And Alvarez knew him, too.

When the lawyer said the friend's name, the owner of Kim's house, it was a shock. Alvarez had taped her talk with LoPriore and received the automated transcript back in minutes. She was wishing that Conklin were sitting across from her, but when Brady came through the gate, she was glad.

Alvarez stood up, said, "Lieutenant. We've got a Code 3 on the Swanson case."

Brady sat down in Boxer's chair, and Alvarez told him what she had just learned.

"I'm feeling it, Lieutenant," she said. "I think this mess is starting to make some sense."

Brady said, "Conklin and Boxer are on their way up. Fill them in fast and take Conklin with you when you pick this guy up. When you've got him in the box, call me. Make sure Conklin is with you for the interview. Good work, Alvarez."

CHAPTER 84

ALVAREZ FOUND THE hidden squib of a street off Columbus on the first try, and then a parking spot opened up within sight of the bar. Conklin gave her a high five, and the two got out of the squad car and entered North Beach on the Rocks.

Lunch was on. There were a dozen people at the bar, and the tables were filled with a loud, happy crowd.

Today's barkeep was a blue-eyed blonde wearing a man's undershirt over her jeans, her arms tastefully inked with flowering vines. She recognized the two cops and said, "He's in his office. Go on back."

Conklin followed Alvarez through the dark bar, past the mermaids, down the hallway to the closed door marked PRIVATE in blue paint.

Alvarez knocked and heard the sound of chair legs scraping back, heavy footsteps, the turn of the doorknob—and then she stared up at the looming figure of Jimmy Ransom in the doorway.

"Inspectors?"

"We need a few minutes of your time, Mr. Ransom."

"Jimmy," he said, stepping back, waving them in.

Alvarez and Conklin settled into the chairs across from Ransom's desk, turned down his offer of refreshment, and waited a beat before starting to question him. But Ransom spoke first. "I was about to call you. It's very strange. I can't reach Kim."

Alvarez nodded and said, "When you called us four days ago—"

"I was *right*?" Ransom asked. "Ted was murdered?"

Conklin said, "Actually, no. No signs of foul play. But we did go see Kim."

Alvarez said, "There's sad news on that front, Mr. Ransom. Maybe you heard about a police action in Bayview."

Ransom had distractedly begun tidying his desk. He tossed an empty bottle into the trash, and Alvarez waited until it had clunked into the can. When Ransom looked up, Alvarez said, "I'm sorry to tell you that Kim was involved in that action—and there's no good way to say this—"

Ransom paled. "She's dead?"

"Passed away in the ambulance."

Ransom raised his voice in protest. "No-no-no. That can't be right. Kim's a stay-at-home mom. Why would she be...? No. Had to be someone who looked like Kim."

"Lily made a positive ID."

Ransom's face buckled with emotion. Tears sprang from his eyes.

He was saying, "Poor kid. How did this happen—" when Alvarez interrupted him.

"Jimmy. When you told us about Kim marrying Ted Swanson, you left something out."

Ransom looked in the general direction of Alvarez, dazed, seeming not to remember what he had said or neglected to say.

Alvarez took out her phone and opened the photo gallery. She swiped the screen and, after a few long seconds, found what she was looking for.

"You recognize this child?" she asked.

Ransom took the phone and looked, then gripped it with both hands.

"Tommy. He's my son. Please. Don't tell me something happened to him, too."

Alvarez explained that he was physically fine and at Child Protective Services with Lily. "Jimmy, I'm going to be straight with you. I don't understand the arrangement you had with Kim, but here's how things stand right now. Time is racing ahead of us. Lily and Tommy are going into foster care by close of day."

"Tell me. What I can do about Tommy."

"As of now, he'll be in the system for the next sixteen years," Alvarez said. "But help us, we'll help you. If you're his father, your DNA checks out, your record is clean, and you're solvent, I think we can turn this around."

"Tell me what to do."

Alvarez said, "Come with us to the station. Tell us everything you know about Swanson, any activities he may have been involved in while in prison. Do that, get on the right side of Child Protective Services and the SFPD. You'll have a good chance of getting your son."

CHAPTER 85

BRADY AND I were behind the one-way mirror in the observation room, watching Alvarez and Conklin in the box with Ransom. Ransom was a weeping mess, but he was trying to pull himself together. He had tissues. He had water. He asked if preparations had been made for Kim's burial. And he asked if he needed a lawyer. He cried, again, for Kim.

Conklin said, "Jimmy, you're not under arrest. But it's past four, and CPS closes at five."

"What do you want? What do you want from me?"

"We think Ted Swanson had a significant side hustle going on even in prison. Tell us about that."

"Why do you think that?"

"Cops have been killed. Several of them knew Ted. They were killed for talking about something big. We think Ted was involved, but he may have been a middleman. Now Ted is dead. Chen is dead. And Kim is dead, too. You're part of that group of people who had violent deaths in the last *week*. Do you feel safe? How are you going to protect your son?"

Ransom looked around the small room. At the camera. At the glass, at the people behind the glass. He turned back to Conklin and Alvarez.

"I don't know about any grand plan," he said. "I loved Kim. She didn't love me. She loved Ted. I don't understand what she had going with Chen. I didn't want to know. What the fuck. I'm glad he's dead. But why take Kim with him?"

Alvarez said, "Kim was armed. She fired the gun. Ted's gun. Her prints were on that gun. Shell casings were all over the street and inside the officers' car."

"Oh, my God. Oh, my God. This is not like her."

Conklin waited a moment, then, "You saw Swanson every month."

"He paid me to keep an eye on Kim and Lily," Ransom said. "To make sure they had everything. He sent money for me to buy the house—you can check that out. A guard gave me notes from Ted that I passed to Kim."

Alvarez asked, "Notes? What kind of notes?"

Jimmy didn't speak. He blinked.

"You read them, right? Come on, Jimmy."

Ransom said, "Some of it was personal. But there were parts that made no sense. Numbers and sentences that looked like code. I'd reseal the envelope and give it to Kim. Look, it was none of my business. Money showed up in my checking account. Enough for all of us. I paid insurance. Doctor's bills. Taxes—" Alvarez interrupted.

"Name of the guard who passed the notes, Jimmy. Let me guess. Arthur Guthrie?"

"He's talking? What did he say?"

"He's dead. His body was found on the Larkspur ferry."

"Christ. I had no idea."

Alvarez asked, "What about hits, Jimmy? Did Swanson ask you to put anyone down?"

"No. Are you crazy? Inspector. You ride in a squad with a guy for five years, and you know each other. He would never ask me to do that and I would never do it. Never."

Conklin said, "Did you ask Kim to decode the notes?"

"I worked for Ted. Kim was raising my only kid.

"Okay. I asked her one time. She gave me a look. Like, *Be serious.*"

Long pause from Ransom. Then he said, "I followed her once about a month ago. Listen. I'm cooperating. Shouldn't you call someone? Put the brakes on the foster home."

"We're getting there, Jimmy," Conklin said. "You were saying. You followed Kim."

"She had the kids with her. She pulled off the highway at a truck stop just outside Upton called the Round Two. Another car pulled into the lot from the opposite direction and nosed its window up to hers. I parked out of direct view, but I got a look at the driver for a few seconds."

Conklin said, "Who was it, Jimmy?"

"If I tell you, I'm going to die. I could die for being here." He looked at the glass and jabbed a finger toward us.

"Hear me? If I talk, I'm going to die."

Alvarez said, "Jimmy. It's ten to five. Speak now and you get protection. Otherwise, you're free to go."

Conklin stood up and opened the door.

Jimmy said, "Wait."

CHAPTER 86

CONKLIN HELD THE door for Brady, who entered Interview 2, took the chair next to Alvarez and across the table from Ransom. After introducing himself, Brady took the lead.

He said, "As I understand it, after receiving sealed envelopes from Ted Swanson by way of prison guard Arthur Guthrie, you gave them to Kim Swanson."

Ransom threw a sigh, then said, "I didn't think it was a crime."

Brady rapped his knuckles on the table and kept going.

"Then you tailed Kim to a truck stop outside of Upton. A car pulled up to Kim's car so that they could speak through the car windows. And you recognized this person."

"Right. That's right."

Brady asked, "And did Kim give him an envelope?"

"I can't swear, but I think so. It was a short meeting. A minute."

Brady asked, "What kind of car?"

"Could have been a Mercedes, but I got a two-second look before her car blocked my view. I couldn't pick it out of a lineup."

"Were you seen?"

"If he'd seen me, I'd be underground. This man has eyes everywhere. He could snuff me like that. And then what will happen to Tommy?"

"Get his tags?"

"No."

Brady said, "Let me see if I've got this right. Swanson deposited money into your account every month. Essentially child support."

"It was autopay," said Ransom. "Ted's name wasn't on the check."

"Who was the issuer?"

"Banco de México," said Ransom.

"And the sum?" Brady asked.

"Four grand."

Brady said, "So you were getting forty-eight thousand a year for Kim, child support, and the mortgage on the house, which belongs to you."

"That's right."

"And you were being paid for services rendered—notes being passed from Ted to Guthrie to you to Kim and finally to this guy at the truck stop."

Ransom looked abashed. He nodded yes.

"In your opinion, is that man at the truck stop the boss?"

"I'd say so, but I don't know."

"Okay. What's his name?"

Ransom said, "I want protection. Me and Tommy, and I want Lily, too. Out of town. Out of state. I want them made available now. Make the calls and I'll give you the name when we get to the airport."

Brady said, "That's going to take a little time. A judge is going to have to weigh in on your paternity, your fitness to parent your own child as well as his half sister."

Ransom muttered, "I'm dead."

Said Brady, "Here's what I'm offering. You leave here in an armored car. We'll take you to a hotel and put protection on your room. Tomorrow we'll transport you to a closed courtroom, here, with all the protection we'd give to the queen of England."

"What about the kids?" Ransom asked.

Alvarez said, "They have a small bedroom and sitting room at CPS. They'll be kept there with a TV and a crib, patrol cars outside, and officers inside, too, until we square this away. One way or the other."

"One way being, I move somewhere with the kids. The other way being, I go back to my bar and the children are put in foster homes."

"What I'd do," said Brady, "is choose plan A. Give us the name. Also your house key and address, and we'll go pick up some things for you."

Ransom said, "I can see the bullet hole in my head right now." He tapped his forehead. "Don't say you weren't warned."

Brady turned to the mirror and said, "Cut the cameras and the sound to the observation room."

I followed orders but could still see through the glass as Brady pulled a pad of paper and a red grease pencil out of the single drawer in the interview table.

Ransom produced his keys. Wrote down what looked like his address and a short list that might be clothing and personal items. Then he passed the pad back to Brady.

Brady skimmed the list, then said something to Ransom that could have been "Write down the name."

Ransom picked up Brady's grease pencil, wrote two words, closed the pad, placed the pencil on top.

Brady got up, reached over, and shook Ransom's hand.

Then he opened the door, and I heard him say, "Stay put for now, Jimmy. I got to do some work on this. You should call in sick so your staff doesn't call the cops. Conklin, keep Mr. Ransom company."

Then, after leaving the interview room and opening the door to the observation room, he said, "Boxer, my office. We have some calls to make."

CHAPTER 87

THE GIRLS—CLAIRE, Yuki, Cindy, and me—were sitting shoulder to shoulder in our booth at Susie's Café. Richie was there for Cindy and had a chair at the head of the table, where he got continually bumped by a line of customers and waitstaff.

He took it well.

Yuki had ordered margaritas all around, and although it's not my favorite drink, it's hers and she deserved it. Claire asked for tea, and Rich ordered beer on tap. I went with the tequila, and Cindy sipped her margarita through a straw. Lorraine delivered baskets of corn chips and lava-stone bowls of guacamole to our table. We could hear the steel band tuning up, all perfect for a predinner snack.

One drink later laughter ricocheted around our booth. Excepting Claire, we'd all been in court to witness Yuki's tour de force.

I put on a Texas accent and said, "Let's hear it, Ms. Castellano," and got a good laugh for my imitation of Judge Brookman. "You have until I put this here glass down."

I put it down hard. Yuki cracked up and so did Claire, who'd missed all of this in person.

Yuki said, "Judge puts down his glass, takes a good look at black-and-blue Cindy and at the defendant's gauze-wrapped hand…well, he had to let me speak. Had to. I didn't wait for *permission* or *forgiveness*. I told the judge the full one-minute version of Anthony Ruffo's unprovoked, brutal assault on Cindy. Ruffo's father tried to break in, but Brookman said, 'Let her talk.' And so I tied it up with a bow: 'Your Honor, we ask that the defendant be remanded into custody until trial.'

"And where is Anthony Ruffo now? The men's jail, where I'd say he's looking at one to five years."

Cindy hugged Yuki and said in a blurry voice, "My hero."

Claire lifted her cup of tea and said, "To Yuki."

We all clinked glasses, and Yuki accepted a nice round of applause before passing me the talking stick—actually a breadstick—saying, "Your turn."

I hadn't figured out how to tell about the afternoon with Jimmy Ransom, and so I passed the stick to Claire—and then I thought I was hallucinating.

Joe came toward us along the pass-through from the front room to the back. When he reached our table, he said, "Sorry, everyone, but Clapper needs Lindsay and Rich. Task force meeting."

I blurted, "Now?"

Rich asked Claire, "You mind driving Cindy home?"

"Not at all."

I tucked some folded money under the empty pitcher of margaritas, but Yuki pushed my cash back into my hand and signed the air, the universal signal for *Check, please*.

Rich and I followed Joe out to the street, all of us wanting to know, "What now? What happened?"

CHAPTER **88**

CLAPPER PAUSED AS Joe, Rich, and I took seats along the window wall of his office.

"Good. We're just getting started."

When we'd settled in, he said to the seven of us in the illegal-gun task force, "Another cop has been murdered. Sergeant Royce Bleecker of the San Diego PD."

The whiteboard was still where it had been in our last meeting three days ago. It showed the timeline of the murders on the left-hand side. To the right were four enlarged ID photos staring out at us. Below the portraits were morgue shots showing three of the dead men with their lips stapled together.

Clapper added Royce Bleecker's head shot to the macabre display, then, beneath it, pictures taken by the ME. Duck lips, bullet hole in the forehead, and the words *You talk, you die* written in marker pen on his neck.

Our chief explained, "Sergeant Bleecker lived in San Diego, and his chief, Lawrence Milton, knew him, as well as his friends and his enemies. Bleecker had more of the former than the latter.

"Chief Milton says he's heard rumors more times than he can count of an upcoming sizable guns-and-drugs payload coming through cross-border tunnels to San Diego. And we've all seen photos of those tunnels, which range anywhere from thirty feet in diameter down to spider holes with beams holding up walls no more than three feet across.

"San Diego PD went through Bleecker's house and garage. Weapons were found. Military variety. A ton of them." He slapped up more photos of M4s, AKs, and automatics of all types.

He continued. "Bleecker's girlfriend was questioned. She claims she knew nothing of this operation, but she was cooperative. Detectives on the case gave her Bleecker's cell. She had his password, and under questioning, she eventually turned up a page of text. It seems to be a half-assed code that might contain the time and date for the departure of the contraband gun train. We have that unverified information and that's all."

Alvarez asked, "Chief. What's the plan?"

"Keep your phones charged and be ready to move."

After Clapper dismissed the meeting, I stayed behind with Joe and Mike Wallenger.

"Charlie," Joe said. "The FBI should be in on this."

"I agree. I'll call Steinmetz now."

Joe asked, "You know the name of the quarterback?"

"We think we do."

"Shouldn't the FBI pick this person up?"

Clapper said, "Not yet, Molinari. But soon."

CHAPTER 89

CLAPPER GOT CRAIG Steinmetz, section chief of the local branch of the FBI, on the phone.

"Craig, Charlie Clapper. We have a situation and possibly a break in how to deal with it. I'm in a car downstairs. Care to take a drive?"

"Describe the car."

"Gray Audi. I'm alone."

"I'm coming down."

Steinmetz left a message with the control room saying where he'd gone, with whom. He set the recorder in his watch, then he left his office and took the elevator down to Golden Gate Avenue. He peered into the Audi and saw Charlie Clapper behind the wheel. The door lock snapped open and Steinmetz got in.

Said Steinmetz, "How're things, Charlie?"

"News every day that reads like a Marvel comic book." Then, "You know, Craig, I have the same watch as yours."

He showed it to Steinmetz, who smiled and undid the clasp

of his watch. Clapper did the same, saying, "I have a gym bag in back."

Steinmetz reached behind him, brought the gym bag forward, and dropped his watch and phone inside. Clapper did the same and covered the electronics with a towel.

Steinmetz said, "I've been sitting all day. Let's take a walk."

Clapper locked up the car, set the alarm. This was a rough neighborhood, but the sky was still light and both men were armed. They set off in a northerly direction.

Steinmetz asked Clapper, "Is this about the upcoming drug-and-gun exchange of world-class proportions?"

"It is," said Clapper. "It feels like it's ready to blow."

"You have the head of the snake?"

"In sight, but no proof."

"More on that," said Steinmetz.

"That's it," said Clapper. "We have a witness to an exchange of information. And now that person, the go-between, is dead."

Steinmetz said, "What do you want to do?"

"I'd like to bring the suspect in, get a confession of intent to transport contraband, with a side of terrorism, but dead witnesses don't talk," said Clapper. "We're working leads that may bear fruit."

"You want us to step in?" Steinmetz asked.

"Not yet. If we move too fast, the whole deal will fold."

Steinmetz said, "And so?"

"We put eyes on him. We keep up the pressure on CIs and patrol cops for information," said Clapper. "I'm hoping your people can decode something we found on a murdered cop's phone."

Steinmetz said, "The dead cop. 'You talk, you die'?"

"Afraid so," said Clapper. "This dead cop is in San Diego and may have been the last man in the chain. Possibly the head is rolling up all the witnesses. That page of text may be the code for time, place, and location."

"That's balancing a whole lot of plates on the tip of a toothpick."

"I know it. I know it, but assuming we're right, we have all of San Diego PD working with SFPD. Still, the Bureau should be in on the takedown and make the arrests."

"Agreed."

"I like Molinari and Wallenger."

"You've got them. Others can be made available if necessary."

"Thanks," Clapper said. "And I need another favor. I have to get people into witness protection probably by end of day tomorrow."

"I'll need to pull strings, but it's doable. Might cost you a dinner, though."

"Thanks, Craig. Name your steak house. I have the dead cop's phone in my car."

Clapper dropped change into a beggar's cup as the two men walked back toward the FBI building.

CHAPTER 90

CINDY WAS AWAKE at just after five and unable to fall back to sleep. She was left with the fragment of a dream, the feeling of hands around her neck. Squeezing.

This was because of the book. She was researching and writing down the words in the voice of a serial killer she'd actually known. The man and his story consumed her even while she slept.

She got quietly out of bed and slipped on her pink cotton bathrobe, went into the kitchen. She leafed through a boxed assortment of tea bags and made a selection. When the cup of herbal tea had steeped, she cooled it off in the freezer for a moment, then poured the tea into an adult sippy cup with a couple of ice cubes.

The apartment had only three rooms. In one, Rich was sleeping soundly, sprawled out across the entire bed. The living room was still dark, the morning light not yet breaching the blinds across the front window. Cindy switched on the table lamp, did the same to her laptop and scanner, and got herself in touch with the waking city.

She sat at her table and listened to the police scanner, which chattered companionably. Car radios calling in codes and addresses, dispatch sending cars to scenes of break-ins; a loiterer or a drunk sleeping under a delivery truck had been dragged and an ambulance was needed. Another patrol car was dispatched to a domestic violence call that had spilled out of doors onto the Haight, and yet another sped to a traffic accident in Union Square.

Cindy touched her face with the pads of her fingers, gauging the depth of her pain. She dialed down the police scanner, then opened her email inbox, and deleted her spam and the new ads that had sprung up overnight in one long block.

Now it was 5:35. She sipped her tea, thought about bacon and eggs, and looked out the window at the still-dark street while considering going back to bed, snuggling up to Richie without waking him.

But a silent alarm had gone off in her head.

She had a book to write and this was a good time of day to do it.

Opening the computer file marked *Burke's Last Stand*, Cindy urged herself into a serial killer state of mind. She reread her introduction to the true-crime work she was hoping to complete in the near future.

This is what she had written months ago:

A crime reporter for the San Francisco Chronicle, *I had reported on several murders that seemed to be the work of a pattern serial killer. This person, presumably a man, had a penchant for young women. If there is a class of serial murderer who preys on young women, this unknown subject was its archetype. I had followed and documented five of his killings in the* Chronicle, *and they all scared me. The victims could have been my cousins or sisters. They were young, trim, and perhaps more like me than I knew. They were trusting.*

As I reported on these victims, I wanted to discover how they'd intersected with their killer. I wanted to write about this professional-grade murderer as a posting to other young women. As a posting to myself. When the killer was finally identified, he denied the charges and took his own life. Only then was it learned that he hadn't been the killer at all.

The real killer was still out there.

While I was covering this predator and his crimes, he had his eyes on me. Not for his usual reason, perhaps. He wasn't looking for a victim. He was looking for a biographer.

He'd read my work. He'd saved it. When he was finally caught by the brave men and women of the San Francisco and Las Vegas Police Departments and the San Francisco branch of the FBI, he stunned us all. None more than me.

He told me that he was the greatest killer of all time, and to prove it, he produced the evidence. He gave me the key to his trove of souvenirs, photographs, maps to the graves of his victims. Over time he also gave me interviews, both over the phone and monthly in person, with the two of us separated by bars. And he left me both a gift and a heavy responsibility to tell his story.

I hope this killer's own words will serve as a warning that men like Evan Burke walk the same streets as we do, go to our schools and parties and ball games—yet we simply don't recognize them.

Burke's 103 victims never suspected that he was the last person they would ever see, touch, hear, or kiss.

Cindy corrected some typos, saved the file, and then clicked on her news feed. The leading headline had just come in: *Automatic Long Guns Confiscated at a Multilevel Parking Lot in Los Angeles.*

And there was more. At around midnight a car had hit a van parked near Fisherman's Wharf. The van's owner had been called, but before he arrived, the local cops had opened the buckled doors of the van and checked inside for injured passengers. Instead they'd found a cache of long guns, automatic variety.

Cindy opened a new folder for gun news, then checked out front-page headlines in other cities — Portland, Kansas City, Chicago, New York.

Gun headlines jumped out at her from all of them. What was happening?

Had getting her face busted shifted her so far out of the loop she'd lost track of the story of the day? Were illegal guns being discovered in so many cities by coincidence? Or was this a coordinated effort? One big bang of guns being distributed across the country?

It was almost 6 a.m.

She went into the bedroom and woke Richie up.

CHAPTER 91

OUR TASK FORCE had again assembled in Clapper's office on short notice. It was 7:45 a.m., and technically I was late, but as I'd been the last soul in the squad room at 1 a.m., I met Clapper's gaze and gave myself a pass.

Conklin was on his feet, reading aloud headlines: "'Police Discover Cache of Military Weapons in Trunk of Car.' 'Fifth Grader Brings AK17 to School.' 'Parks Department Finds Automatic Weapons in Work Shed.'

"Cindy pulled another dozen stories like these from coast to coast, all dated within the last three days."

Rich sat down beside me, and Clapper said, "What do you make of this? Anyone?"

I said, "Bayview was three days ago. So it could be that while we were there, the gun deal went down elsewhere."

Clapper said, "Worst-case scenario. The party went on without us."

I said, "Or maybe these weapons showing up all at once, hundreds of miles away, is a feint to get us off their trail."

Clapper nodded, said, "Both are possible."

He assigned two teams to calling the PDs in those towns and getting an update. Then he got out from behind his desk and stepped to the whiteboard. He stared at the faces of the dead men, who stared sightlessly back at him.

I could read his mind. We were nowhere, but not for lack of trying. Every cop in the Bay Area was working the homicides. The families, friends, neighbors, and coworkers of the deceased had given us everything they had, and we burned through manpower following dead-end leads.

And we were heading toward worse to come.

Alvarez spoke up. "What if we put out the word that the deal did go down? That we bought it?"

"I like that," Chi said. "We missed the boat. Guns landed on the beach. No one is watching us now, and we continue to work this deal as before."

"This time without Kenny Chen's pointers," said Conklin.

He was going for a laugh and got one, but Brady and I exchanged eye contact. I was still feeling the effects of the shoot-out in Bayview. I'd fired. Jammed on the gas. People had died.

"I'm not done with this," said Clapper, "and you people are not quitters. Stay alert even in your dreams."

We said "You bet" and "Yes, sir," but I was swimming in place. I wanted to ask what we could have left out, overlooked, dropped? What was the truth about the monster gun run? Would we solve the homicides that were at square zero and going cold?

CHAPTER 92

KATIE LOOKED UP from her desk as Clapper came back from the washroom.

"Chief, I've got Section Chief Steinmetz on hold."

"Thanks."

He leaned over her and picked up the call from her console. He and Steinmetz exchanged a few words.

"Sure, Craig. I'll be there at ten."

By 9:50 Clapper was parking his car on Eddy Street, two blocks from the FBI building. It sounded like Steinmetz had news and Clapper was optimistic.

Last year at this time he'd been in charge of two hundred lab techs and CSIs, had a hands-on investigative role when required and time permitted, but at a nice clean remove. He was Forensics. Cops were assigned to cases.

Now those cops reported to him.

He slept less, had quadruple the responsibility, and had no one to share the angst with. He liked working with Steinmetz. More than liked it. Steinmetz gave him hope.

The round-faced and portly FBI section chief opened the car door and got in. He grinned widely.

"What's funny, Craig?"

"Wondering who's going to say it first."

"You are."

"We've got to stop meeting like this."

They both laughed and there it was. Steinmetz giving him hope.

"Talk to me," Clapper said.

Steinmetz reached into the breast pocket of his jacket and pulled out a sheet of paper that had been folded into thirds.

He said, "Here's the memo we captured from Royce Bleecker's phone. It's half a loaf, but it's more than we had before. Here's your copy. Mine's in my head."

Clapper unfolded the paper slowly, noting that it was covered with hieroglyphic-like markings. As he stared at the page, the top-to-bottom, wall-to-wall rows of letters and numbers broke into abbreviated words. It was a puzzle, not the report he was hoping for.

"You have a spare decoder ring?"

Steinmetz said, "Not on me. It's part alphanumeric, part mish-mash code. The bad guys used a book as the basis for this crapola, and we don't know which one. Still, it's pretty primitive. This part, four inches down and one inch in, refers to 'the tunnel.'"

"So, the cross-border underground."

Steinmetz nodded. "I expected that, but which tunnel? Looks to me like the final selection was still undecided when Bleecker was capped. But there is some joy in this report, Charlie."

"Don't hold back."

"Here. The date of the operation seems nailed down. Tomorrow the drugs depart from Tijuana. Discounting accidents and incidents, intel from the San Diego division has identified the two most promising locations in Otay Mesa.

"Here. Numbers tell us that the target time for the drugs to leave Tijuana is 9 p.m. Should be arriving at their destination about a half hour later. Given the millions at stake, I'm inclined to believe that the target time is correct."

Steinmetz went on. "Trucks, likely already loaded with weapons, should arrive at one of these two locations to pick up the drugs. Our people should be in position and under cover by dusk, say 6:00 p.m., and be prepared to watch and wait, all night if that's what it takes."

"Sounds right," said Clapper.

"Oh, two numbers in this page of rubble could be initials. Right here."

Steinmetz took the paper out of Clapper's hand and circled the two short sets of numbers with his pen.

"Does 6-2 mean something to you?"

Clapper considered the almost childlike code, then said, "I'm thinking the sixth letter of the alphabet is *F*. The second letter is *B*."

Steinmetz: "I'm thinking you'd be right. FB."

Clapper thought about James Ransom, the North Beach barman who'd witnessed Swanson's wife passing messages to ATF chief Fred Braun at a truck stop on a strip of highway in no-man's-land. Braun, that twisted bastard. Betrayed his agency. Betrayed all of them, and still his initials were found on a dead man's phone.

Clapper and Steinmetz spoke for another few minutes, Steinmetz saying that Ransom and the two kids had been successfully relocated. And that ten agents had been assigned to Wallenger to help FBI's San Diego division with the "tunnel fandango."

"Thanks, Craig. Steak dinner coming up with a side of onion rings. Also, good Scotch and chocolate cake with a cherry on top."

Steinmetz laughed. "Happy?" he asked Clapper.

"More like dazed and elated," Clapper said.

Steinmetz said they'd see each other virtually and soon.

Clapper said, "Braced and girded."

They shook hands, Steinmetz got out of the car, and Clapper watched him walk smartly up the street.

Clapper thought of himself as a meticulous man, a forensic scientist and investigator who required evidentiary proof before making a determination. Now he was in a world of encrypted codes and virtual information, working with people who had decades, lifetimes, in the clandestine services, often with military backgrounds and expertise. San Francisco was under siege—maybe. But Clapper trusted Craig Steinmetz.

Clapper was newly energized as he drove back to the Hall.

CHAPTER 93

SAN QUENTIN'S WARDEN, Frank Hauser, said good-bye to Chief Clapper and clicked off. He walked out of his office, down the hallway to the locked door to the common room. He opened the door and stood below the tiers, giving himself a moment to think. Prisoners would be having their evening meal in the next hour, but things were quiet now.

Back inside his office, Hauser called ATF chief Fred Braun's cell number.

Braun answered, "Yes?"

Hauser said, "Fred? Frank Hauser. Is this a bad time?"

"I'm in the car," said Braun. "What can I do for you?"

"I'm holding something here that may interest you. An envelope addressed to you from Theodore Swanson, deceased, that we found with his personal belongings. He has no living family or adult heirs, so either I hand this off to you, or I send it to Clapper for handling and disposition."

"An envelope to me from Ted Swanson? I didn't know the man."

"You never met him?"

"Once. When he was a cop and we were working the same case. Before he went dirty. I know nothing about an envelope."

Hauser said, "We put it through black light and the metal detector. It's just paper and now it's yours. Either you want it, or I'll messenger it out to the HOJ in the morning and Clapper can take it from there."

"Can you have someone bring it out to me?"

Hauser kept his mouth shut.

"Is that a no?"

Hauser said, "Braun. I'm already going out of my way. I must hand it to you sealed. You have to sign for it."

"I'll come out and get it. Be there by five," said Braun. And he hung up. Hauser said to the dead line, "You're welcome."

*　　*　　*

Braun parked in the driveway in a nice neighborhood near Golden Gate Park. He left his briefcase in the car and went through the garage into the house, where he found his wife, Greta, at the stove, stirring one pot, turning up the heat on another.

He kissed the side of Greta's neck and gave her a squeeze while doing the math. It was a twenty-minute drive to San Quentin. Say another fifteen minutes for the frickin' rigamarole to sign in and another fifteen to accept Ted frickin' Swanson's letter. Then the drive back, another twenty minutes depending on traffic.

Braun said to Greta, "I have to go out for an hour or so, due to some bullshit at the prison. Ted Swanson seems to have left me a fond farewell. Pain in the butt, that guy, alive and dead. You eat. I might get held up."

Braun got back into his car and took off, wondering if Swanson

296

had had a last-minute change of mind before he swung himself from the bars. Or had he passed on valuable intel?

What the hell. He was chief of the San Francisco ATF, now chasing an unopened envelope from a dead man who'd talked to the cops and taken himself out. The letter was probably an eff-you. Or. It might actually hold important information.

Braun stepped on the gas.

CHAPTER 94

I WAS BEHIND the wheel of an armored Chevy Suburban with Joe beside me, both of us geared up and watching everything as we cruised through a residential neighborhood in the Richmond District.

Wallenger and Conklin were a few car lengths behind. SWAT was standing by in the park, a quick two minutes out from Twenty-First Avenue, the target location.

Joe saw it first: Braun's car speeding away from the blue two-story house up ahead in the middle of the block. It was upmarket but not over the top, one house in a row of twelve similar houses.

Kids on bikes whizzed past us, lights flashing between their spokes. Up ahead, Braun's car turned the corner and was quickly out of sight.

Mike Wallenger's voice came over the radio.

"Let's hit it," he said.

Wallenger passed us and backed into Braun's driveway, positioned to chase Braun if we had to go to plan B. Plan A was to serve the warrant on Mrs. Braun and thoroughly search the house before Fred Braun's lizard brain picked up that he'd been gamed.

As we got out of our cars, a lace curtain in the front first-floor window parted. Greta Braun was peering out, watching us. I waved and smiled, a cheery deflection to stop her from calling her husband, saying, "Get back here. Quick."

She kept her eyes on our four-person unit as we walked along the poured-cement path, up a three-step set of stairs to the front door. Conklin reached around me and pressed the doorbell. Chimes rang inside. I patted the warrant in my breast pocket, touched the grip of my gun in my shoulder holster, and braced to kick in the door.

The lock rattled and the front door opened enough for me to see a woman of fifty with gray-streaked hair, glasses on a long chain, and suspicion flickering in her eyes.

"What can I do for you?" she asked.

I held up the folded document signed by federal judge Philip R. Hoffman confirming that we had reasonable cause for the search.

I said, "Mrs. Frederick Braun?"

"My husband ran out to do an errand," she said. "He'll be back in an hour. Maybe sooner."

I leaned against the door so she couldn't close it and introduced our task force in a few words, giving her a clear view of our heft and authority.

"This is a warrant to search your premises," I said. "That includes your vehicles. We're also authorized to seize your computers and phones."

Fear flashed across Mrs. Braun's features, but she opened the door. I stood beside her as the men moved in. She was saying to herself, "I don't understand. I don't understand."

I didn't say that that was the idea.

I was high on excitement and I believed we were about to crack open this frustrating, multipronged case.

I was with great people I knew and trusted.

And I was feeling lucky.

CHAPTER 95

MY TEAM AND I were in the Brauns' neat, squared-away living room, furnished in sturdy catalog furniture with a narrow view of the bay. From what I could see, it would be a snap to search these eighteen hundred square feet in half the time allowed. The construction was so clean, there were damned few places to conceal anything.

Wallenger said, "Conklin and I are going out to the garage. Lindsay, stay with Mrs. Braun, okay? Joe, you take the office."

The men swarmed out, methodically tossing drawers, opening closets, tapping walls, floors, and ceilings. Moving on.

Mrs. Braun followed me around the living room. I guessed my blond ponytail and big smile had disarmed her. She told me that her husband was head of the US government's Bureau of Alcohol, Tobacco, Firearms, and Explosives. That he was going to "have a fit" that we hadn't waited for him to come home.

I muttered, "Mmm-hmmm. It will be all right. We know him," and she cooperated. Opened the broom closet. Showed me where she kept the ironing board. Showed me their wedding picture in the bedroom and their daughter's college graduation photo.

I checked my watch. Our window was closing. Fred Braun was likely coming back over the Golden Gate Bridge by now, looking out at the water, raging about the worthless trip, the waste of time.

Here, at the blue house, Conklin and Wallenger returned from the garage to the main room. Mrs. Braun was unable to see over their shoulders, but the rest of us pressed around Conklin as he swiped through the pictures on his phone.

I saw shot after shot of illegal automatic weapons standing neatly in tool closets, strapped around the inside walls of a large RV. I recognized these long guns as the same makes and models as the weaponry found in Royce Bleecker's garage. They were high-quality reproductions of American guns, but these had been made in the Czech Republic, Mexico, Poland, Russia.

Mrs. Braun edged into our scrum, wrapped her fingers around Conklin's wrist, and angled the phone so that it faced her.

"Those guns are from his work," said Mrs. Braun, stepping away, turning on the lights, turning down the oven. Joe spoke to Mrs. Braun's back, saying that it was not customary to seize weaponry and store them at home. That foreign weapons meant that they had been illegally obtained.

Greta Braun muttered that that was impossible. Then she stopped speaking when she heard a car speeding up the street. Time had gone quickly, but in fact, the timing was perfect.

"Fred," she said. "Fred's home."

CHAPTER 96

THE SITUATION ESCALATED automatically, dramati-
cally, quickly. Wallenger and Conklin left by the sliders to the
back deck, went down the outer stairs, and took up positions at
the rear of the house. I stayed beside Mrs. Braun, prepared to
restrain her, and Joe exited by the front door.

Mrs. Braun broke for the curtained front window, so I went
with her. Together we watched Braun slow to pull into his driveway, avoiding Wallenger's Suburban, which took up most of the
two-car space.

Standing on the front steps, Joe helped him navigate, waving
him in.

Braun inched ahead, braked hard, then got out of his car. He
looked up toward the front door and at Joe. I thought he was
gauging Joe's expression, the time it would take, the distance.
Could he make it back into his car?

Three black armored SUVs cruised up Twenty-First Avenue
and stopped to block off the Audi's exit. Braun was boxed in, but
he got back into his car. I saw him reach across the front seat

to the glove box, and Joe, seeing that, too, leapt down the steps and reached Braun's car door in a split second. Braun's left leg was still outside the car, being used for leverage. Joe slammed the door closed with his hip, crushing Braun's leg between door and frame.

Braun screamed.

Joe pulled his gun, gripped it in both hands, and aimed at Braun's face.

"Hands up, Fred. Show me your hands."

Braun raised them and Joe eased up on the door. Wincing with pain, the ATF chief said, *"Molinari.* What the *fuck* are you doing?"

Joe was calm, almost friendly.

He said, "We've executed a warrant to search your house, your vehicles, and to take possession of your files and electronics."

"Why? What the hell is this about?"

Joe pulled open the driver's-side door, still keeping up the pressure on Braun. "Keep your hands up. Out of the car."

Reg Covington, head of our SWAT unit, approached with five men on his team. They were now on foot, guns ready.

Joe said, "Fred Braun, you're under arrest for the possession of illegal weapons with intent to sell. You have the right to remain silent—"

"The hell. Anything illegal on my property, you planted it."

"Hands behind your back, now."

"Up your ass."

Joe spun Braun around, flattened him against the Audi, and pressed his gun to the man's neck. SWAT cuffed, then frisked, Braun, relieved him of his ankle gun, the piece in the glove box, and the phone in his pocket, then bundled him into an SUV.

I let Greta Braun call her daughter, and then I confiscated her phone, too. We couldn't get on the road fast enough for me.

Joe and I brought up the rear as we headed to the FBI office at 450 Golden Gate Avenue, where Braun was taken to be processed. An hour later, still handcuffed, the ATF chief was seated at a metal table in an interrogation room.

My observation? Braun looked pissed off enough to have a heart attack.

CHAPTER 97

CONKLIN AND I were in an observation room at the FBI, close to the glass, watching Joe and Wallenger interrogate Fred Braun. Braun offered no records of the guns we'd found in his garage and said nothing about the kilo of heroin SWAT had found in the trap under the Audi's dash.

He didn't even try to explain.

What he did was curse, stonewall, threaten payback, and jump his chair legs against the floor while the tape rolled, recording his tantrum and vehement denials.

I almost felt sorry for him. Well, not sorry, but I understood that he'd never expected to get caught left of boom because of a weak code on a dead cop's phone.

When Craig Steinmetz sat down at the table across from Braun, his mild features hardened. I saw in him the man Joe had described to me: a former USMC lieutenant active during Desert Storm; a high-ranking captain at Quantico; now director of the FBI's SF division.

Steinmetz said, "Fred, you're wasting our time and yours. Do yourself a favor. Tell us the location of the tunnel exit in Otay Mesa and the names of whoever killed five men, three of them former cops, one a guard at the Q. I give you my word that if you cooperate fully, I will go to bat for you. We all will. You could be looking at doing comfortable time somewhere your wife can visit."

"I'm not guilty of anything, Craig, and you should know that about me. I'll take my chances in court."

"You're making a mistake, Fred," Steinmetz said. "We have proof of your principal involvement in a major cross-border shipment of illegal arms and drugs due to launch tomorrow. It took a grade C tech to unencrypt the code, and he did it in ten minutes."

"So run with it, Craig."

"Hey, Fred. What happened to you? Greed? Stupidity? Or were you Ted Swanson's houseboy? Actually, I don't care why. You have a one-time offer to turn your treachery into helping us, because you're an honorable man on course to make a big mistake."

"Save it."

"Got it, Fred. And you get this. I will be at your arraignment to tell the judge why you should be denied bail. My word will trump yours, and both before and after trial, I'll make sure you're housed in general pop and that it's known you talked to the FBI. Get me? You talked."

Braun stared at his folded hands. "I want my phone call."

Wallenger—square jawed, heavily muscled, trained in martial arts—leaned in.

He snapped, "Braun, are you kidding me? This is a freaking lifeboat. Give it up or we will fucking nail you for the guns, drugs, and five homicides if it takes us the rest of our lives."

Braun's laughter cracked before it escaped his throat. He blustered and swore and spat. Then he took a deep breath.

"I've had those weapons in my garage for years. They're not for sale. They're souvenirs. That's the truth."

Steinmetz said to Wallenger, "You can't cure stupid."

Braun said again, "I need my phone."

Wallenger got up from the table and returned with Braun's iPhone. He said, "Direct me. I'll dial."

Was Braun going to give in or lawyer up? I'm a good reader, but I couldn't tell.

It was just after 8 p.m. A plane was standing by to take Mike, Joe, and other FBI agents to San Diego. If Joe and Mike weren't at the airfield by 10:00, the plane would leave without them.

Braun looked at the phone in Wallenger's hands. Then he glanced up at the blinking red light in the corner of the room.

"Keep the recorder on," said Braun. "I don't want to defend made-up bullshit."

Joe said, "Where does the tunnel exit? Precisely."

Braun rotated his shoulders forward, then back, to take the pressure off his handcuffed wrists.

"Open my phone and hit Map," he said to Joe.

Wallenger tapped the phone and put it down in front of the angry ATF chief, who was looking at a small screen and nothing but regrettable options.

CHAPTER 98

THE MORNING AFTER busting Braun, Joe awoke at dawn in a room at the Holiday Inn just off I-5 near San Diego. He'd dragged a standing lamp over to the rickety table by the window and was on his laptop, going over the schematics he'd just received from the FBI.

At the back of the room, Mike Wallenger kicked the blankets off his bed, yawned loudly, and said, "Morning, Butch. How'd you sleep?"

"Like a kitten, Sundance."

Wallenger swung his legs over the bedside, toed his feet into paper slippers, and shuffled over to Joe. He looked down at the laptop screen showing an aerial shot of the factory district in Otay Mesa.

"This one is circled," Joe said of Vytek Machinery on Customhouse Court. "And this one." He put his finger on a warehouse with a callout beside it reading *Blue Bell Apparel*.

Wallenger grunted. "Good. Same as on the phones."

"And now they're confirmed. I just heard from Steinmetz. San

Diego FBI has had air coverage and ground-penetrating radar on these sites for twenty-four hours, both locations. They went in with warrants and wired them with CCTV."

"Pretty damned glorious," said Wallenger.

"Makes me realize I've been bored for a while," Joe said.

He tapped a couple of keys, and the image on the screen broke out into six segmented views of a factory floor.

"Here's Vytek," Joe said.

A wooden staircase linked the ground floor to the loft. Two forklifts and loaded pallets banked the north side of the ground floor. He enlarged all the shots, pausing on the view marked *4,* saying, "This is the street side, and the tunnel comes up here."

He made an *X* with his forefinger.

Wallenger said, "What's the floor look like? Plywood sheets?"

"Can't tell. But it's flimsy," said Joe. "The hydraulic lift rises from the tunnel to the factory floor. It pushes up the flooring, lifts the drugs, and the mules. Mules load the drugs onto hand trucks, trundle them out these doors to the parking lot. Easy breezy."

Wallenger looked at each of the interior pictures, asked Joe to show him views of the Blue Bell building. They looked at each view, compared them, flipped from overhead views to ground level. The spaces were clean. A battlefield with few obstacles.

There were a few box trucks in each of the parking lots, with the company names and logos painted on the sides.

"We could hide in those trucks. Bore peepholes in the sides," Wallenger said.

"After dark," Joe said. "I like it. You?"

"Tremendous. If Murphy leaves his law at home."

Joe grinned. What they said in the military: No plans survive first contact with the enemy.

CHAPTER 99

JOE'S PHONE BUZZED with an incoming text. He glanced at it, got up, and parted the curtains at the front of the room before opening the door. Special Agent Cortland James, sniper and undercover specialist, was there.

He was five ten, with dreadlocks hanging below his shoulders and many commendations that he kept to himself.

He said, "Hey, Molinari. Long time."

"Too long," said Joe.

The two shook hands and caught up while looking over the schematics on the laptop. Minutes later Wallenger joined his colleagues at the table, asking James, "How does all this strike you?"

"I like both sites," said James. "Let's go for a drive."

James gave Wallenger and Molinari a droll guided tour of Otay Mesa's factory district, then drove with them to the FBI's San Diego office on Vista Sorrento Parkway. After signing in, all three were shown to a large conference room, half the size of a high school basketball court.

A hundred chairs pulled back from the table as SWAT commanders, special forces, FBI agents from San Diego and San Francisco, sniper and surveillance team leaders, and several heads of violent crimes squads all got settled in. When the table was full, more operatives filled the chairs banking the sides of the room.

People Joe hadn't seen since his time with DHS called out his name, came over to say hello. And then the room quieted as Special Agent in Charge Analise Thompson limped to the head of the table and turned on the computer.

An attractive woman of sixty, SAC Thompson had been injured when her chopper was brought down in Afghanistan. After returning to the States, she'd devoted her life to the FBI. She greeted the men and women in the strike force, then said, "We've never attempted an operation of this size in so little time. So, wasting none of it…"

The lights went down.

Joe, Wallenger, and about ninety other agents watched the laser end of the pointer as Thompson began her talk. She showed a cross section of a tunnel used to traffic drugs, weapons, and people under the border between Mexico and the USA.

"Like most of these tunnels, this one has lights, fans, and a miniature railroad that runs its length.

"Why this tunnel? Because two years ago, in an attempted drug run, shit happened. The payload was at midpoint when the smugglers met with a counterforce. Shots were fired. Half the drug load—about six hundred pounds, worth millions—was pulled back to Mexico. All of the runners escaped. But we did learn something.

"For the last twenty-four hours we've taken over the factories and have eyes on the trucks."

Thompson flicked a button and a schematic came up on the big screen.

"Let's call this Tunnel #1," she said. "It travels north under José de Gálvez, runs two hundred yards, takes a quarter turn under La Media Road, and exits in the northwest quadrant of the Vytek Machinery factory. There won't be lights or HVAC in the building after 6 p.m. There may be a few vehicles in the lot. The lock on the gates in the chain-link fence has been cut.

"Tunnel #2 runs twice that distance and exits inside a warehouse owned by Blue Bell Apparel. The building is virtually empty and looking for a tenant."

As Thompson spoke, Joe took in the sheer amount of manpower involved: surveillance assets, air assets, and SOG, the Special Operations Group. San Diego FBI, like other divisions, had their own air wing, and they would be called in. Not drones or choppers, but two-engine Mitsubishi planes flying in silent circles above a five-mile center on the targets. They would be feeding information back to the command post here in this building, as well as to the mobile unit and surveillance squads. Intel had it that the trucks had California plates and would be under surveillance once they crossed the border into San Diego.

Fred Braun couldn't have masterminded a plan of this complexity without a large organization of people and at least one partner on the other side of the border.

If that was true, there was another enemy. A major brain. Was that person still involved? Or had he ditched the plan when Braun stopped answering his phone as of six o'clock last night?

CHAPTER 100

TWENTY MINUTES INTO her tactical briefing, Special Agent in Charge Thompson reviewed the organizational chart showing which teams would be operating where and reporting to whom. She said that she would be watching everything.

"Something goes wrong," she said, "I'm going to see it and let you know. Mobile coms posts will also be getting the play-by-play, as well as the head of the San Francisco branch. Snipers will be positioned at both locations. You will not want for backup. And we have picked up chatter that cartel chief El Carriola will be sending his son, Pepe, into the tunnel. He's twenty-two or -three. According to accounts from those who know, he has notched a dozen kills into his belt. This is his photo."

The photo showed a tall, good-looking Mexican twentysomething kid gassing up his car. Looked to be an American-made pickup, blocked 95 percent by the angle of the shot. No way to read the make, model, or plates.

Thompson went on. "He calls himself El Diablo. If you see

him, treat him with extreme caution. We would rather have him in custody than in the morgue, but we'll take the morgue if that's the best option.

"So let's take another look at the locations."

Joe studied the blueprint of the Vytek factory on the big screen. Thirty thousand square feet of concrete block building surrounded by a larger parking area. Thompson waved the laser over the area where the trucks would likely be parked.

"The arrival of trucks at night is going to be our true confirmation. There's almost too much at stake for these desperados, you know, so expect thousands of weapons, hundreds of kilos of drugs—a fight.

"Once we're good to go, outbound undercover agents and SFPD will replace the drivers and take the loaded trucks to the drop point, here on Potrero Hill, where we believe the buyers will be waiting. SFPD will take their money and arrest them. All of this will be recorded."

She held up crossed fingers and smiled.

Joe had medium confidence in this plan. They had inside people, live technology, FBI expertise, and military backup. Thompson was first rate, and he was proud to be in the company of these incredibly skilled and dedicated men and women.

But the mental notes he'd made three hours ago at the motel had added up to a potential mountain for error that had only increased as he'd come to understand the magnitude and number of moving parts.

He tuned back in to what Thompson was saying.

"As I said, it's unlikely these highly motivated smugglers are going to see us and say, 'We give up.' There will be a confrontation. But we lose half the value of this operation if the offenders drop back down into the tunnel and run back to Mexico. We want to hold them, interrogate them, lock them up."

Joe had an idea. Infallible? No. But there was time to cut off the escape route once the smugglers were in the building and send them running out the exits and into the arms of the FBI.

When Thompson asked for questions or comments, Joe raised his hand.

Thompson called on him, addressing Joe by his former Homeland Security title. "Deputy Director?"

"Commander, I have a thought."

She nodded, and in a few words Joe laid out a plan.

CHAPTER 101

I WAS IN the dark, sitting in a camp chair inside a box truck that had been parked—or abandoned—outside the Blue Bell Apparel warehouse. The FBI had wired up the warehouse for sight and sound, and Mike Wallenger's idea to drill holes in the truck's body and implant pinhole cameras had made sense. Techs had affixed a screen the size of an iPad inside, so that I was connected to the AV of the building inside and out.

Everything was quiet. Nothing to see.

It was 9:30 p.m.

The over-three-hour wait time inside the empty truck had been expected, but I was still jumpy from the Bayview shootings four days ago. My fight-or-flight instinct responded to every dog bark, car horn, radio blast, even the distant whoosh of traffic on the 905 Freeway.

I wanted to call Joe, but that wouldn't do. He was posted at Vytek Machinery and needed all his attention on the job. I needed all my attention on mine. Joe and I had separated deliberately, to halve the risk of Julie becoming orphaned tonight. It was the prudent thing to do.

But, man, did I ever want to talk to Joe.

I was ripped from my dark cloud by the roar of a truck rolling into the parking lot. I peered at the screen, but the truck sped by too fast for me to describe it or read the tag numbers, and the pinholes had too narrow a range. Then I saw the truck park lengthwise against the building as Thompson had predicted. Close to the exit, so the drugs could be loaded into the rear compartment and the driver could make a fast getaway.

I swiped the see-all screen to get a view inside the warehouse, but still the infrared CCTV showed me nothing. Not even a mouse. I swiped back to the parking lot view and saw a second truck arrive, this one larger than the first.

I texted SAC Thompson, who was already on it. Her text back was a blast to thirty men and women at this location: *Stay sharp, everyone. It's starting.*

The second truck parked nose-to-tail to the first. The cab door opened, and a man got out, walked to the building, and faced the wall. After he'd taken his leak, he was joined by the driver of the first truck. Their voices were muted, but they were speaking English. These were the guys meant to drive to San Francisco and exchange the truckload of unknowable millions in drugs and guns for cash.

We had other plans.

SAC Thompson was in my ear. "Sergeant Boxer. Stand by."

After three hours in solitary came a light tap on the rear doors. A voice spoke through the door.

"It's SA Cortland James," he said. "Friend of Joe's."

He held his FBI badge up to a pinhole camera.

I said, "Cort, right? Have you seen Joe? Is he okay?"

"He's good," he said. I released my breath and let him inside. "Nice to finally meet you, Lindsay."

"Same here," I said.

We shook hands. James opened a folding chair and pulled it over to the screen.

He said, "Here comes number three."

This truck had a Fresh to You logo on the side, and it parked in line behind the other two.

James said, "They could stuff any number of people in those box trucks. Any movement inside the plant?"

I looked at the screen, at all six interior views, but saw nothing. I was about to say so when I noted a disturbance in the farthest northeast corner. The ten-foot square of flooring was coming up in one flat piece.

"Cort," I said, "check this out."

Thompson joined the conversation.

She said, "I see the floor lifting. Now I see drugs being handed up in one-key packets. I can't read the writing, but I'm thinking fentanyl. Still coming. Stay put until those men are out of the tunnel," she said.

Focusing on the unbelievable, I watched a small platform lift rising into the warehouse with a payload of drugs, enough to blanket the great state of California. Men climbed out of the hole and began stacking bricks of drugs efficiently onto a pallet, then filled the next and the next. One of those men climbed into the open cab of the forklift.

Cort and I watched the eerie infrared images on the screen. I counted ten men who'd clambered out of the hole. They'd extracted the haul, stacked the pallets, and now formed a loose huddle, speaking Spanish. I had about a dozen words in my Spanish vocabulary. I vowed to study up when we got out of there. Were the runners making a plan to return to Mexico the same way they'd come?

I never found out.

Thompson said, "On my count. Three. Two."

"*Wait,*" I shouted.

A man appeared on the lift, half out of the tunnel, using his hands on the floor beside it to lift himself out.

Thompson said, "One."

A loud boom rumbled, and I could feel the vibration inside our truck. Then I saw the blast.

And with it, the consummation of Joe Molinari's excellent idea to explode and collapse the tunnel behind the mules. The screen went white as the cameras were destroyed by the explosion.

Cort James said, "Boxer. Let's go."

I stayed long enough to swipe the screen so I could see Blue Bell's exterior view. Exit doors were being kicked open as almost a dozen men poured out into the lot.

CHAPTER 102

I FOLLOWED SPECIAL Agent James, jumped down from the rear of the truck, misjudged the distance, stumbled, found my feet, and pulled my gun.

Dozens of agents wearing FBI windbreakers over their vests and tactical gear shouted orders at the mules. "Hands up!" "Drop the gun!" "On your knees!"

Some of our team were yelling in Spanish. The mules were dazed by the explosion that had collapsed the tunnel, surprised by the number of cops everywhere, and trapped by the locked chain-link fence.

This was not in their plan.

SWAT tossed flashbang grenades. Blinded and deafened, most of the suspects were down, flat on the asphalt, arms outstretched. They were going nowhere, and that nowhere was made even clearer by the wattage coming from overhead. The police chopper lit up the whole crisis site bright enough to find a dropped contact lens.

While most of the mules submitted to cuffs and capture, others scattered, ducking behind the Fresh To You trucks, climbing inside. They buzzed down the windows and fired, their muzzle flares showing us just where they were.

An FBI agent was hit. He dropped to the ground, and return fire was leveled at the truck. The chatter of AKs filled the air as a fusillade of bullets punctured steel and flesh. The gunfire and screams were chilling.

I was using the box truck I thought of as "ours" as a shield. My feet were on asphalt and I was yelling my lungs out at a drug runner heading toward the chain-link fence. I shouted, "Drop the gun!" When my order was ignored and a gun was aimed at me, I fired. I saw my target grab a shoulder, spin, fold to his knees, and keel over.

Cortland James went to the man, kicked his gun away, felt for a pulse.

"He's breathing," he said.

He rolled him over and cuffed him. Thompson's voice was inside my ear as she called for medics.

James was talking to the downed drug runner, telling the guy not to move, then snapped his head toward me. He yelled, *"Boxer. Behind you!"*

I spun around, saw a man behind the wheel of our truck. My Glock was like a part of my hand. I shouted, "Drop it! Now! Hands up!"

Instead the mule got off a burst of shots, puncturing the truck, missing me.

I returned fire, but the mule had ducked and scrambled to the other side of the truck. And that's when one well-aimed shot came from the roof of the building.

The mule grabbed his throat and fell. And as fast it had started, the gunfire stopped. I ran to the man behind the truck. Blood was bubbling out of his collar. I kicked his gun away and made contact with Thompson. "Man down. I'm losing him."

Ambulances stationed at the outer perimeter tore around the corner, got an okay that the scene was secured, then entered the lot.

Thompson's voice was in my ear, "Sergeant. Watch your ass. That mule is the jefe's son. Don't take your eyes off him. If he touches his gun, shoot to kill."

My face got hot, but she was right. I did what Thompson said. I put my back to the truck and held my gun on the man, now gasping at my feet. He was young. Twenties. Dying.

"Hang on. It's not your turn to die," I lied.

Sirens looped, wailed, burped, and flashers made a dizzying strobe light display in red and blue. I waved an ambulance in, made sure the EMTs got to El Carriola's son, whom a sniper had drilled with a single shot from the warehouse roof 300 yards away. As El Diablo was lifted onto a stretcher, one of the EMTs said to the other, "This one is gone."

CHAPTER 103

ONCE THE LOT was quiet, I climbed back into the truck and sat in my chair. I swiped the view screen to see the other location in our sights, Vytek Machinery, only two miles away from Blue Bell. The building was square, redbrick with small-paned windows and a razor-wired fence enclosing the narrow yard.

It looked like a pen for the criminally insane.

I saw the three trucks parked with their tailgates to the loading dock, reducing the parking lot to a horseshoe of buckled asphalt maybe thirty yards wide. There was one light over the main entrance. Otherwise, Vytek was in shadow.

The trucks told me that the site was in play and Joe was there.

I swiped the screen to the CCTV transmission from Vytek's interior. All six views showed that the enormous space was empty. And then it wasn't. As I watched, a platform rose up from the mouth of the tunnel. A string of ghostly-looking drug runners climbed out, bearing bricks of drugs by the armload. They wore headlamps, and the lights whipped around the cavernous space as the mules stacked their loads on pallets.

Even though I expected it, I was still shocked when the boom reverberated through my earbuds and a whiteout obliterated my view of the factory floor as Vytek's tunnel blew the hell up.

The exterior view of Vytek showed that the mules found the exits and kicked, wrenched, or butted the doors open in their frenzy to escape.

The deputy agent in charge shouted, ordering the mules to throw down their weapons. To get to their knees. Some did as they were told, others found cover and fired.

Flashbang grenades exploded. Mules dropped and submitted. My blood was hot with fear for Joe, who figured to be in the thick of this action. I couldn't do a thing but pray that he'd be safe.

Just then the rear door of my truck wrenched open. My gun was in my hand. I yelled at a shape, a silhouette boosting itself onto the floor of the truck.

I shouted, *"Stay where you are! I'm armed."*

"Boxer. It's Cortland James. Hold your fire."

The silhouette materialized.

The voice in my head was saying, *God, oh God.* I lowered my gun.

"Rookie move," Cort said. "I should have announced myself. If you'd shot me, it woulda been my fault."

He reached out his hand, and I grabbed it and helped him to his feet. We stood next to each other and watched the view on the small screen. I was shaken and Cort knew it.

"It's okay, Lindsay. You've been at war all week."

I said, "I could have shot you. God loves us, Cort."

"Nothing happened. We're both here. It was my fault."

I nodded and tried to slow my breathing as we watched the starbursts of gunfire at Vytek, and then the police chopper dropped the bright, wide circle of light on the field. The light revealed the various-size trucks and the stampede of drug mules wearing caps with lights, gun belts strung across their chests. This was a different crew, run by a different chief.

We'd believed that the operation would be confined to one factory or the other, and not knowing which, we'd covered both. But it hadn't been a choice of Blue Bell or Vytek.

"Cort. I get it now. They chose both locations."

"They sure did. Twice the odds of getting the payday or twice the haul. A bonanza."

CHAPTER 104

THE POLICE VAN arrived moments after the scene was secure. The handcuffed, shackled, uninjured mules were loaded into the van, and the ambulances took the injured away. One bus took the dead, including the deceased heir to El Carriola's criminal enterprise. I was sure there would be payback for that. Automobiles at the edges of the crisis field started up, moved out. Cops heading back to their offices or homes.

There was a knock on our truck's rear doors. James pushed a door open, reached down, and helped someone up. By the dimmest light of the viewing screen, I saw his height, his hair, and he saw me. We went into each other's arms.

"You okay?" Joe asked.

"I need a beer."

"I second that. Our ride's outside."

He turned me loose and hugged Cortland James. "Thank you," he said.

"Your lady didn't need me. She has a steady hand and first-class response inhibition, or I'd be dead."

I took in what Cortland had said. *Response inhibition. Steady hand.*

And I realized that Joe had been watching his screen. He'd heard his old friend warn me that there was someone behind me with a gun. A sniper had taken the guy down, but if Cortland hadn't warned me, I wouldn't be in Joe's arms.

I stepped in and gave James a hug, too.

"We'll have to do this again sometime," Joe said.

We all grinned. And then Thompson's voice came through our earbuds.

"Boxer, Molinari. Brady's setting up for the meet. You can get there in time, even if you stop for a beer. Good work, everyone. We've got a total of twenty living drug runners, six injured, six bodies, and, after we pick up the pieces, a boatload of narcotics. Take good care of the guns."

We signed off with Thompson, said good-bye to Cortland and the empty truck. Joe pointed out the gun-laden truck that was now our ride. Thirty feet long. Green, with Fresh to You logos on the sides. I opened the rear compartment and saw the long guns strapped to the truck's walls. Guns that would never find their way onto the streets of San Francisco.

"I'll drive," I said, wondering if I could.

"You sleep," said Joe.

We closed the rear doors and latched them, then climbed into the cab. I took the passenger seat. We buckled up and Joe inserted the key into the ignition.

"Hey," I said. "You're a genius, you know. Blowing up the tunnels."

"I knew you were watching. It was a good feeling, Blondie."

I put my hand behind his neck and kissed my husband with a

328

ton of feeling. He returned that kiss and held me for the best long moment of the whole stressful day.

He drove the truck out of the lot and onto Customhouse Court. I leaned my head against the window, and as we got onto the highway, my eyes closed. I didn't open them again until my phone rang just north of LA.

It was my sister, Cat.

"What's wrong?" I said.

"I want to go home."

It wasn't Cat. It was Julie.

CHAPTER 105

IT WAS AFTER one in the morning when I pressed the Talk key on my phone and heard my daughter not just crying but sobbing.

"Julie. Julie, what's wrong?"

Joe shot me a look as we sped along I-5.

"Are you *hurt*, Jules? Are you *hurt*?"

I asked her several times, but she just kept crying.

Then a long, pitiable wail. "I want to go home!"

"Soon, honey. Dad and I are really far away."

"I don't care."

I heard Cat in the background. "Julie, who are you talking to? Give me the phone. Now, Jules." Then to me, "Who is this, please?"

"Cat, it's me. Julie called. Is she sick?"

"Homesick, I'd say."

I said to Joe, "Julie wants to go home. Cat, did something happen?"

"Not exactly. But listen, I've got this."

I persisted. "What happened?"

"Oh, God. Well. Nothing actually happened. The girls are going to school, and Julie is home with me and Martha. Meredith and Brigid both have friends and after-school activities and secrets. You know?"

I was getting it. Julie felt left out. She was only four, and I no longer knew what we'd been thinking by leaving her with my sister. It was unfair to all concerned, but we'd committed ourselves to a big goddam life-endangering deal that was threatening California and, from there, points east.

Could we possibly get Julie now? And then what? Ditch the meeting on Potrero Hill? It would be unforgivable. It would impact my job, effective tomorrow morning. Some of the brass hadn't quite bought the Bayview incident, and I guessed they'd put asterisks on my file. I tried to stop my racing thoughts. Julie was safe. Upset. But safe.

"Cat, I need a minute." I didn't wait for her to answer. I clapped my hand over the phone and said to Joe, "Here's the situation."

We kicked it around in shorthand. We were six hours out from the presumed meet with the buyers, driving a truckload of assault weapons and enough fentanyl to kill tens of thousands. Joe looked half at me, half at the road, took his hands off the wheel for a second to shrug.

Then he said, "I'll talk to her."

I put my ear to the phone and heard Julie wailing in the background.

"Cat?"

She said, "Sis, just tell me when you're coming for her and I'll calm her down. I've done this before, you know."

I gave her my best estimate and told her I had to turn off my phone at 7 a.m.

"Joe wants to talk to her," I said. "Thanks, Cat."

There are a lot of people who don't think I'm doing my child any favors by being a cop. Right then I agreed with them all. I'd done well at Blue Bell. I didn't need to justify that. I'd saved lives.

But the job wasn't done. And now I had to choose between work and my baby girl.

Joe took the phone. He said, "Julie. Are you in bed?…Good. Go back to sleep. We'll see you soon, but not now.…Just because. I'll explain when I see you, but right now give the phone to Aunt Cat."

He said, "Cat, we're sorry and we owe you. We can't get away from this right now.…Good. Thank you. We'll call you when we kick free."

No sooner had he hung up with Cat than my phone rang again. This time it was Brady. I gave him our location and ETA and the plate number of our truck, carrying multimillions in illegal goods.

Brady said, "You're on schedule. See you soon."

"My turn to drive," I said to my amazing husband.

Joe pulled over at the next gas station, and we gassed up, changed out of our tactical gear and into jeans, sweaters, canvas jackets, baseball caps. We looked like long-haul truckers.

Then we changed places.

Soon Joe was sleeping, and I was heading west toward San Francisco, and I felt resolute. We *had* to do this.

My hands were steady, and my mind was on the road.

CHAPTER 106

JOE AND I alternated sleeping during the long drive from Otay Mesa to the outskirts of San Francisco. We met up with Wallenger at Harris Ranch in Coalinga. We had coffee and a few anxiety-relieving laughs and got back on the road.

At 6 a.m. Brady called me from another crumbling factory area, this one called Potrero Hill in the outskirts of San Francisco. He described his vehicle, its placement at the gates to the factory, and told me where the rest of the team were positioned. SWAT was inside the factory across the street, within easy reach and ready to roll.

At ten minutes to seven, with Joe at the wheel, we pulled up to the designated parking lot where trucks loaded with weapons and drugs would be on offer. Naturally, the would-be buyers didn't know that the gatekeepers and truck drivers were FBI and local law enforcement.

Joe honked a short blast at the entrance to the parking lot, and Brady got out of his car and threw the double gates open. He stepped up on our truck's running board and told us that the potential buyers had been shown the manifests of each of six trucks up for sale. Four of the six trucks had been spoken for and the "drivers" had accepted the cash. The remaining four would-be purchasers would bid against one another for the two unbought trucks.

One of those trucks was ours.

Brady gave the manifest to me.

He said, "Here's what you're carrying. Here's the expected sale price. Any trouble, just speak in a normal voice saying that's below the required offer. I'll hear you, so will Steinmetz, Clapper, and Covington, and that's the signal for SWAT to roll in."

I had two guns and a Kevlar vest. Joe had the same. The buyers could have howitzers. What could possibly go wrong?

The gates closed behind us. The sun was just up, giving us a romanticized view of a peak-roofed wooden building, four stories tall, dilapidated, deserted, and surrounded by other buildings of similar age and wear.

I inventoried the vehicles inside the lot. Four trucks, and we made five. Fourteen family-style vans and SUVs were parked side-by-side across from the trucks. Honestly, I didn't like it. I knew that cops surrounded the lot, but the opportunity to pull a double-cross and abscond with the cash and the truckload might be too much for criminals of this magnitude to resist.

I squeezed Joe's knee as we rolled toward the far side of the lot and the last truck moved in behind us.

When both of the trucks were within locked gates, Brady used his megaphone and read out the plate numbers of the fifth and sixth trucks. High beams of a dusty Ford 4 x 4 flashed. The truck driver got out of his Fresh to You box truck and walked to the flashing headlights. I recognized him as Northern Station's

Lieutenant John Bainbridge. He spoke with the driver, who got out and walked back to the truck with Bainbridge to inspect the merchandise.

Bainbridge accepted the satchel of cash, swapped keys to the Ford pickup for keys to a large box truck full of contraband. A station wagon and a panel van both flashed their lights, and Joe said to me, "Here we go."

He got out of the truck and met the owners of those cars flashing their interest. Two men joined Joe and the rear doors opened. I heard an offer, and the haggling began. When one man outbid the other, Joe took a bag of cash. He gave it a look and came around to open the passenger-side door for me.

I grabbed Joe's duffel and mine from the footwell and hopped down out of the truck. Joe clenched his hand around the keys to the station wagon as the losing bidder said, "I hope I didn't blow the opportunity of a lifetime."

To which the successful buyer said, "I think you did."

Joe and I got into the station wagon and locked the doors. Now that the last purchase was completed, I watched and waited for the third act to begin.

CHAPTER 107

BRADY BROUGHT THE megaphone to his mouth and pulled the trigger, and the feedback squeal got everyone's attention.

He said, "This is Lieutenant Jackson Brady of the SFPD. By purchasing or attempting to purchase illegal guns and drugs, you have broken the law. If you're not wearing a badge, you have a choice.

"Best one: if you're armed, leave your guns in your vehicle, get out with your hands up, and don't resist the police officer who will place you under arrest. This choice gives you the lawful right to a phone call, a lawyer, a chance to make your case at trial.

"Your other choice is to make a break for it. The gates are locked. Law enforcement outnumbers you six to one. We are all armed, and if necessary, we will shoot. The FBI is filming. Police officers are wearing body cams. The roads are blocked with police vehicles. There is no escape.

"So, guns down, out of your vehicle with hands up. Or die tonight resisting arrest.

"You have one minute to decide. Starting now."

One of the new drivers of a Fresh to You truck shouted, "This is entrapment!"

Brady said through his megaphone, "Tell that to your lawyer."

Truck engines revved and one of the oversize box trucks, avoiding other vehicles, slammed into the old chain-link fencing, then backed up and did it again. SWAT team vehicles stormed out of the adjacent factory and shot out the truck's tires. Cops who'd been parked on the street in unmarked cars quickly surrounded the lot, guns drawn. First one, then another, of the drivers got out of their trucks with hands held high.

They were flattened against the sides of their trucks and placed under arrest. Then one of the drivers, a weedy-looking guy in a leather jacket, vented loudly about his rights under the Second Amendment and got back into the truck.

Was he crazy, or did he have perfect timing?

Brady and Chi had just opened the gates for the police van, and the renegade driver made a suicide run for the gates.

There was room for only one vehicle to come in the gates at a time. The truck driver leaned on his horn, and when the van was partly inside, the truck rushed the gates, knocking the van onto two wheels, and bulled his way through.

Brady, Cappy, and Chi used their hoods as gun braces and fired through the truck's windshield.

Although I was half a lot away, I heard the driver howl and curse before crashing into a parked vehicle. Cappy dragged him from his truck, disarmed and cuffed him, and kept him under watch as I used my phone to call dispatch.

"Sergeant Boxer calling from 1240 Pennsylvania Avenue. We need an ambulance. Send two."

As the downed man lay on the ground bleeding, he managed to say, "I want to talk to Wallenger. And Molinari."

What? What was that? I didn't like it.

I said into my mic, "Joe Molinari. The driver of the runaway truck just asked to speak with you and Mike. He's injured. I called it in."

Joe said, "On my way."

He walked the fifty paces to the man lying on his stomach on the asphalt. He stooped and they exchanged a few words. Leaving Wallenger with the injured man, Joe came back to me and Brady.

Joe said, "That's Alejandro Vega."

I said, "The gun show guy? The one who was taken into custody by *federales* and locked up in Mexico?"

"The same."

Joe asked Brady, "How badly is he hurt?"

"All I know is he can speak."

Joe said, "If he can be patched up, we need to interrogate him. Today."

CHAPTER 108

VEGA HAD TAKEN a shot in his right shoulder, and the round was a through-and-through, making Vega a lucky man.

The ambulance took off in the direction of Metro Hospital, and Joe and Mike took one of the squad cars.

I joined the squad loading mules into the police van. When it took off, I leaned against the station wagon. Clouds scudded overhead. Scraps of newspaper blew like tumbleweeds across the pavement.

I wondered how Vega fit into this sprawling enterprise. Was he a mule? Was he a buyer refreshing his stock? Or was there more to Vega than we knew?

Brady came over to where I was leaning on the car.

"You all right?" he asked.

"Yes, thanks. Not sure what to do now. Can I take this station wagon home?"

"Let's not complicate things. Cappy is going to drive you to the Hall. Sleep in, Boxer. Take the day off."

Brady handed me a set of keys.

"What are these?"

"Cappy," said Brady, calling my colleague over. "Take good care. Both of you."

Were these the keys to a squad car? Was Cappy driving me to the Hall? And then what? I didn't get the chance to find out. Cappy asked, "Those bags belong to you?"

"They do."

He picked them up, and I walked with him beyond the gates to the row of unmarked cars. Cappy settled my bags in back, me in the passenger seat, then turned on the scanner, which obliterated all chance for conversation.

I dozed during the ride to 850 Bryant until Cappy said my name and I woke up. I remembered broken pieces of a dream. There'd been a lot of shooting and screaming and bombs. I looked at my watch. It was nine thirty. My husband was at the FBI office, and Brady was still doing mop-up on Potrero Hill.

Cappy asked, "You still have those keys?"

Oh. I pulled them out of my pocket and jingled them.

"There's your ride," he said, pointing to the car parked next to ours in front of the Hall. It was a blue Explorer. Like my old car, and my old car before that.

"My ride…for the day?"

"Yours was killed in the line of duty. This is your replacement. To keep, Boxer."

He grinned, got out, and walked around to my side of the squad car. He opened the door with a flourish. I got out and inspected the Explorer. It wasn't new, but it was newer than the one I'd left on the field at Bayview.

I opened the driver's-side door and got behind the wheel. Cappy put the duffel bags in the passenger side as I buckled up. I didn't even need to adjust the seat. I started 'er up and saw that the tank was full. The engine gave me a welcome-home-Lindsay purr.

Cappy said, "Bon voyage."

I grinned and put the car in gear. I was in my high seat. Looking through my broad windshield. It felt as roomy as a living room sofa.

I loved my new old car.

I was back.

CHAPTER 109

JOE MOLINARI AND Mike Wallenger were in Craig Steinmetz's office, sitting in the chairs facing the director's desk, waiting for him to speak.

Steinmetz twiddled a fountain pen, thinking. Finally he put down the pen and clasped his hands together on his desk.

He said, "Vega says he doesn't care what book we throw at him, as long as he lands in the US. He says he wants his wife and kids relocated here, too, but I don't even believe *that*. He's done everything possible to make sure he never sees them again. Get ready for this weasel to try to break your hearts. I say, break his."

Joe thought, *Direct order.*

Vega was in the interrogation room. Steinmetz went into the observation room and checked that the volume was on, then Mike and Joe went in to the interview room, said hello to Vega, and sat down across from him.

Vega's injured arm was bandaged in a sling across his chest, and his good arm was cuffed to the hook in the center of the table. Chains rattled around his ankles.

Joe said, "Last time we saw you, you were on your way to a Mexican federal prison. What happened?"

"Tunnel," said Vega. "El Chapo style."

"Figures," Joe said. "I'm amazed at the ingenuity."

Vega said, *"Gracias."*

Joe said, "So tell us. What did you have to do with this very elaborate gun-and-drug-running scheme?"

"Hard to say in a couple of sentences. I'm in some pain, you know."

Wallenger crumpled a paper cup, balled it up, slammed it into the trash basket across the room. "That's tough, Vega. This is your one and only chance to talk. Do a good job, we'll talk to the prosecutors, and in a couple of days you'll be having huevos rancheros in your cell. Otherwise—you don't need me to tell you otherwise, do you?"

"You'll beat me up and throw me in solitary until I talk."

The look on Vega's face told Joe that Vega wasn't opposed to that idea. Must be whatever drug the hospital had given him for pain.

Joe said, "Mike here would be glad to give you a beating, Al. A lot of people died tonight on account of you. So what you want to do is tell the truth, nothing but, and tell it to us now. Your opportunities fade by the second."

Vega sighed. "Does the name Ted Swanson mean anything to you?"

Joe said, "Crooked cop, corrupted about twenty cops on the SFPD, stole drugs from a cartel jefe, worth many millions. Body count due to his psycho activity numbered almost two dozen dead. Half were cops and the others were innocent victims. Is that the Ted Swanson you mean?"

"Yeah. It looked like a good deal. We set this up."

Wallenger said, "You and Swanson set this up? He's been in the Q for three years."

"He had a partner here, and they had some form of communication, I don't know how. They called each other Mr. Inside and Mr. Way Inside."

Nobody laughed.

Vega continued, "Swanson's plan. His partner was with the ATF. Fred Braun. He made the gun truck arrangements from this side.

"I was the tunnel guy. And recruiter. And scheduler, but I can't take credit for everything. Listen," said Vega. "This plan was solid. What did we do wrong?"

"You overestimated yourself, Vega," said Joe. "But let's stick to the subject. You're looking for a way to get yourself located near your family. That's going to take giving us whoever took out five men—"

"'You talk, you die.' I heard there was a hit man. Wasn't me. I don't even think it was Braun."

"No games, Vega. And do not try to tell me that Swanson was the hit man's point guard. If we don't solve those murders, you get no deal."

"What if I don't know?"

"You know."

"I want a deal in writing. I mean official from the Department of Justice. And if you can't get me that, I say nothing."

Steinmetz came into the room.

"Say your prayers, Vega. We no longer care."

CHAPTER 110

WALLENGER STOOD UP and said, "Director, if you can spare a few minutes. Privately."

Steinmetz scowled at Vega, said "Okay" to Wallenger, and together they left the room.

When they were gone, Joe said to Vega, "Al, this office is going to fill up with FBI agents in about ten minutes. Steinmetz owns you, body and soul. Wallenger can't stand you. I'm the one who got you a door-to-door drive to Guadalajara, and I brought your letter to Ana. When I walk out the door, you're on your own. Speak or don't."

Vega said, "Forget DOJ. Get me a letter from Steinmetz that says, 'In consideration for information given of his own free will, I have promised Alejandro Vega to let him serve his sentence in California.' Something like that."

Joe said, "I'll try. Stay put."

He left the room, walked into the observation room, and said to Steinmetz and Wallenger, "Write something like that on your letterhead. Means nothing. But if he gives us the killer or killers..." Joe shrugged.

"I already wrote it. Let him sweat for a few minutes. Maybe long enough to think you've gone home."

He gave Joe the letter on the cream-colored paper with the dark-blue-and-gold emblem of the FBI.

"He'll go for it," said Wallenger. "He's just faking himself out."

"Take all the fun out of this, Sundance."

Joe read the letter. It wasn't verbatim, but it was good enough for a desperate man who was about to live in a max-security prison until he died. Provided Vega couldn't tunnel through a cement floor.

"Okay," he said. "I'm going with this."

He walked the twenty steps back to the door of the interrogation room, knocked, replaced the guard, and sat down at the table. In the few minutes Joe had been away, Vega's face had changed. The bravado was gone. The man was in pain.

"Here you go." Joe put the page down so Vega could read it.

"That's his signature?"

"I watched him write it and sign it. And now. Who killed Brian Donahue, Roy Abend, Carl Barrows, Arthur Guthrie, and Royce Bleecker?"

"I'm going to pay for this," said Vega. He tried futilely to stretch his good hand over to his bad arm. "You think I could have some water?"

"Al. I want names. And I'm going to check them out. And if they check, you get water, and another shot of painkiller, and a clean hospital bed, okay? If you're nice, I'll call Ana and tell her that you're alive."

"He's my cousin," Vega said. "My father's youngest sister, Julia. Married an American."

"Name."

"Ruffo. Anthony Ruffo."

Joe had been interrogated more than once and had done the same to numerous bad guys. He felt a shock from the blue, like he'd been blindsided, but he gave nothing away.

He said, "Ruffo. I think I know that name."

"Probably because the kid's father, Anthony Ruffo Sr., is a lawyer."

"The son. Junior. You're saying he killed all those men?"

"He has a few pals. I think he paid them. Look. He didn't tell me everything. Sweat him. You know how, right?"

Joe stood up. "I'll get you that water now, Al. By the way, do you happen to know what kind of car your cousin drives?"

"BMW. Black one. Belonged to his old man."

Bingo. Joe asked the guard to step in, then went back to the observation room and said to Steinmetz, "I know this Ruffo kid. He's been charged for pistol-whipping a friend of ours, breaking her nose. He's awaiting trial in the men's jail. I'm pretty sure he's also the one who threatened me and Lindsay in Sacramento.

"There's audio tape of some of that and a police report. Also, he stalked us and our neighbor. Patrol officers have his ID and that of his posse from a week ago."

"I remember now," said Steinmetz. "Nice catch, Joe. Well, now we know where to find him. Conveniently in the pokey."

Joe said, "Craig, about Vega. Can you give that dirtbag some water? I promised. And now I've got to go."

CHAPTER 111

JULIE, MARTHA, AND I were in the big bed at home. Joe hadn't called, his phone was off, and I didn't know where he was. Furthermore, Julie was in a state. Even a visit from Mrs. Rose hadn't mollified her.

So what tragedy had befallen her?

She'd left her stuffed cow doll, Mrs. Mooey Milkington, in Cat's car. There had been a lot of excitement when Cat and I met at the halfway point between Half Moon Bay and Lake Street. Martha was joyous. Julie was, too, but between grabbing the doggy, the kiddo, her bag of clothing, her barrettes and socks from the car floor, and her car seat, and cleaning out all the discarded trash she had spread around the back seat, no one noticed that Mooey had gotten stuck under the front seat.

"Julie, I know you miss her. Is there anyone else you could play with until we can get her back? Baby Bumpkin? Floppers?"

"Mooey doesn't know where I am."

"Fine. Can you get me my phone? Please?"

Julie went out to the living room, brought my phone back to

me. I texted Cat. Told her that Mooey was in the car and to please tell her that Julie was home, and we'd bring her back soon.

Cat texted me back, *Hahahahahahahaahah. Okay. Consider it done. Thanks, I'll tell Julie.*

Cat sent me a string of emojis, some laughing, some growling, some sticking out their little tongues, one with a halo, then a string of hearts.

I texted, *Back at you. Thanks.*

I said, "Aunt Cat is telling Mooey now, okay?"

Julie was still unhappy.

I said, "Will you do something for me?"

"What? Okay."

"I need you to read to me, Jules. I haven't slept in so long. Days and days, and it will help me calm down if you tell me a story."

"Brigid said I was a brat."

"Okay, honey. That wasn't nice. But she's not used to having company, you know?"

"She gave me a coloring book."

"Now, that was nice. Let me see."

Julie went into her room and returned with a coloring book, got into bed again, and began to read the way she does. The pictures were of jungle animals, and Julie started with the elephant. And then she made up a story.

"This is Milly," she said. "Milly has a baby named Blimpo. See, Mom? Milly eats chocolate-covered leaves...."

I put my arm around Julie's waist, and she told me about another few animals and I heard them in my sleep. It was Joe who woke me up. I sat up. Julie wasn't there.

"I took her to school."

"You did?"

349

"It's a school day. She missed her friends."

"Good, Joe. Great idea."

I looked at the clock. I'd gotten two hours of sleep, not in a truck but with a mattress and pillows and blankets. I needed more.

Covering a yawn, I said, "What's happening, Joe?"

"Big news, Linds. Vega fingered the guy he claims is responsible for all of those unsolved homicides of yours."

"You're serious? How does he know? Tell me everything."

Joe kicked off his shoes and got into the bed, and as I had held Julie, my husband put his arms around me. He told me the tangled story of Ted Swanson and Fred Braun and their Mexican-American recruiter and tunnel man, Alejandro Vega. And he told me about a presumed killer I'd almost given up on finding.

"Anthony Ruffo Jr. With the BMW. The one who threatened me and attacked Cindy?"

"That's him."

I said, "He told Cindy to pass a message on to me. That it wasn't over yet, remember? That nasty kid. I got a very bad vibe off him. Like what I've seen in hard-core criminals. We gave him a citation for parking in a no-parking zone. Damn it. That's all we had."

Joe said, "If it can be proven that he was a hit man responsible for the 'You talk, you die' homicides—"

"Please, God. Joe. Does Cindy know about this?"

"Doubtful," said Joe.

"Any reason I can't tell her?"

"Just make sure she knows it's off the record."

I didn't know I had any laughter left in me, but I couldn't stop laughing until Joe held my face with his hands. He said, "What's funny?"

"We always tell her it's off the record. Always. She hates that. Says, 'You know what I do for a living?'"

Joe said, "Why do you smell so good?"

"Soap and water. Shampoo. Mouthwash."

"I'm going to get me some of that."

"Before or after?" I said to my dear husband.

"You choose."

"As you are. I love the smell of flashbangs in the morning. Just take off your clothes."

CHAPTER 112

CINDY WOKE UP at the crack of dawn. Again.

How could she sleep with all that she had going on in her mind? Lindsay's call a week ago about Ruffo had kept her awake until three. And then there was the meteor-size thing that had been keeping her up every night for months. *Burke's Last Stand.*

She had finished writing the first draft of the book and read it to Richie, and he was biased, but they both thought it was a winner. She'd emailed it to her agent/lawyer, Bob Barnett, four days ago, and he hadn't acknowledged receipt.

That was excruciating. He had been excited by the concept. He'd followed her writings about Burke in the *Chronicle* day by day, but she hadn't heard back from him.

Rich had gotten home late last night, and thank God he was okay. But if she kept tossing, he wouldn't get as much sleep as he needed.

Her robe was hanging over the footboard. After slipping out of bed, Cindy put the robe on over her nightgown and walked quietly into the bathroom. She looked in the mirror and touched the bridge of her nose. It was barely tender, and her doctor said it was more of a crack than a break. She'd always have a little bump, he'd told her, but not so anyone would know anything had happened.

Cindy washed, brushed, went to the kitchen, and made a cup of green tea in a flowered china mug that had belonged to her grandmother. Sometimes just holding this mug calmed her, but not today.

Why hadn't Barnett called her?

It was just after six fifteen here in San Francisco. Which meant it was after nine in DC, where Barnett lived and worked.

He should be in his office now.

Did she dare?

She sipped her tea and took her seat at the table she used as a desk. She reached across the table and palmed her phone from where it had been charging. She had some unanswered calls, none from Barnett. She had some unopened emails, none from the *Chronicle*. She put her mug on a coaster, then opened the address book on her phone. She pressed the button that dialed Bob Barnett.

As the call rang, she braced herself for rejection. She took a better angle on that and figured he'd tell her he'd been working on some notes for her, changes in the structure of the story line.

After two rings Bob answered.

"Cindy? I was going to wait until sunrise on the West Coast to call you."

"Everything okay, Bob?"

"With me? Yes. And you?"

Cindy wasn't sure how to answer. She was a wreck. The nose. Her friends and lover at risk nearly every day and night. Her fear that she had oversold this book. Was it too savage? Too gory? Was there still a market for books about serial monsters?

"I'm fine, Bob. Been thinking about Evan Burke. He gets word to me every couple of days. You can imagine. 'How's it going?' with an unsubtle subtext, 'I've killed a lot of women, you know.' What a pen pal."

She tried a laugh but couldn't quite pull it off.

Barnett said, "Next time he calls, tell him that I love it. And as for you, Cindy, I read slowly because I didn't want the book to be over. I finished it last night and wanted more."

Cindy put her hand over her heart and smiled.

"Oh, good. Thanks, Bob. That's so good to hear."

"Of course, Cindy, but then let me thank *you*. I know how much you put into this work. It's palpable. And, Cindy, why I was going to call you. I want to gather up some folks here and have a Zoom meeting. We should talk about publishers. And of course money. I'll get back to you later today. I'm very excited about your book, Cindy. I cannot wait to get it into play."

After she and Bob signed off, Cindy sat in her chair for a long time, not moving, just taking it in. The book was good. The worry she'd been carrying around for so long was gone—and she kind of missed it. That lump of a book for a killer wasn't inside her anymore.

Now came the good part and all that went with it.

Was she ready for that? Praise. Book signings. Maybe her name on the bestseller list.

She went into the bedroom, where Richie had taken up the entire bed and was snoring. *Sorry, Rich. Gotta do it.*

"Honey? Richie?"

"What time is it?"

"Rich, I just spoke with Bob. He loves it."

"Awww, Cindy. I told you. I knew he would."

"He's scheduling a meeting to discuss plans to sell it."

"Now?"

Cindy laughed. "Not now."

She melted down into the bed next to Rich, and he made room for her. He got himself comfortable with his arms around his love, and together they fell asleep.

ACKNOWLEDGMENTS

We are thankful to our researchers, advisors, and friends who shared their time and expertise with us in the creation of this thriller. The real Rich Conklin also shared his name. In real life, Captain Richard Conklin is with the Bureau of Criminal Investigations, Stamford, Connecticut, Police Department. Special thanks to Michael A. Cizmar, Special Agent FBI, retired, and private military contractor in Afghanistan. He had boots on the ground and cell phone in hand while this book was in progress. Thanks, too, to Steven Cerutti, retired Special Agent, Homeland Security Investigations, our friend and advisor throughout. Steve Rabinowitz, PLLC, in New York, was, again, our first-class legal advisor.

Armloads of thanks to Ingrid Taylar, photographer and our insightful researcher, for once again guiding us through the secret lanes and roller coaster streets of San Francisco. Thanks, too, to J. A. Duffy and Heather Parsons for their help with the unseen underground and to Mary Jordan who uses crazy glue to hold the pieces and parts together. We also wish to thank Team Patterson at Little, Brown, who convert our typewritten pages into actual books. Thank you, all.

ACKNOWLEDGMENTS

Why everyone loves James Patterson and the Women's Murder Club

'It's no mystery why James Patterson is the world's most popular thriller writer. Simply put: **nobody does it better**.'
Jeffery Deaver

'**Smart characters, shocking twists . . .** you count down to the very last page to discover what will happen next.'
Lisa Gardner

'No one gets this big without **amazing natural storytelling** talent – which is what Jim has, in spades.'
Lee Child

'**Boxer steals the show** as the tough cop with a good heart.'
Mirror

'**Great plot**, **fantastic storytelling** and characters that spring off the page.'
Heidi Perks

'Patterson boils a scene down to the single, telling detail, the element that **defines a character** or moves a plot along. It's what fires off the movie projector in the reader's mind.'
Michael Connelly

'James Patterson is **The Boss**. End of.'
Ian Rankin

Have You Read Them All?

1ST TO DIE

Four friends come together to form the Women's Murder Club. Their job? To find a killer who is brutally slaughtering newly-wed couples on their wedding night.

2ND CHANCE
(with Andrew Gross)

The Women's Murder Club tracks a mystifying serial killer, but things get dangerous when he turns his pursuers into prey.

3RD DEGREE
(with Andrew Gross)

A wave of violence sweeps the city, and whoever is behind it is intent on killing someone every three days. Now he has targeted one of the Women's Murder Club . . .

4TH OF JULY
(with Maxine Paetro)

In a deadly shoot-out, Detective Lindsay Boxer makes a split-second decision that threatens everything she's ever worked for.

THE 5TH HORSEMAN
(with Maxine Paetro)

Recovering patients are dying inexplicably in hospital. Nobody is claiming responsibility. Could these deaths be tragic coincidences, or something more sinister?

11TH HOUR
(with Maxine Paetro)

Is one of Detective Lindsay Boxer's colleagues a vicious killer? She won't know until the 11th hour.

12TH OF NEVER
(with Maxine Paetro)

A convicted serial killer wakes from a two-year coma. He says he's ready to tell where the bodies are buried, but what does he want in return?

UNLUCKY 13
(with Maxine Paetro)

Someone returns to San Francisco to pay a visit to some old friends. But a cheerful reunion is not on the cards.

14TH DEADLY SIN
(with Maxine Paetro)

A new terror is sweeping the streets of San Francisco, and the killers are dressed in police uniform. Lindsay treads a dangerous line as she investigates whether the criminals are brilliant imposters or police officers gone rogue.

15TH AFFAIR
(with Maxine Paetro)

Four bodies are found in a luxury hotel. Lindsay is sent in to investigate and hunt down an elusive and dangerous suspect. But when her husband Joe goes missing, she begins to fear that the suspect she is searching for could be him.

Discover the newest thriller from James Patterson,
coming November 2022

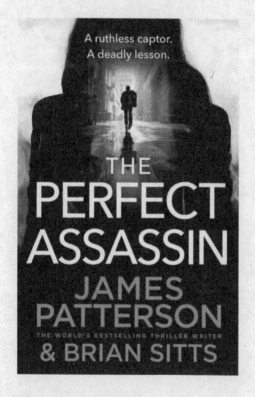

A ruthless captor.
A deadly lesson.

THE
PERFECT
ASSASSIN

JAMES
PATTERSON
THE WORLD'S BESTSELLING THRILLER WRITER
& BRIAN SITTS

Read on for an exclusive extract . . .

ONE

A MOTHER CAN sense a disturbance in her world, even in her sleep.

Marisha did.

The late-night snowfall made the small village on the Kamchatka Peninsula look like a cozy Christmas painting, but the wind was harsh. It whistled around the cottage and seeped through the walls of the tiny nursery where the six-month-old twins slept in a single crib, spooned together for warmth. Like tiny dolls. They were just five minutes apart in age, with matching features and the same delicate, pale skin. But the similarities stopped at the top of their heads. One girl had her father's dark, straight hair. The other had lush copper-colored curls, like nobody else in the family.

Marisha was a physicist. Her husband Mikhail was a mathematician. In their courting days at the university, they had long talks about what extraordinary children they would have together. And that's exactly what happened. Two in one day. The babies were remarkable—so beautiful and loving. And now, at just half a year old, already advanced for their age. They were everything a parent could wish for, and more.

Mikhail had put the girls down just after seven. At 2 a.m., Marisha woke suddenly. Something was off. She could feel it. She pushed back the covers and slipped out of bed, not bothering to nudge her husband or find her slippers. She grabbed her robe from the wall hook and wrapped it hastily over her nightgown as she hurried down the short hallway, feeling the cold tile against her bare feet.

When she opened the door to the nursery, a waft of frosty air crossed her face. In the next second, she felt a matching chill in her gut. She took a step toward the center of the dark room and inhaled sharply. Snow dusted the floor under the half-open window. Marisha grabbed the side rail of the crib with both hands, then dropped to her knees and screamed for her husband. Mikhail stumbled into in the doorway seconds later, his eyes bleary and half closed. He saw his wife on the floor and then—the empty crib. His eyes opened wide.

"They're gone!" Marisha wailed. "Both of them! *Gone!*"

TWO

A MILE AWAY, two thickset men in heavy wool coats were making their way up a rugged slope. The village lights were already fading behind the scrim of windblown snow. The footing was treacherous, and they were not familiar with the terrain.

Bortsov, the taller of the pair, used a heavy hiking pole to probe the path ahead. Gusev, the shorter partner, carried a high-powered hunting rifle. In their opposite arms, each man carried a tightly wrapped bundle. The men were killers by trade, and this was their first kidnapping. In fact, it was the first time either of them had held an infant. They clutched the sixteen-pound babies like rugby balls.

After twenty minutes of steady hiking, they were out of sight of the village. Still, Gusev kept looking over his shoulder.

"Stop worrying," said Bortsov gruffly, pointing at the trail behind them. "We were never here." He was right. Just a few yards back, the snow was already filling their tracks. The search would begin at dawn. By then, it would be no use.

Bortsov had scouted the campsite the day before. It was

a natural shelter beneath a rock overhang. He'd even taken the time to gather wood for a fire. By the time the kidnappers reached the spot, it was nearly 4 a.m. They were both exhausted from the climb and their arms were cramped from gripping the babies. Bortsov walked to a snowdrift about ten yards from the shelter. He bent forward and set the bundle he'd been carrying down in the snow. Gusev did the same with his.

They stepped back. The twins were about four feet apart, separated by a snow-covered log. They were both squirming under their tight wraps, their cries muffled by wool scarves around their heads. Bortsov pulled a handful of coins from his pocket and placed them on a rock in front of the baby on the left. Gusev placed a bunch of coins in front of the baby on the right. Then they shuffled back toward the shelter and started a fire.

When the wood caught, flames and sparks illuminated the small recess. The kidnappers tucked themselves under the rock and pulled their thick coats up around their necks. Gusev fished a flask of vodka out of his coat pocket, took a deep gulp, and passed it to his partner. A little extra warmth. Before long, their eyes were glazed. Soon after that, their stupor faded into sleep.

The babies, left in the open, were no longer crying.

THREE

MORNING. GUSEV WOKE first, stirred by an acrid waft of smoke from the smoldering fire. He brushed the snow off his coat and shook his flask. It was empty. Gusev's head throbbed and the inside of his mouth felt thick and pasty. He glanced across the small clearing to where the two babies lay silent in the snow. He elbowed Bortsov in the ribs. Bortsov stirred and rolled over. Gusev nodded toward the twins.

Both men rose slowly to their feet and walked on unsteady legs to the snowdrift. Over the past few hours, the wind had blown a fresh coating of white over both babies. Bortsov pulled the stiff scarves away from their faces. In the dawn light, their skin was bluish, their lips and nostrils coated with frost. Obviously dead. A total waste of a trip.

"Weak! *Both* of them!" said Gusev, spitting into the snow.

Bortsov turned away, snarling in frustration. "Food for the bears," he muttered.

As Gusev retrieved his rifle, he heard a small mewing sound. He turned. The baby on the left was stirring slightly.

Gusev hurried back and knelt down. He pushed the frozen scarf back off the baby's head, revealing coils of copper hair.

"We have one!" Gusev shouted, "She's alive!"

Bortsov tromped over. "Mine!" he called out with a victorious sneer. He scooped both sets of coins from under the snow and pocketed them. Then he lifted the copper-haired girl from the snowbank and tucked her roughly under his coat. Gusev gave the dark-haired baby one final shake, but there was no response. He kicked fresh snow over the tiny corpse, then followed his partner up the mountain, cursing all the way. He hated to lose a bet.

The walk down the other side of the mountain was even harder than last night's climb. Bortsov's knees ached with every step, and Gusev was coughing in the thin, cold air. But they knew the effort would be worth it. They had conducted the test with the babies, side-by-side, as they had been instructed. A survivor this strong meant a big payday, maybe even a bonus. An hour later, Bortsov and Gusev pushed through the last of the tree line into a rolling snow-covered valley.

Straight ahead was a campus of sturdy buildings made of thick stone. A few simple balconies protruded from the top floors, and most of the windows were striped with heavy metal grates. In the early morning, a light glowed from a corner room, where they knew the headmaster would be waiting for the new student. Bortsov pulled the copper-haired baby out from under his coat as they approached the imposing school gate. He knew the headmaster would be pleased. This child showed exceptional promise.

PART 1

CHAPTER 1

University of Chicago
Present Day

I'D FORGOTTEN HOW much I hated first-year students..

I'd just finished a solid fifty minutes of a cultural psych lecture, and I might as well have been talking to a roomful of tree stumps. I was already pissed at Barton for asking me to sub for him at the last minute—and a 9 a.m. class, no less. I hadn't taught this early since I was an anthropology TA. That was twelve long years ago.

Barton's lecture notes were good, but since I'd actually written my thesis on South Pacific cultures, I was able to ad lib some interesting insights and twists on tribal gender roles. At least *I* thought they were interesting. Judging by my audience, not nearly as interesting as TikTok.

After class, the students moved toward the door with their eyes still glued to their screens. I felt like I was forgetting something. *Shit. The reading assignment!* I scrolled through Barton's notes. *Jesus. Where is it? Right here. Got it.*

"Sorry!" I called out to the departing crowd, "Listen up, please! Reading for next class!" I held the textbook over my head like a banner. It was as heavy as a brick. "In Muckle and

Gonzalez! Chapters Five and Six, please!" Most of the students just ignored me. I tried to catch their eyes as they walked past, but up-close contact has never been my strength. Lecturing to a class of a hundred, no problem. Just a faceless mass. Close up, I tended to get clammy.

Sometimes I thought I might be on the spectrum. No shame in it. So was Albert Einstein. I definitely met some of the criteria. Preference for being alone? Check. Difficulty in relating to people? Check. Stuck in repetitive patterns? Check. On the other hand, maybe I was just your garden-variety misanthrope.

I plopped the textbook down on the lectern. Two female students were the last to leave. I'd noticed them in the back row—way more interested in each other than in my cogent analysis of the Solomon Islanders.

"Awesome class," said the first student. Right. As if she'd heard a word of it. She was small and pert, with purple-streaked hair and an earful of silver rings. "So interesting," said her blond friend. Were they trying to suck up? Maybe they were hoping I'd be back for good and that I'd grade easier than Barton, who I knew could be a real prick.

"Good, good, thanks," I mumbled. I stuffed Barton's iPad and textbook into my briefcase and snapped it shut. Enough higher education for one day. Out of the corner of my eye, I saw Purple Hair nudge her partner. They looked over their shoulders at the whiteboard, where I'd written my name in big capital letters at the start of class.

DR. BRANDT SAVAGE

Purple Hair leaned in close to the blonde and whispered in a low, seductive voice, "I'll *bet* he's a savage!" She gave her friend a suggestive little hip bump. Nothing like freshman

10

sarcasm. Make a little fun of the gawky PhD. Got it. And not the first time somebody had made the point: I was about as far from a savage as a man could possibly get.

I headed down the hall to the department office to pick up my mail. As I pushed through the heavy oak door, I could hear Natalie, our department admin, helping a student sort out a snafu in his schedule. When she saw me, she held up her index finger, signifying "I need to talk to you."

I liked Natalie. She was all business, no drama. Quiet and efficient. Herding cats was a cinch compared to keeping a bunch of eccentric academics in line, and she did it well. The student jammed his new schedule into his backpack and headed out the door. Natalie leaned over the counter in my direction.

"So where will you be going?" she asked, flashing a knowing smile.

"What do you mean?" I asked. My only travel plans involved heading home and heating up some soup. Natalie leaned closer and looked both ways, as if she were revealing a state secret. She gave me an insider's wink and held up a slip of paper.

"Your sabbatical." she whispered. "It's been approved!"

CHAPTER 2

HOW THE HELL did *that* happen, I wondered? I headed down the corridor with the slip in my pocket, dodging students as I went. I'd put in the sabbatical request eight months ago and hadn't heard a thing. The university system was definitely not built for speed. Ulrich, my department head, was unearthing a crypt somewhere in the Middle East. I'd given up on an approval until he got back. Had somebody gotten to him? I guess miracles do happen.

My only problem was that I hadn't really given any thought to a destination. All I knew was I'd earned six months of peace and quiet. Now I just had to figure out where to spend it.

I pushed open the main door and stepped out through the Gothic stone front of Cobb Hall. My glasses were immediately speckled with falling snow, and the cold cut right through my overcoat. That Chicago wind everybody talked about was no joke. I put my head down and almost banged into two students rushing up the steps.

"Sorry," I said. "My bad."

Even on sub-zero days, I looked forward to the

twenty-minute walk to my apartment. Time to clear my head. A break from crowded classrooms and talky colleagues. As I headed toward East 59th, my shoes lost traction on the sidewalk and I had one of those real-life cartoon moments, where your arms flail in the air while you try to keep from falling on your ass and you hope to hell nobody is watching. Once I got my footing again, I walked the rest of the way across campus with short, careful steps. Like an old man with an invisible walker.

I dipped my head into the wind and headed up the city sidewalk, squinting to keep the snow out of my eyes. Most people who passed me from the opposite direction gave me wide berth, probably because I looked half blind. The next time I looked up, I saw a young woman in a puffy parka headed toward me through the snow.

She was walking at a quick pace, staring straight ahead. As she passed, our elbows bumped.

"Sorry, sorry," I mumbled. I was a real menace to humanity today.

The woman stopped and turned abruptly. "Don't apologize!" she shouted.

The shock froze me in place. Before I could open my mouth again, she grabbed my upper arms and turned me to face the curb, like a cop getting ready to frisk a suspect.

Adrenaline shot through me. "Hey!" was all I could get out. I saw a green van with an open cargo door right in front of me. She shoved me forward, and I sprawled into the van head first. My face slapped hard against the rubber floor liner. When I flipped myself right side up, the door was sliding shut.

My heart was beating so hard I could hear my pulse in my ears. This had to be a prank, or some terrible mistake. I kicked against the inside of the door, but my rubber soles didn't even make a mark. A second later, I heard the passenger door open. There was a thick divider between the cargo section and the front seats. It was black metal at the bottom with thick, clear plastic across the top. I saw the woman slide into the driver's seat. I pounded on the plastic with my fists. She ignored me and turned the key in the ignition. She cranked the wheel and pulled out onto the street. Then she floored the accelerator. I fell backward against the rear door. I didn't bother trying to stand up. I crawled forward on my hands and knees.

"Hey! What are you doing??" I shouted, "Where are you taking me??"

My face was jammed right up against the plastic. The woman stared ahead, arms straight out on the steering wheel, weaving through the morning traffic like an Indy racer. We were heading north, out of Hyde Park. I turned to the side and started pounding on the sliding door. I twisted the door handle back and forth. It wasn't just locked. It was unscrewed. Totally useless. I tried the rear door. Same thing. I put my face against the cold metal of the truck wall. "Help!" I shouted. "I need *help*!"

"No whining!"

It was her. She was shouting at me from the front seat. Her voice cut right through the divider.

I kept on yelling. Every true-crime show I'd ever watched flashed through my brain. Rule Number One: Never get into a stranger's vehicle. Once you're taken, your chances of survival go way down. Why hadn't I put up a fight? Because it happened so fast, that's why. In real life, you don't get time to think about it. All I could do now was keep making noise and hope that we'd pull up next to a police car. *Any* car. But when

14

I looked out through the plastic, I could see that we were now on a deserted street, or maybe in an alley. There was nobody around.

I kept pounding and shouting for dear life anyway. Suddenly I felt the van pull over and skid to a stop. I flew forward and my shoulder banged hard against the partition. I was frantic, confused, terrified. My knuckles were bruised and bloody. As I got up from the floor, the cargo door slid open. The woman was outside, leaning in.

She had a no-bullshit look on her face. Her voice was low and even.

I said, "no whining."

The punch came so fast I barely saw it. There was a sharp pain in my jaw and I felt my head snap back. I was out cold before I hit the floor.

Also By James Patterson

ALEX CROSS NOVELS

Along Came a Spider • Kiss the Girls • Jack and Jill • Cat and
Mouse • Pop Goes the Weasel • Roses are Red • Violets are
Blue • Four Blind Mice • The Big Bad Wolf • London Bridges •
Mary, Mary • Cross • Double Cross • Cross Country • Alex
Cross's Trial (*with Richard DiLallo*) • I, Alex Cross • Cross Fire •
Kill Alex Cross • Merry Christmas, Alex Cross • Alex Cross,
Run • Cross My Heart • Hope to Die • Cross Justice •
Cross the Line • The People vs. Alex Cross • Target: Alex Cross •
Criss Cross • Deadly Cross • Fear No Evil • Triple Cross

THE WOMEN'S MURDER CLUB SERIES

1st to Die (*with Andrew Gross*) • 2nd Chance (*with Andrew
Gross*) • 3rd Degree (*with Andrew Gross*) • 4th of July
(*with Maxine Paetro*) • The 5th Horseman (*with Maxine Paetro*) •
The 6th Target (*with Maxine Paetro*) • 7th Heaven (*with Maxine
Paetro*) • 8th Confession (*with Maxine Paetro*) • 9th Judgement
(*with Maxine Paetro*) • 10th Anniversary (*with Maxine Paetro*) • 11th
Hour (*with Maxine Paetro*) • 12th of Never (*with Maxine Paetro*) •
Unlucky 13 (*with Maxine Paetro*) • 14th Deadly Sin (*with Maxine
Paetro*) • 15th Affair (*with Maxine Paetro*) • 16th Seduction (*with
Maxine Paetro*) • 17th Suspect (*with Maxine Paetro*) • 18th Abduction
(*with Maxine Paetro*) • 19th Christmas (*with Maxine Paetro*) • 20th
Victim (*with Maxine Paetro*) • 21st Birthday (*with Maxine Paetro*) •
22 Seconds (*with Maxine Paetro*)

DETECTIVE MICHAEL BENNETT SERIES

Step on a Crack (*with Michael Ledwidge*) • Run for Your
Life (*with Michael Ledwidge*) • Worst Case (*with Michael
Ledwidge*) • Tick Tock (*with Michael Ledwidge*) • I, Michael
Bennett (*with Michael Ledwidge*) • Gone (*with Michael
Ledwidge*) • Burn (*with Michael Ledwidge*) • Alert (*with
Michael Ledwidge*) • Bullseye (*with Michael Ledwidge*) •
Haunted (*with James O. Born*) • Ambush (*with James
O. Born*) • Blindside (*with James O. Born*) • The Russian
(*with James O. Born*) • Shattered (*with James O. Born*)

PRIVATE NOVELS

Private (*with Maxine Paetro*) • Private London (*with Mark Pearson*) • Private Games (*with Mark Sullivan*) • Private: No. 1 Suspect (*with Maxine Paetro*) • Private Berlin (*with Mark Sullivan*) • Private Down Under (*with Michael White*) • Private L.A. (*with Mark Sullivan*) • Private India (*with Ashwin Sanghi*) • Private Vegas (*with Maxine Paetro*) • Private Sydney (*with Kathryn Fox*) • Private Paris (*with Mark Sullivan*) • The Games (*with Mark Sullivan*) • Private Delhi (*with Ashwin Sanghi*) • Private Princess (*with Rees Jones*) • Private Moscow (*with Adam Hamdy*) • Private Rogue (*with Adam Hamdy*)

NYPD RED SERIES

NYPD Red (*with Marshall Karp*) • NYPD Red 2 (*with Marshall Karp*) • NYPD Red 3 (*with Marshall Karp*) • NYPD Red 4 (*with Marshall Karp*) • NYPD Red 5 (*with Marshall Karp*) • NYPD Red 6 (*with Marshall Karp*)

DETECTIVE HARRIET BLUE SERIES

Never Never (*with Candice Fox*) • Fifty Fifty (*with Candice Fox*) • Liar Liar (*with Candice Fox*) • Hush Hush (*with Candice Fox*)

INSTINCT SERIES

Instinct (*with Howard Roughan, previously published as* Murder Games) • Killer Instinct (*with Howard Roughan*) • Steal (*with Howard Roughan*)

THE BLACK BOOK SERIES

The Black Book (*with David Ellis*) • The Red Book (*with David Ellis*) • Escape (*with David Ellis*)

STAND-ALONE THRILLERS

The Thomas Berryman Number • Hide and Seek • Black Market • The Midnight Club • Sail (*with Howard Roughan*) • Swimsuit (*with Maxine Paetro*) • Don't Blink (*with Howard Roughan*) • Postcard Killers (*with Liza Marklund*) • Toys (with Neil McMahon) • Now You See Her (with Michael Ledwidge) • Kill Me If You Can (with Marshall Karp) • Guilty Wives (with David Ellis) • Zoo (with Michael Ledwidge) • Second Honeymoon (with Howard Roughan) • Mistress (with David Ellis) • Invisible (with David Ellis) • Truth or Die (with Howard Roughan) • Murder House (with David Ellis) • The Store (with Richard DiLallo) • Texas Ranger (with Andrew Bourelle) • The President is Missing (with Bill Clinton) • Revenge (with Andrew Holmes) • Juror No. 3 (with Nancy Allen) • The First Lady (with Brendan DuBois) • The Chef (with Max DiLallo) • Out of Sight (with Brendan DuBois) • Unsolved (with David Ellis) • The Inn (with Candice Fox) • Lost (with James O. Born) • Texas Outlaw (with Andrew Bourelle) • The Summer House (with Brendan DuBois) • 1st Case (with Chris Tebbetts) • Cajun Justice (with Tucker Axum)• The Midwife Murders (with Richard DiLallo) • The Coast-to-Coast Murders (with J.D. Barker) • Three Women Disappear (with Shan Serafin) • The President's Daughter (with Bill Clinton) • The Shadow (with Brian Sitts) • The Noise (with J.D. Barker) • 2 Sisters Detective Agency (with Candice Fox) • Jailhouse Lawyer (with Nancy Allen) • The Horsewoman (with Mike Lupica) • Run Rose Run (with Dolly Parton) • Death of the Black Widow (with J.D. Barker) • The Ninth Month (with Richard DiLallo) • Blowback (with Brendan DuBois) • The Twelve Topsy-Turvy, Very Messy Days of Christmas (with Tad Safran)

NON-FICTION

Torn Apart (with Hal and Cory Friedman) • The Murder of King Tut (with Martin Dugard) • All-American Murder (with Alex Abramovich and Mike Harvkey) • The Kennedy Curse (with Cynthia Fagen) • The Last Days of John Lennon (with Casey Sherman and Dave Wedge) • Walk in My Combat Boots (with Matt Eversmann and Chris Mooney) • ER Nurses: True stories from the frontline (with Matt Eversmann) • James Patterson by James Patterson: The Stories of My Life • Diana, William and Harry (with Chris Mooney)

MURDER IS FOREVER TRUE CRIME

Murder, Interrupted (with Alex Abramovich and Christopher Charles) • Home Sweet Murder (with Andrew Bourelle and Scott Slaven) • Murder Beyond the Grave (with Andrew Bourelle and Christopher Charles) • Murder Thy Neighbour (with Andrew Bourelle and Max DiLallo) • Murder of Innocence (with Max DiLallo and Andrew Bourelle) • Till Murder Do Us Part (with Andrew Bourelle and Max DiLallo)

COLLECTIONS

Triple Threat (*with Max DiLallo and Andrew Bourelle*) •
Kill or Be Killed (*with Maxine Paetro, Rees Jones, Shan Serafin
and Emily Raymond*) • The Moores are Missing (*with Loren
D. Estleman, Sam Hawken and Ed Chatterton*) • The Family Lawyer
(*with Robert Rotstein, Christopher Charles and Rachel Howzell
Hall*) • Murder in Paradise (*with Doug Allyn, Connor Hyde
and Duane Swierczynski*) • The House Next Door (*with Susan
DiLallo, Max DiLallo and Brendan DuBois*) • 13-Minute Murder
(*with Shan Serafin, Christopher Farnsworth and Scott Slaven*) •
The River Murders (*with James O. Born*) • The Palm Beach
Murders (*with James O. Born, Duane Swierczynski
and Tim Arnold*) • Paris Detective

For more information about James Patterson's novels,
visit www.penguin.co.uk.